A note from the author.....

I hope my readers enjoy the travel to Australia. While living abroad in Queensland, I have seen some amazing sites and breathtaking scenery. Many thanks to Graeme Bowden, Anne Brown and Graeme & Wendy Sutton, book store owners, who have opened their doors that allowed me to meet and talk with the locals about my writing. It has been an amazing journey.

I took the cover photo on Moreton Island, the second largest Sand Island in the world, located just off Brisbane's shore. Special thanks to my son Dylan and his Aussie friend, Dearne, for posing along the beach and helping me find the perfect spot for the photo. Also to Maud Caldarola, Foreign Exchange Student from France and an AP Art student from Granbury High School, who sketched the mystery man. Maud plans to continue the study of art when she returns home to France. Last, thanks to my loving husband Steve who continues to support my work.

Novels by Tonya Sharp Hyche

Swept Away

Just For You

Breathless

Fearless (September 2012)

Acclaim for Tonya Sharp Hyche

Just For You

"Tonya's grip on human emotion entwined with a fast moving crime story kept me enthralled from start to finish. Written in a refreshing and smooth flowing style. One of the best crime books I've read. Looking forward to the next one."

DENNIS ALLATT
ARTIST
PELICAN WATERS, QUEENSLAND

"Just as with Swept Away I could not put Just For You down. Another unpredictable, fast-paced, page-turner leaving me gasping for breath. Interesting characters both good and evil. This book will meet all your expectations of a suspenseful crime thriller. Tonya Sharp Hyche has become my new favorite author."

MARION HARPER
TEXAS

"If you love mysteries *Just for You* is a must read for 2012. You will be propelled thru the book to only find out at the end what you thought you had figured out is not true. This book is a real page turner and leaves you wanting more. Exciting, thrilling and surprising!"

PAULA ROESKE
PRESIDENT & CEO OF PRK PRODUCTS, INC

"*Just For You* is a riveting page turner. Hyche intertwines the different characters' lives in fascinating ways. The suspense is unrelenting."

SARAH GRENZ
THE WOODLANDS, TEXAS

Swept Away

"...I was very impressed...Strong characters with great understanding of police and detective work. Nice environment change from hard city life to beachy atmosphere. Good, fluent read and can't wait to read her next..."

"...read Swept Away and couldn't put it down... Loved the twists and turns and you never really knew who people were until the very end. ...you know how to keep your readers engrossed. Can't wait to read Just for You."

Breathless

TONYA SHARP HYCHE

ISBN-10: 1470026147
ISBN-13: 9781470026141
Library of Congress Control Number: 2012903121
CreateSpace, North Charleston, SC

Chapter 1

Melissa slowly opened her eyes and looked around a strange room. Blue curtains were hanging down from a circular silver rod, and she instantly knew she was in a hospital. Slowly she leaned upward and looked over her body. She was covered with a blanket except for her arms and hands lying on top. Noticing tape, she studied her hand and saw that she was hooked up to an IV. Melissa followed the line up and found it attached to a bag of clear liquid hanging on a metal stand. Leaning forward more, she felt sudden pain exploding in her head, so she stopped and gently lay back down on a pillow.

Closing her eyes, she tried to concentrate on what had happened that had landed her in this condition. Suddenly, a memory flashed before her eyes. She remembered driving her husband's Mercedes, sliding down a steep hill, and hitting a tree head-on. She was alive, but what about her husband of three years, Quinton Pierson?

Melissa fought through the pain and forced herself to sit up in the bed. Carefully with her other free hand, she stretched over her chest and pressed the nurse's call button and patiently waited. Scanning her body once more, nothing looked broken. Next she moved her toes and then felt her head for damage. On the left side, she found bandages, and her hair felt gritty. Looking downward and pulling on her long blonde hair, she was finally able to look at her once-golden locks. Now they were spotted with brown, matted crust. She thought, *Is that blood?*

Did I cut myself? She once again felt around her head, and the bandaged area was sore. Just then a hand touched the curtains and then pulled them back and revealed an older woman who was dressed as a nurse.

"Oh, sweetie, don't touch your head. Here, you need to lie back down."

The nurse took another step and gently pushed Melissa back onto the pillow. She stated, "I'm Shea, you're in a hospital. Do you know who you are?"

"Yes, Melissa Pierson, but that's not important now. Where is my husband? Why isn't he here with me?"

Shea looked away slightly. "Let me get the doctor."

As the nurse turned around, Melissa yelled out, "Wait...is he okay?"

Shea turned back around with pleading eyes and said, "The doctor will be in shortly, and he can answer all your questions."

Melissa opened her mouth to respond, but couldn't form the words, and the nurse left.

A tear rolled down Melissa face as she closed her eyes and prayed, "Dear God, oh please, please let him be dead."

Chapter 2

Melissa Brock Mason was sitting on a couch eating popcorn and surrounded by her two best friends, Alison Roeske and Amanda Fields. They were watching Julia Roberts's movie *Sleeping with the Enemy* for the first time. Even though the movie came out in the nineties, none of the girls had seen the film before, until now. Tonight was unusually quiet for the campus of Ole Miss. The Rebels were playing an away football game on Saturday at Auburn, a college in Alabama. Most students had left for the weekend for the big game, and only a few remained.

The movie ended, and Alison was the first to comment. "You have got to be joking! Why didn't she kill that SOB the first time he hit her?"

Melissa threw popcorn at Alison. "If they did that, dummy, it wouldn't be a movie!"

Amanda chimed in, "Yeah, the movie would've been over after five minutes."

"Guys, I know, but I'm just saying, she is the stupid one for not killing him to begin with."

Melissa thought about the statement. "You're right. She should have planned his murder and then taken all his money."

"Exactly! Did you see that house on the coast? What a house!"

"I would have drugged him and then, when the other guy wasn't looking, pushed him overboard into the water. He wasn't wearing a life jacket," stated Amanda.

Melissa stood up, tossed her hair over her shoulder and playfully batted her eyes. "Yep, then she would have remarried, and they would have lived happily ever after in his house."

All the girls giggled.

"So what is the next movie?" asked Amanda.

"*Pretty Woman*, it's an all-night marathon starring Julia Roberts."

Amanda exclaimed, "Yes! I love that movie!"

"You would, and you—" But Melissa stopped in midsentence when the doorbell rang.

Everyone got real quiet and looked around. Suddenly Melissa burst out laughing. "What? It's a crazy man at the door?"

Melissa got up off the couch and made her way over to the front door of their home, Phi Delta. Turning around once, she could see how the girls were slowly following her but at the same time smoothing down their hair and checking out their outfits. Melissa rolled her eyes and thought, *That didn't last long. Mr. Killer just turned into a hoped-for date.*

Melissa reached out and twisted the antique doorknob just as the doorbell rang again. Pulling open the door, she was immediately greeted by a stranger, who happened to be Mr. Tall, Dark, and Handsome.

Opening the door wider for her girlfriends to see, Melissa asked, "Can I help you?"

The six-feet-two sandy-brown-haired, brown-eyed gentleman replied, "Yes. I'm looking for Melissa Mason."

Melissa quickly answered, "She isn't here. Can I take a message?"

The tall stranger looked into her blue eyes. "That won't be necessary, Melissa."

Taking a step back, she said, "Excuse me?"

The stranger looked past her and over toward the other college girls and said loudly for all to hear, "Is she normally like this? Because if so, I'm gonna have to call her grandma back and say thanks, but no thanks."

Melissa's face turned a shade red, and she blurted out, "What has Nana gone and done now?"

For the first time, the stranger smiled, and then he held up a picture of a beautiful blonde-haired, blue-eyed girl wearing a dark green designer dress, standing in front of the spiral staircase of a house built in the mid-1800s in Jackson, Mississippi.

Amanda and Alison quickly made their way over, and Alison grabbed the picture. "Pretty! Melissa, I haven't seen this one before."

Quinton Robert Pierson met Melissa's gaze and smiled.

Chapter 3

"Nana! Where are you?" Melissa was running up the wooden stairs in high heels, wearing only a full-length satin-and-lace slip.

"Shh! Stop your hollering, young lady. The guests will hear you," replied Virginia Leigh Mason.

In a much quieter voice, she said, "Nana, I can't find my garter."

"What? Well it has to be somewhere. What else are you going to use at the reception?"

Melissa stated, "I guess we will just skip that tradition and go straight to throwing the bouquet."

Virginia Leigh turned white and grabbed her throat. "Like hell you are. Now find that damn garter. It couldn't have gone far."

Just then, Alison walked in wearing a red velvet floor-length dress and swinging a lacy garter around her finger. "Look what I found on the floor by the bathroom. This could have been ugly if I hadn't had to pee and stumbled across it."

Virginia Leigh closed her eyes and whispered a prayer, "Thank you Jesus," and then reached out and grabbed the flying garter with her white satin gloves. Then she looked into Melissa's face and stated, "Get your butt ready. No wedding at my house will fall behind schedule."

Melissa grabbed the garter and then took off running on the third floor, with Alison by her side, yelling, "Amanda! I need help with my dress!"

Virginia Leigh was a few steps down the stairs and then turned back around and said, "Shh! Melissa, the guests will hear you."

Alison placed a hand over her mouth and started giggling. She quickly took Melissa's hand and guided her into Melissa's old bedroom.

Outside, beside the four-acre lake, stood Quinton Robert Pierson beside his father, Robert Theodore Pierson, his best man. Behind the elder Pierson stood Quinton's three best friends from Ole Miss, Brad, Phil, and Mark. Quinton looked at the men standing beside him and then around until he saw his grandfather, George Robert Quinton, whom he had been named after. The seventy-year-old gray-headed man held his stare and then smiled. Quinton returned the smile and then looked over toward the lady sitting beside him, his mother, Janella Pierson. The Mrs. George Robert Quinton had died last year of cancer, and all felt a void that hadn't yet been replaced.

Quinton looked down at his watch and saw that it was 3:58. Soon it would begin. There was no doubt in his mind the wedding would begin at four o'clock sharp. He had known Virginia Leigh Mason now all his life, and she had never held any event that turned out disastrous or late. Quinton thought back to the Fourth of July party that was held at the Mason estate last year. For weeks the place was pampered and prepared for over five hundred guests. There were to be fireworks, music with a band, and fine Southern cuisine for all. A week before the party, a hurricane hit Biloxi, but somehow nothing was broken or bent, and the whole affair went off without a hitch.

Quinton looked at his watch one more time and saw that it was now four o'clock. He quickly looked over to find Virginia Leigh sitting in the front row on the opposite side of his family. She was dressed in teal blue silk two-piece suit, and not a strand of her blondish-gray hair was out of place, as it was wrapped up into a French knot on the back of her brilliant mind. She smiled at Quinton and nodded her head, and then like magic, the music began.

Four bridesmaids walked down the white tapestry that ran the length of the rows of chairs set up for the twelve hundred guests in attendance. Quinton smiled at each of the lovely ladies he had known now for the last four years, Amanda, Michelle, Beverly, and her maid of honor, Alison. All the girls wore their hair high up on top of their heads. He thought, had Virginia Leigh not allowed anyone to cut their hair in the last twelve months?

Soon the thoughts of hair and friendship left his mind when he saw his future bride dressed in white satin and lace walking toward him down the white cloth pavement. Melissa was escorted by her grandfather, Redford William Mason, who looked into Quinton's eyes and then beamed with pride. Quinton felt a sense of relief wash over him. Winning the trust and admiration from the Mr. Mason of Jackson had been a long, hard struggle that he'd eventually won just two years ago.

Melissa must have seen his expression because she cracked a big smile that could be seen underneath the sheer white veil three feet away. As Melissa and her grandfather made the final steps, all music stopped, and the ceremony began.

The minister said, "Who gives this bride to the groom, Quinton Robert Pierson?"

Mr. Mason stepped forward and stated, "I, Redford William Mason, in memory of my son, Jonathan William Mason."

Slowly the veil was raised to reveal the future Melissa Mason Pierson.

Four hours later, music was playing as people danced and drank under the setting sun. The lake shined under the pink-and-orange sky as if it had been ordered specially for Melissa's wedding.

Looking out the glass window on the third floor, Melissa asked Alison, "So what did my Nana promise God to get this incredible sunset?"

Alison walked over and placed a hand on Melissa's arm. "Nothing. That's your mama and daddy smiling down on you tonight."

Instantly Melissa's eyes grew moist, and she broke her gaze from the sunset and turned to face Alison. "I can't believe they are not here to share this day with me. Lord knows I had five years to prepare myself, but—"

"Oh, Melissa, I'm sorry, I didn't mean to bring it up. That was stupid of me. Today is a happy day. Look, you're married!"

Melissa turned away and looked into the light shining over the lake and said, "No. Don't apologize, you're right. I feel them. They are happy for me." Turning back toward Alison, Melissa wiped under her eyes. "So, I think it's time for me to get dressed now, and we better hurry before Nana comes running up here shooing us!"

Alison quickly walked around her and began to unzip Melissa's $3,500 wedding dress. Carefully the zipper was lowered to not snap one of the thousands of small pearls that were embedded in the white satin. Melissa placed a hand on Alison's shoulder for balance and then gingerly stepped out. When her left foot was almost over the side of the dress, her high heel caught a bead and snagged it.

"Oh shit!"

Melissa said, "It's okay, Alison, the wedding portraits are over. At least I made it this long without damaging it."

"If you say so." Bending over, Alison picked up the dress and then carefully carried it over to the white wrought-iron bed and laid it down, smoothing out the creases as she went. Turning back around, she stopped suddenly and said in a raised voice, "Melissa! What happened to your back?"

Standing in her matching lace-and-satin bra and panties, Melissa turned back around and found a mirror and looked intently at her image. A memory flashed through her mind of her and Quinton fighting last night. She eventually shook her head and replied, "It was a silly accident."

"Accident?"

Melissa turned back around and faced her best friend since childhood and tried her best to downplay the incident. Smiling, she said, "It just happened. I tripped over a shoe last night, and I fell and hit the small coffee table on my way down."

"Does it hurt? I mean, it looks like you could have broken a rib."

"Alison, honestly, do you think I would've been running around all day if I'd had a broken rib?"

"No, especially not up all those stairs, but—" Alison walked closer and placed a hand on Melissa's large bruise—"it has to hurt."

"Ouch! Only when you touch it!"

"Sorry. Are you gonna have it looked at when you're on your honeymoon?"

Melissa shook her head. "In Costa Rica? No, I will be fine, and it will fade in another day or two."

"Well, just make sure you don't get any pictures from behind in your bikini. Then you'll end up having to explain it to everyone."

Melissa frowned. "No kidding. Look, enough, help me finish dressing."

Alison walked over and opened Melissa's deep walk-in closet and removed a fitted white linen dress wrapped in a canvas bag. Clasping the hanger on the doorknob, she unzipped the bag and removed the dress and walked it over to Melissa, who was inspecting her bruise once again. Turning around, she stepped into the dress and pulled it up. Alison walked behind her and then pulled up the zipper, and the bruise disappeared.

Next, Melissa stepped into some new heels and said in a tender voice, "Thanks for everything! I wouldn't have known what to do today without you. I love you, my dearest best friend."

Alison's eyes grew moist, and she reached out and hugged Melissa. "Where else would I be? I love you too, sweetie."

The best friends were still embracing when Nana opened the door and stated, "Girls, it's time. Hurry down!"

Alison pulled away from Melissa. "Yes, Mrs. Mason."

Nana walked over and placed a hand on Melissa's cheek and said, "Are you okay? You look tired."

Melissa laughed out loud and stated, "I am! But Nana, it has been well worth it," and she reached out and gave her loving grandmother a hug. "Thanks for a wonderful day. I'll never forget it."

Nana pulled back and grabbed her hand and said, "I'm glad. Let's go on down. It's time to say good-bye to the guests."

Melissa followed Virginia Leigh out the bedroom door and down three flights of stairs. When she was at the last landing, she stopped when her eyes met her husband's face. He was smiling, and his eyes were sparkling from the light of the large chandelier that hung in the foyer. Pushing all insecurities away, she smiled back and then continued down the stairs and into his muscular arms.

Chapter 4

HONEYMOON
COSTA RICA

Quinton and Melissa arrived at the Liberia National Airport one day after their wedding. Both stepped off the plane exhausted but ready for their three-week adventure in Costa Rica. An experienced travel agent had put the entire package together that included all the different sceneries, from the Pacific Ocean in the west to the Caribbean Sea in the east. But first, five days and four nights would be spent in the province of Guanacaste, along the northern coast of the Pacific Ocean, at The Palms, a five-star resort.

After clearing customs and retrieving all their luggage, the happy couple was greeted by Ralph, a driver of a private limousine company. Quickly, bags were packed away and Quinton was handing Melissa a glass of champagne in the backseat.

"To my beautiful bride and our new and exciting adventures in Costa Rica!"

Melissa touched his glass and then took a sip, and Quinton removed his shoes and then leaned back and stretched out on the leather seat. Placing an arm around Melissa, he brought her closer, and she was soon leaning against him and stretching out as well along the seat.

"I cannot wait to stretch out on a lounge chair and soak up some rays."

Quinton said, "Me neither. Who knew a wedding would be so stressful?"

Melissa looked into his big brown eyes. "You're joking! We were both warned by several of our friends."

He smirked, "Yeah, I know, it's just I didn't want to believe them. I honestly thought they were exaggerating."

"It was beautiful, though, so many people. Did you see the gifts that were left in the foyer?"

Quinton replied, "Yeah, I'm sure Virginia Leigh has already had them delivered to our new home by now."

"Oh, I'm sure she has already opened them and has created a list for the thank-you cards."

He smiled. "If she went ahead and mailed them, do you think it would look suspicious since we will be out of the country for the next three weeks?"

"Oh, she won't do that, but they will already be addressed and stamped, waiting on my handwritten note in the inside."

Quinton commented, "We could stay longer. How about the entire summer?"

Melissa laughed out loud. "The sign has already gone up: Quinton, Pierson, and Pierson Family Law."

He frowned. "You're right, I'm sure by the time I get back there will be a stack of paperwork waiting just for me."

Quinton and Melissa had agreed to move to Jackson, where he would practice law with his father and grandfather. It was already an established business, and the money was too hard to turn down. At least for now, they would start their marriage in Jackson and reevaluate after another year. When the engagement was announced nine months ago, Melissa and Quinton began looking at house plans and bought a two-acre lot in a well-established neighborhood north of the city limits. Soon construction began, and they were able to close on the house a week before the wedding. For months, Melissa picked out furniture and designed each room of the four-bedroom two-story home. Quinton was in charge of the grounds, including the design of the outdoor kitchen and the swimming pool. After the honeymoon, Melissa would finally spend her first night there and begin to enjoy all her hard work.

The white limousine came to a complete stop outside a large resort with a circular drive. The door was opened, and a hand was extended to help Melissa get out of the vehicle. Stepping out in a pale pink sundress with strappy heels, Melissa was immediately hit with the warm rays of sunlight.

"Greetings, welcome to the beautiful Palms. My name is Juan, and I will help you with your check-in and bags."

Quinton stepped out behind Melissa wearing a light blue knit polo shirt and khaki pants. He was just as beautiful to look at as Melissa. The pair did make a striking couple, and they caught several glances from other tourists and staff who were walking around them.

Quinton replied, "Thanks, it's great to be here. This is my beautiful wife, Melissa, and I'm Quinton Pierson."

The man smiled and said, "Of course, we are expecting you. Come follow me."

Quinton took Melissa's hand, and they followed Juan through the open oak double doors that led to a large foyer that held the reception. A man wearing a white linen resort uniform walked over and offered a welcome glass filled with red punch.

Melissa took the offered glass and said, "Thank you," and watched as Quinton did the same. By the time they arrived at the counter, a lady was waiting with a smile and holding their check-in papers.

"You must be the Piersons."

"We are," responded Quinton.

"Welcome to The Palms. I have put you in our finest ocean villa accommodation, number seven." Melissa looked at the resort map the woman was holding as she explained, "It's located on the northern end of the resort, with spectacular oceanfront views and your own private pool and hot tub."

Melissa smiled and said, "Sounds heavenly! Thank you."

Quinton signed some paperwork and handed it back. Then he placed a hand on Melissa's waist and turned to follow Juan to their waiting villa. As they walked through the resort, Juan talked and pointed out all the amenities and restaurants. There were two large pools for the 355 rooms, and five different restaurants to choose from, including room service anytime of the day.

Melissa continued to hold Quinton's hand as they followed Juan down a winding pathway surrounded by beautiful hibiscus trees and tall palm trees swaying in the light breeze. Soon they stopped at a large villa painted light blue, and Juan produced a key.

Opening the door, he stepped to the side and motioned the happy couple inside. Soon two men followed in with their luggage and then quickly left. Juan thanked the men and then stepped into the room and began to point out the stocked bar, pool towels, and a basket with sunscreens, lotions, and local maps.

Next Juan motioned toward the back of the villa and said, "Follow me."

They all stepped out through the sliding doors and saw the beautiful white, sandy beach with a nice cushioned lounge bed covered with a straw roof. Beside the bed were two lounge chairs with a small table for drinks. All had a towel rolled up and were waiting just for them.

Taking Quinton's hand, Melissa exclaimed, "This is amazing!" Then she turned around. "Where is the pool?"

Juan pointed to the left and said, "Come, I'll show you."

Pushing a heavy wrought-iron gate, they entered into a small courtyard, surrounded by thick, lush palms, that contained the pool, hot tub, and a few chaise lounges. There was a door that also led back into the side of the villa.

Juan looked at the couple and winked. "The pool was designed for privacy."

Quinton quickly responded, "Thank you. That will be all, Juan."

Melissa looked from Juan to Quinton, and then back to Juan, and added, "Thanks for your help."

Juan politely nodded. "Enjoy your stay, and don't hesitate to ask the front desk for assistance. Good-bye now, I will leave you." Then he turned around and left through the open gate.

Melissa said, "He didn't mean anything by that."

Quinton looked hard into Melissa's blue eyes, "Sweetie, we are on our honeymoon, remember?"

Melissa smiled then and said, "Let's go change. I can't wait to walk barefoot on the sand!"

Soon bags were unpacked and Melissa stood in her underwear, holding up three swimsuits, and asked, "Which one?"

"The one I picked out, the hot pink."

Melissa threw the other two in a drawer and then turned around and faced Quinton, who had already changed into a pair of blue trunks. Melissa's heart missed a beat as he stood before her with his hard, muscular bare chest and golden tan. His sandy-brown hair had some light highlights he had picked up from the sun over the last month working on their new outdoor kitchen. To Melissa, he resembled Ken, and she had to smile at the many references people often made about them, "Ken and Barbie."

"What are you grinning about?"

"Oh, just how Barbie can't wait to get Ken alone for a solid twenty-four hours!"

Quinton walked forward, touched Melissa's face, and then moved his hand down her body, but stopped when he got to her waist. Gently he turned her around and placed his large hand over her ugly bruise. In a quiet voice, he spoke. "I'm so sorry about that, Melissa. Please, please forgive me and let me make that up to you."

Melissa removed his hand with hers and then slowly turned around and faced Quinton. "I have. Now let's not discuss that anymore. I know it was an accident. I want to forget about it, please."

Slowly he bent forward and embraced her face with his large, strong hands and began gently kissing her. Soon the kissing led them to the king-size oak bed, and it would be another hour before Melissa finally touched the sand with her bare feet.

For the next five days, Melissa and Quinton spent the days lounging in the sun, frolicking in the waves, taking long walks along the beach, and just relaxing. Their nights were spent alone around the pool and hot tub, away from all others. So far, Quinton had done exactly as he'd said: *"Let me make that up to you."*

Chapter 5

On day six of their honeymoon, luggage was stored at The Palms, and Quinton and Melissa headed toward the airport for their twelve-day ecotour adventure. From Liberia Airport, they flew first class again to San Jose. From there they bordered a chartered plane and flew to their first destination, a village located in Tortuguero. For four days and three nights, they would explore the secluded evergreens, swamps, and beaches located along the northern coastline of Costa Rica, which bordered the Caribbean Sea. Two days into the ecotour, there was hardly any evidence of a bruise left on Melissa's back.

Throughout their stay, the couple watched the many different birds and photographed the popular toucans and parrots. They were even lucky enough to see the poison dart frog, which is often known as "blue jeans" due to its red-orange body with dark blue legs and hands. They had spotted the unusual frog along one of their self-guided hikes through the jungle on the second day. There they stood and watched in awe, taking turns snapping photos of the odd creature. Several hours later, with several hundred photos, the couple arrived back at their private hut located in Tortuguero's village.

The next day, Quinton and Melissa hiked Tortuguero Hill and had a picnic near the top. Sipping wine and eating cheese, the couple talked about their plans for the future.

"I think I want four kids, three boys and one girl."

Melissa laughed out loud and said, "Oh really, what happens if I have three girls? Are you going to dare go for a fourth?"

"Absolutely. If I had four daughters, I would be the envy of every man because no doubt they would look just as beautiful as their mother."

"What if I get all fat after the first child? Will you still love me?"

Quinton lost the smile on his face for a moment and then finally responded, "That's a ridiculous thing to say. Of course you're not going to get all fat."

Melissa narrowed her eyes and said, "Oh, but I might."

"Then I will divorce you and move on."

Melissa searched his face for a wink or a smile, but saw neither. She looked away and then got up and stated, "You're right, it's impossible for Barbie to get fat."

Melissa looked away as she frowned and took one step before she was immediately picked up and swung around in his arms. She looked up and saw his face, and he was smiling.

"Melissa, Melissa, I love you no matter what!" He bent over and kissed her, then sank to his knees, laid her back down on the quilt, and began undressing her. For the next thirty minutes, Quinton and Melissa made love overlooking the village of Tortuguero in broad daylight.

On their last full day, Melissa and Quinton slept in and had breakfast in bed. It was twelve o'clock when they finally emerged from their hut to embrace the day ahead. A local man greeted them around twelve thirty and then took them on a long boat ride through the canals. On this adventure, they spotted crocodiles and watched in amazement as the man threw them chicken to eat. The crocs opened their mouths to reveal their sharp teeth and quickly snatched the waiting meat and splashed away in the water. Two hours later, both Melissa and Quinton were relieved to find a quite beach with no lurking crocodiles.

Along the beach, a table had been set up in a remote area, and the two enjoyed a meal with candlelight as the sun began setting over the land filled with evergreens. The sky turned a shade of pink over the ocean, and the two were happy to sit quietly, just absorbing God's beauty. Finally, after dinner, the man who had taken them on the boat tour arrived again to take them on another adventure, turtle watching. Melissa and Quinton were led to the water, and all three boarded a small canoe. The man began rowing along the coast. May was nesting season, and one could view the turtles only from the water, as the beaches were protected at night from visitors. From the canoe, a light was shined across the shore, and Melissa watched in wonder at the sight of the turtles. They were amazing to watch. This was one of the most protected natural environments for sea turtles in the world, and the Piersons felt honored to be a part of it for just one night.

On their fourth and final day, Quinton and Melissa spent the morning shopping in Tortuguero's village. They bought souvenirs for themselves as well as for their family. Quinton picked out another swimsuit for Melissa, and she picked out a brown hat for him to wear on their next adventure. With gifts packed away, they checked out of their villa and caught a ride back to their charter plane to make the flight back to San Jose. From there they took another small plane to Quepos with four other couples. Once they landed, they were then taken by a car to a small beachside cottage and left there for the rest of the day.

Melissa and Quinton spent the remaining day exploring the beach and found a small bar to dine and have drinks in. They laughed and talked for hours and even danced several songs to a local band. Four hours later, the two were walking hand in hand back to their private beachside cottage. Melissa thought, *I can't possibly be any happier, can I?*

Quinton opened the door and then bent down and picked up Melissa and stepped into the two-room cottage. Gently he placed her down and kissed her forehead. "I'm beat. Let's get a shower and get to bed."

Melissa looked back into his eyes and was going to comment, but noticed he was serious. She instead said, "You're right. Tomorrow is a big day. We are going to hike the rain forest."

Quinton stepped away and made his way toward the shower. He turned on the water and stripped down. Then he felt the water temperature and walked in and shut the glass door behind him. Melissa turned around and wandered over to her purse and pulled out her BlackBerry to see if their limited service had picked up any e-mail. Right when e-mails started popping up, her hand was hit, and her BlackBerry went crashing to the floor.

Spinning around, she said, "What the hell?"

Quinton grabbed her wrist and lowered his face within inches of hers. "Why does my wife stand out here looking at e-mails instead of joining her new husband in the shower?"

Melissa spoke in a shaking voice. "I-I thought you wanted to be alone...I didn't..."

Quinton released her hands, wrapped his arms around her, and squeezed her into his wet, naked body. Melissa was trembling as he lowered his mouth to hers. Slowly he pulled away and then turned around and headed back toward the shower without another word spoken as Melissa watched speechless.

Chapter 6

Eleven days into their honeymoon, Melissa felt lost. She thought, *How could this man make me feel so many different emotions? I'm breathless, excited, happy, and sometimes frightened by his actions. Over the last year, since we announced our engagement, he has slowly changed, becoming more and more possessive.*

Melissa replayed in her head the many times she had changed clothing at his request. If she wore something conservative to hide her curves, he asked her to change. If she bought a dress that showed off her curves, he asked whom she was trying to impress. Lately, she had just given up and let him pick her clothing. It just seemed easier that way.

Standing in their room, she asked, "What should I wear today for our hike?" and she held up some options.

"Either looks fine to me."

Melissa bit her lip to keep her from stating what was on her mind. Quickly she picked the khaki shorts and black shirt. As she was dressing, Quinton pointed out the fact that today was their fifth day of their ecotour adventure and they were setting out to explore Manuel Antonio, which was located in North Puntarenas, along the Pacific Ocean in the middle of the country of Costa Rica.

Just as they were locking up, Quinton said, "I think that black shirt will make you hot. You probably should wear a lighter color."

Not wanting to fight, Melissa opened the door back up to change just as a four-wheel drive pulled up. As she changed her top, Melissa could hear Quinton talking through the open window.

"She's still changing. You know women, can't ever decide what to wear."

Melissa rolled her eyes and felt her face flush with anger as the men laughed at his comments.

Pulling her shirt down over her chest, she stormed over to the mirror to take a look at her reflection. Turning sideways, she looked at her stomach and smoothed out her shirt. Had she gained weight? Immediately she thought of Quinton's comment he'd made the other day.

As she turned back around, she looked hard into the mirror and said quietly, "Well we will never know. I have no intentions of getting fat or pregnant anytime soon."

"Melissa! You coming, or changing everything?"

Angrily Melissa grabbed her ponytail holder and walked outside to join them.

Quinton introduced her to the gentleman as Peyton, their tour guide. The older gentleman smiled at Melissa and said, "You look great! You ready to go on an adventure, little lady?"

Melissa nodded and then climbed into the backseat through the open door of the four-wheel drive. It took over a half hour before they arrived at the rain forest. During that time, Melissa spoke very little and tried to push the bad thoughts out of her mind.

When the four-wheel drive came to a stop, Peyton jumped out and then popped the rear hatch. He handed them each a small backpack that contained water, snacks, insect repellant, and a small first aid kit. Soon they were on their way.

As the hours passed by, Melissa forgot all about the black shirt and Quinton's odd behavior from the night before. He was attentive, loving, and full of entertaining conversation. Together they hiked and explored the rain forest and found more exotic birds as well as the popular white-faced monkeys that lived in the forest. At the end of the day, Peyton took them to a small hut that housed a monkey and allowed them to feed it and get pictures with the tamed animal. They laughed and smiled as they played with the exotic monkey for about thirty minutes. Eventually it was time to leave, and Peyton escorted them back down the path that led to their waiting all-terrain vehicle.

It was five thirty when Peyton pulled away and said his good-byes. He promised to return tomorrow, same time, for another fantastic adventure that awaited them. "Don't forget to wear your swimwear under your clothing!" Then he pulled away and left them standing alone in front of their cottage.

"Well, he was quite the character!"

Quinton nodded in agreement and turned to face Melissa. "I have a surprise for you."

Melissa looked into his soft brown eyes and smiled. Quinton took her hand and led her around the cottage to the beachside. After a few steps, her heart stopped as she saw a small table for two set up with three men off to the side with musical instruments. As soon as the men saw them, they started playing.

Melissa turned to Quinton and said, "Mr. Pierson, you take my breath away," and then lifted up on her tippy-toes and kissed him on the lips.

Quinton touched her back softly and held her in a touching embrace. Time stood still as Melissa absorbed her husband's loving arms and the wonderful memories of the day.

The next morning, Melissa threw on a swimsuit and a tank top with cutoff blue jeans shorts on top. Today they were going on a river-rafting adventure that promised to be exhilarating.

"Are you ready, little lady?" Peyton asked as he held the door opened.

Melissa forced a smile and said, "Absolutely," and then jumped inside the four-wheel drive and snuggled up to her husband.

The next hour was passed holding on with one hand to Quinton and the other hand on the handrail by the door as they continued to climb uphill on a washed-out dirt road. Finally they arrived at their destination and saw two other vehicles.

Quinton opened his door and then held out a hand for Melissa and asked with a grin, "Are you okay?"

"Yes. That was a fun ride."

Peyton spoke up. "You haven't seen nothing yet. Wait till you're holding on for dear life racing down that there river."

Quinton and Melissa looked at where he was pointing and both thought silently, *What the hell have we been signed up for?*

Melissa looked at Quinton, and instantly knew they had read each other's mind. Both smiled and reached out for each other's hand and then slowly followed Peyton toward the river's edge, where other guests were patiently waiting.

A taller man was standing in front of four strangers talking when he made eye contact with Quinton and Melissa. He paused and then said, "Welcome, you must be the Piersons from Mississippi."

Melissa spoke first. "Yes, we are, we made it."

The man stuck out his hand and said, "I'm JP. Are you two ready for the ride of your life?"

Melissa looked up into Quinton's smiling face and then turned toward JP and replied for the second time today, "Absolutely!"

The man smiled back and quickly introduced them to the two couples, then handed them their life jackets. "Put these on, and make sure they fit, and follow me over to the raft."

Peyton yelled out, "I'll pick you two up downriver. Have a blast!"

Melissa just smiled at Peyton and then followed JP down the small embankment and saw the red inflatable raft with paddles. She listened as JP continued on with some directions, and in a matter of two minutes flat, they were seated and then pushed off into the rushing water.

The first rapid was small, and Melissa thought to herself, *Okay, this is doable. I can relax and enjoy this.*

Two minutes later, another rapid appeared and left Melissa breathless and shaking. As she held on tight to the side handle, she looked over at Quinton. Immediately she saw the fire in his eyes as he was wrapped up into the thrill of being swept away without any control. She continued to watch his movements and thought, *He's alive with this. He undeniably loves this adventure.* With each turn and rapid, he looked even more relaxed than before. *Wow, he loves being reckless! I knew he was adventurous, but had no clue he thrived on completely letting loose and diving straight into the unknown.*

Quinton met her gaze and grinned ear to ear. He shouted above the loudness of the water, "This is awe...some!" His words were broken up with another dip into the water.

She responded, "Yeah, it is awesome!"

He shouted, "Whooo hooo!" and they went plunging headfirst into the biggest drop-off yet. He steadied his balance and looked over at Melissa. "I love you, babe, and I promise our marriage will be just as wild of a ride!"

The other couples laughed, and JP responded, "You haven't seen nothing yet. Wait till the next one."

Melissa looked forward and saw the water disappearing over an edge and felt woozy. Quinton shouted out, "Hold on!" and then grabbed her arm with his free hand and held her in place with his body strength as they went sailing over and landed with a whoosh.

Melissa closed her eyes and tried to breathe. *Oh my God, I'm going to die in Costa Rica.*

Quinton leaned over and yelled, "You okay? You look a little funny."

Melissa was drenched, and her blonde hair was stuck to the side of her face. She looked down at her tennis shoes and saw that they were inches deep in water. She looked over at Quinton and forced her winning smile that everyone fell in love with and replied, "Absolutely!"

Another ten minutes passed, and all of a sudden, the deafening sound of the water faded as they drifted downstream into calmer water. Melissa shouted, "What's happening?"

JP answered, "No need to shout, missy, everything is fine. We are now at the turn of the river, where it is flat for the next half mile."

Melissa turned a shade pink when she realized she had shouted. She quietly said, "Oh."

JP continued, "Okay, guys, we are going to paddle a bit while the girls catch their breaths."

The young red-haired girl sitting in front of Melissa turned around and said, "Thank God."

Melissa only nodded her head, and JP, watching the two, laughed out loud some more as though they were the funniest thing in the world.

After five minutes of paddling, JP announced, "Look up ahead, everybody. This is the best part of the trip."

Melissa silently cringed and forced herself to look toward the direction of JP's outstretched arm. Slowly they rounded the corner, and she was immediately in awe of the most spectacular waterfall she had ever seen.

As they neared the fall, the noise of the water sounded louder, and then JP shouted, "We are going to tie up over there, and you guys can swim."

Again, Melissa looked at where he was pointing and saw a picnic area set up with food and drinks. Looking over at Quinton, she saw him raise his eyebrows and point over to an area that appeared to be a swimming hole. She smiled.

When the raft was brought ashore, Quinton reached out and picked Melissa up under her arms and practically lifted her to land. He continued to hold on as Melissa got her land legs back and steadied herself.

JP said, "We head out in two hours, so drink, eat, relax, and go swimming!"

Quinton released Melissa, but quickly reached out for her hand. The others were heading toward the table, and Quinton was quickly leading her away toward the swimming hole. When they were several yards away, Quinton walked behind one of the rocks and quickly scooped up Melissa in his arms and began kissing her madly. Melissa couldn't speak as he ravished her body with his hands and covered her mouth with his. Somehow he had already stripped her down to her black bikini and was pulling her down into the water. Hiding behind two large rocks, Quinton took her right there in lightning speed. Melissa could only hold on as she was wrapped up tight in his embrace and heading toward the sandy edge. Time seemed to stand still as Quinton made love to his wife of twelve days without a care in the world to where he was or who was around.

Slowly Quinton released Melissa and submerged his whole body under the water. She watched as his head disappeared and then took a quick breath of air as he grabbed her waist and pulled her under. Slowly Melissa was brought to him, and he kissed her under the clear turquoise water. An image appeared from above, and Quinton released her and brought her back up and spotted JP smiling down on them.

"You kids gonna eat, or play the whole time?"

Quinton looked over and met Melissa's blue eyes and said with a smile, "I'm famished! Let's eat."

JP stepped to the side as both of them emerged from the water. Melissa looked over at JP, and he was still smiling as he bent down and picked up her tank. "Here, you want this?"

Quinton answered for her, "No. She doesn't need it."

Melissa looked away from JP quickly and then followed Quinton back, still holding his hand.

Quinton grabbed two sandwiches and then whispered in her ear, "You grab the drinks, and let's go over there and sit by the waterfall."

Melissa nodded and grabbed two drinks and then followed him over. They found a flat rock right at the edge of the fall and sat down with their food. She looked into his brown eyes and then placed her hand over his head and smoothed back his wet hair off his forehead and smiled. "You enjoyed that."

With a boyish smirk, he said, "Which part?"

"I think both."

He leaned in and kissed her and said, "Yes, both, equally!"

The two hours that were promised seemed like thirty minutes to Melissa as she was once again strapping herself into a life jacket and holding on for dear life. This time it didn't seem as bad, or maybe she was getting used to it. After another hour, she was just as carefree and reckless as Quinton. After a few more rapids, Peyton's four-wheel drive came into sight. She thought, *Great! Just as I start to relax, it's over.*

The ride back to the cottage seemed to fly by, and once again they were saying good-byes to Peyton as he promised to return in two days. Melissa waved and then turned around and gazed at Quinton. He still was wearing an expression of sheer joy.

"That was a lot of fun. How are we going to top that?" she asked.

He stepped closer. "I'll show you." He picked her up and walked straight toward the ocean, and once again they made passionate love, this time on the white sand with crashing waves at their feet.

Chapter 7

The last day at Manuel Antonio was spent on the beach lazing under the palm trees. Melissa silently counted to three. *Three times today and it's not even noon.*

Turning toward Quinton, she smiled and then traced her finger over his flat chest. He opened his eyes and then grabbed her finger and rolled over on top of her. "You are going to be the death of me."

Melissa said, "Are you hungry? 'Cause I could probably eat."

He looked down and felt her flat stomach. "You probably should before you blow away."

"Oh, I think I've gained weight on this trip."

He looked down and studied her stomach, then felt one of her hips, flipped her over, and rubbed his hands over her ass. "Nope. You haven't." Then he flipped her back over, leaned in, and kissed her all over.

Ten minutes later, Quinton stood and pulled Melissa up into his arms. "Stay right here. I will make us a sandwich and bring us another Corona."

Melissa watched as he walked away, and then she took a few steps toward the ocean until her feet got wet. There she sat in the water and watched as the waves rolled to shore and onto her outstretched legs. She closed her eyes and inhaled deeply of the salt air. *Is this bliss? Is this what marriage is all about? Is there really such a thing as a perfect marriage with no hiccups?*

She thought back to her parents. She remembered some fights, but they were always verbal, not abusive, and the one thing her parents did was always make up. She smiled at the memory of her father bringing her mom a dozen roses and saying, *"Sorry about yesterday, I was wrong."* At the sheer thought of her father apologizing, she realized how rarely Quinton did that, and never had he stated he was wrong. Telling herself it was still early in their relationship, she foolishly convinced her mind that he would soften and change over time.

Suddenly a hand touched her shoulder, and she turned around to find Quinton holding a beer out for her. She took it from him and then began to stand up. He pressed down on her shoulders and said, "No, it's nice here."

Sitting down beside her, he handed her a premade sandwich wrapped in plastic wrap. Someone had stocked their refrigerator for the day yesterday when they were out rafting. So far, everything had been well planned out, just as the travel agent had advertised.

Melissa unwrapped the sandwich and took a bite. Words were not spoken as each sat quietly and watched the beautiful turquoise water lap at their feet. She thought to herself, *Yes, this is bliss.*

Chapter 8

The next morning, Quinton and Melissa packed up once again and were greeted by a joyous Peyton. After loading them up one last time, he drove them to Quepos and then wished them well on their next journey. Melissa boarded another small plane with Quinton right behind her. From here, they were going to Corcovado National Park, which was located in the wild and untamed Osa Peninsula on the southern coastline of Costa Rica bordering the Pacific Ocean.

The plan was to stay one night along the coast and go for two short hikes. Once they arrived, they were once again greeted with a four-wheel drive and their own personal tour guide. As they traveled along, Melissa noted how the national park was secluded and untamed, just as advertised. Also, both Melissa and Quinton were surprised at the amount of jaguars they saw running through the wild forest. Many birds were also spotted as they were told over four hundred different bird species lived at the park.

The night was spent along the coast in a small hut that had been built over the water. Melissa and Quinton laid their sleepy heads down and fell asleep in each other's arms as the waves rolled to shore beneath them.

At two in the morning, Melissa woke to a noise and looked over to find Quinton, but he was not there. Slowly she sat up and looked around, but saw no movement and no husband. Carefully, she stepped out of the bed and went in search of Quinton. There weren't many places to look, as the hut was quite small. After searching the bathroom, Melissa concluded Quinton wasn't here. Turning on the bathroom light, she turned around and walked across the small bedroom and opened the door to the small walkway that led to shore. She took one step outside and looked around. Still, no sign of Quinton.

The printed brochure of Osa Peninsula quickly filled her mind. Words such as "secluded, untamed, wild" flashed through her mind. She shook her head. "Oh, for goodness sakes, Melissa! Get a hold of yourself. He is probably out planning another big surprise, and you're gonna ruin it when he comes back and finds you missing, or worse, worried!"

Stepping back inside the hut, she closed the door and turned the bathroom light back off and then walked over to the bed and climbed in. She pulled the sheets back over her body and thought, *Why am I trying so hard to convince myself that he is out surprising me? Why in God's name would he leave me in the middle of the night?*

Several minutes passed and no sign of Quinton. She was doing her best to try to fall asleep as she concentrated on the waves below. More minutes passed, and still no husband. Just when Melissa was almost back asleep, she heard a noise and jumped. It sounded from below the bed. As she quickly sat up, she heard the noise again. Something seemed to be scraping the pole below the hut. Instantly, visions of black jaguars filled her mind. Shaking her head, she thought, *No, I'm being ridiculous. They live in the wild, not in the water!*

Melissa turned her head toward the door as she began to hear footsteps along the walkway. Quietly she lay back down and pulled the covers back over her. She closed her eyes, facing the ceiling. As she lay there, she listened carefully and barely heard the door open. She slightly cracked open her eyes and saw Quinton's outline from the full moon as he closed the door. Soon he turned toward her and stood there watching.

Moments passed by, and no movement was made by either of them. Finally Quinton moved and walked toward the bathroom. Again, Melissa cracked her eyes and saw him close the door behind him, and a small light escaped under the door. Melissa sat up and stared at the closed door and thought, *I'm being foolish. Why am I pretending to be asleep? This is so stupid.* But still, something tugged at her mind that it was best to remain quiet. As her heart and mind continued to play a tug-of-war, she watched the door in silence.

Several minutes passed as she continued watching the closed door. Finally, she saw the light under the door disappear, and she quickly lay back down in the same position as before. Slowly, Quinton made his way over to the bed and eased down, trying not to wake her. As he settled in quietly, he made no move toward her. Instead, she noticed he faced the opposite direction with his back toward her. Melissa opened her eyes wider and looked over at him and frowned in the dark. Her last thoughts before falling back to sleep were, *I hope the surprise is going to be worth it. Why else would you leave me here alone on an untamed island?*

Melissa woke the next day to an empty bed once again. She looked around the room, but this time she could see clearly. Light was pouring in between the cracks of the bamboo blinds. Sitting up, Melissa stretched her arms up and then stepped out of bed and made her way over to the bathroom. When she stepped inside, she stopped when she saw a drop of blood on the floor. Looking around some more, she found another splatter by the faucet, but none was in the sink.

Turning away, she ran across the room toward the door and opened it up right as Quinton appeared.

"Well good morning, beautiful!"

Melissa watched as he lowered his mouth for a kiss and then stood back to take another look over her body. Suddenly she realized she wasn't wearing anything.

Quinton smiled and said, "Don't move. I'll be right back," and he walked over toward the bathroom and closed the door. Five minutes passed, and he finally opened the door back up. "I have breakfast waiting along the beach. Are you hungry?"

Melissa heard her stomach growl and said, "Yes, um, but, never mind, I just need to use the ladies' room first."

Stepping out of her way, he gestured for her to enter, and she did, closing the door behind her. Immediately she looked for the blood, but this time didn't see any. She asked herself, *Where the hell did it go? Did he clean it up?*

Frustrated and confused, she used the bathroom and then opened up the door and found no Quinton. Next she walked over to the small suitcase and pulled out her orange sundress and quickly threw it on. Hearing a noise outside, she left the small hut in search of what was going on. When she stepped onto the walkway, she saw Quinton pulling a small boat closer to the pole. *That must have been the noise I heard last night.*

Interrupting her thoughts, he said, "Come on, I want to show you something."

Quinton led the way down the walkway and toward the beach. A few feet away was a blanket set up with two tin canisters. Taking a seat, he pulled her down and then lifted the lid and said, "Omelets."

Relief washed over her face as, once again, she realized Quinton had set up another surprise.

An hour had passed by as they relaxed and ate in the morning sun. Eventually Quinton announced, "I have a boat tied up for us to use today. We are going to use it to go around the peninsula to the other side, where there is a small island to explore."

"Oh, that sounds nice."

He added, "We will take all our stuff. We won't be coming back here tonight. Instead we are going to take a late flight to San Jose and stay the night there."

Melissa thought, *I don't remember this part*, but decided it was all too much to keep track of, so she said instead, "What is in San Jose?"

"Lots to see. It is a beautiful city, and we will tour it tomorrow before our six o'clock flight back to Liberia and then on to Guanacaste."

"I'm in your hands. This has been an amazing trip!" Melissa pushed all silly thoughts out of her head and stretched out onto Quinton's lap.

Quinton placed a hand over her forehead and began to smooth out her long blonde hair. She reached up and placed her hand on top of his other hand and felt him flinch. She turned her head toward his hand that was lying beside her and saw that it was bruised and bleeding.

"What happened to your hand?" she exclaimed.

"I smashed it between the boat and the dock."

"When was this? Do we need to have it looked at?"

Quinton removed his hand from her view and then stood up and stated, "No, I'm fine. We should get going."

Taken aback, Melissa stood up and then followed Quinton with a worried expression painted on her face. More questions were going through her mind about his nightly excursion that had obviously resulted in an injured hand. Finally getting up enough nerve, she timidly asked, "Quinton, what happened—"

"Melissa, I'm fine! Don't ask any more questions, okay!"

Melissa listened to his angry words and watched as his expression turned mean. Not wanting to set him off, she whispered softly, "Okay, no more, I'm sorry."

Quinton looked hard into her eyes. Then his shoulders relaxed as he dropped his hands off his hips and turned back around toward the cottage. Over his shoulder he continued, "Let's just pack up."

Chapter 9

"To Melissa! We wish you the best in Birmingham, and we will miss you terribly."

"Hear, hear! We love you, Melissa!"

Shouts were called out among the hundred people who were gathered in the large meeting room on the seventh floor of Guin and Williams Company. Melissa Pierson had been their CFO for over a year now and was giving up her job to move to Birmingham, Alabama. Quinton was offered a job with a top legal firm and had decided it was time to make the break from the family law business in Jackson.

Quinton's real passion was corporate law, not family law, and he had quickly become bored with his job at Quinton, Pierson, and Pierson. At first, Melissa was shocked to hear that he was unhappy and looking elsewhere for something new and more exciting. It took a few weeks for Quinton to finally win Melissa over, and she finally came around and agreed with Quinton that it was time to move on.

It wasn't uncommon for women to give up their job to follow their husband's career, and it didn't seem to matter that Melissa brought home over two hundred grand a year. Growing up in the Deep South, girls were raised at a young age to cater to their husbands, and he would make the ultimate decisions when it came to finances and work. So as a dutiful wife of fourteen months, Melissa agreed to give up her dream job and follow and support her husband with his new job.

"So, Melissa, any news on job prospects?"

Melissa turned toward Kent Barnes, her right-hand man. "Some, but I'm going to get settled first and then get serious about looking."

Quinton stepped forward and added, "Yes, Melissa has a lot to do in the next several months. You've seen her art collection. It will take her at least six months just to get the house organized."

Melissa looked over at her husband. "Well, not that long, but it will take me a good month or two to really settle in."

Kasey, her secretary, asked, "So have you closed on that house yet?"

Melissa nodded. "Yes, just this past weekend. It is truly a nice home with excellent schools surrounding the area."

"That's good. It doesn't hurt to look down the road," and then she smiled and winked.

"Melissa doesn't want kids for at least another two years."

Melissa gave Quinton a quizzical look. "I never said that."

Quinton's face turned a shade pink. "I must have misunderstood. Please excuse me, all. I see someone I need to talk to."

Kent and Kasey exchanged looks and Melissa smirked. "Oh, stop it! He is stressed right now."

Kasey inquired, "So, you do want to start a family?"

She twisted her mouth and pondered the thought for a moment. "No. He is right, not now."

Henry Guin stepped over toward the threesome. "Melissa, we sure are going to miss you around here. I don't know how I'm going to replace you."

Henry Guin was forty years old and recently divorced. He was extremely good looking, and many Jackson women were lining up trying to win him over to become the next Mrs. Guin. Henry was a gifted entrepreneur with a very successful business that would only continue to increase his wealth. He and Melissa had become close over the last couple of months and often had lunch together. Henry had shared with Melissa private things about his divorce, and Melissa had been a good friend who listened and understood.

"Thanks, Henry, it has been a pleasure working for Guin and Williams, and I will miss working here very much."

"Well, just know, if you ever move back to Jackson, you have a job."

Melissa smiled and leaned over and hugged Henry and said in his ear, "Thank you. I will miss you very much, my dear friend."

Pulling away from the embrace, Melissa saw Quinton's frown. She watched as he stepped away from his conversation with two gentlemen and walked her way. Instantly she was reminded of his jealous streak and immediately tried to defuse the situation. Stepping farther away from Henry Guin, she shouted out over the crowd of people, "If I could have everyone's attention please." She saw Quinton stop dead in his tracks, and everyone quickly quieted for her to speak.

"I want to thank everyone for coming out tonight. I appreciate—" She extended her hand toward Quinton, and he then walked forward and grabbed her hand. She continued, "We appreciate all of your support with our new adventure that lies ahead. We promise to drop by on our next visit to Jackson. Thanks again, and good night, everyone."

People clapped and shouts were yelled—"Good luck!"—as Melissa took Quinton's hand and led him toward the exit door. It was nearing six o'clock, and many people were sad to see her leave, but they needed to get home to their own life. Quinton opened the glass door, and Melissa turned once more and smiled and waved to all of her coworkers, many of whom had become her dear friends.

Once Quinton pulled his BMW out of the company parking lot, he tore into Melissa. "What the hell were you doing hugging your boss in front of everyone like that? Were you trying to mock me or embarrass me?"

In an angry voice, Melissa responded, "Oh, you have got to be kidding me. You know there is *nothing* going on between us. How can you think like that? I'm leaving my job to move to another state to be by your side and to support you!"

Quinton slammed on the brakes as the yellow light turned red, and then turned toward Melissa and slapped her hard across the face. "I'm no fool, Melissa. I see the way he looks at you."

Trying to contain the situation before it accelerated into something worse yet again, she pleaded for some reasoning. "Most men look at me that way, Quinton. I'm your Barbie, remember?"

Quinton looked away and stared at the red light.

Another moment passed as Melissa touched her face, and then she slowly stretched out her hand and touched his. "And you're my Ken. Did you not see how all the women were gawking at you tonight? Right in front of me!"

The light turned green. Quinton placed both hands on the wheel and accelerated. "Let's just get home. I'm tired, and it's been a long day."

Melissa turned her head away and looked out her window. *I just gave up my job for this? What the hell am I doing?*

As if hearing her thoughts, Quinton reached over and touched her hand that was resting on her tan silk skirt. Melissa looked down at his hand and then slowly placed hers on top, but not another word was spoken all the way home.

After pulling his sports car into the secure garage, he shut off the engine and lowered the door. Melissa quickly opened her car door but he reached out and closed it back. Pulling away from him, she forcefully opened the door once more and got out. "I'm not going to talk about this in the car."

Since she was closest to the door, she opened it and immediately walked quickly through the kitchen, to the stairs that led to their bedroom. Just as she stepped up the first stair, Quinton picked her up from behind in his strong arms and carried her up the stairs, into their bedroom.

Melissa struggled for him to put her down, but her cries fell on deaf ears. Soon they were in the bedroom, and he threw her down on the bed and started ripping his clothes off. It was not until that very moment Melissa realized he had other intentions instead of using his fist. Suddenly he was on top of her, ripping her fine silk skirt to shreds. Melissa opened her mouth to protest, but was immediately flipped over. With one hand, he ripped off her underwear and with the other lifted her thighs into the air. Instantly Melissa saw stars as her upper body was thrust into the firm mattress.

The next morning, Quinton left at six o'clock for a breakfast meeting downtown. Melissa took the opportunity to sleep in another hour before the movers arrived at eight. At seven o'clock, her alarm sounded, and she reached over and slapped the large snooze button. Before she fell back asleep, the doorbell rang, and Melissa's eyes shot wide open.

"Oh please, not the moving company yet?"

For hours, she had tossed and turned last night on what to do. Should she stay in Jackson and get her old job back? Her heart told her to divorce Quinton, and her mind assured her she was financially sound on her own to make it without his lucrative salary.

Just as the decision was made to leave him, shame immediately washed over her at the negative connotation of a divorce. How could she explain to her Nana and Papa that she was leaving her marriage? They wouldn't understand. They would think she was a quitter. What if she revealed that Quinton had sometimes pushed her around? Would they believe her? If news got out of any type of physical abuse, she would be mortified. Abuse only happened to weak, insecure women, not strong, self-confident executives.

With all the thoughts flashing through her mind, she realized she would have to move from Jackson. It would be too shameful to stay. But where would she go? Then, over the next hour, somehow she had convinced herself that she had gotten too close to her boss, and yes, he had every right to be angry with her for hugging him tenderly for all to see. She cried as she recounted with shame all the lunches they had shared together discussing private, intimate details about his marriage. Was this a true sign that she was unfaithful in a different way other than sexually? Finally, she had given in to sleep as it tugged at her brain without ever making a clear decision about her future.

Pulling the covers off her body, she got up and quickly pulled on her pink cotton housecoat to hide the bruises on her arms. By the time she was within three feet of the front door, the doorbell sounded again.

"I'm coming!"

Unlocking the dead bolt, Melissa swung the door open, only to find her best friend, Alison, standing there holding a brown bag and coffees with a smile upon her face.

"Good morning, sleepyhead! I came to help you."

Melissa stepped to the side and motioned for her to enter. "But you have work today."

"I took off."

"You're the best! I couldn't have a better friend!"

Alison said, "Oh, don't get mushy on me yet. This is hard enough as it is."

"Don't be silly. I'm not moving across the country. It will only be about a four-hour drive, and besides, we now can have girl weekends because of the distance."

Alison tilted her head and said, "Somehow I don't see Quinton allowing you to leave for a weekend without him."

"What? You're being ridiculous!"

"Really? Since announcing your engagement, you haven't been on any trips with me."

Melissa grabbed the coffee and started walking toward the kitchen and said over her shoulder, "Well, he thinks you are going to corrupt me since you're still single."

"Exactly! And you think that will change now?"

Melissa sat down and then opened the brown bag and removed two blueberry muffins. "We will use napkins. My dishes are all clean, ready for the packers."

Alison pulled out the other chair and took a seat and asked, "How did last night go?"

It all came flooding back too quickly, and Melissa's head began to spin, to the point she felt dizzy and light-headed.

"Hey, you okay?"

Melissa forced herself to take a bite and concentrated on breathing. Finally, the only words she was able to speak were, "It was tough. I—"

Alison interrupted and said tenderly, "You will be fine, and you will quickly find another job. You'll see. You are Melissa Brock Mason. Everything you do is perfect. You are perfect!"

Melissa smiled back at her childhood friend and said, "I-I don't know what to do. Quinton is—"

The doorbell rang again, and Alison jumped up. "Go get dressed. I will get them started."

Melissa reached out and stopped her and then hugged her tightly. Alison hugged her back tenderly as the doorbell sounded again. Pulling away, Alison touched her face and said with confidence, "Everything is going to be fine, you'll see."

Melissa allowed her to leave without another word spoken about last night. Slowly she left the kitchen to get dressed. She felt so sore and tired as she climbed the stairs. Rounding the corner of her bedroom, Melissa felt nauseous and immediately placed a hand over her mouth and ran toward the toilet and vomited. For the next five minutes, she was violently sick and dry heaving. Ten more minutes passed as Melissa laid her head down on the cool tile floor. Soon Alison was calling her name, and she found it difficult to sit back up.

Melissa saw her friend round the corner with a look of shock on her face. "Melissa? What is wrong?"

"I...I don't know. I just got sick, and now I feel light-headed and weak."

Alison crouched down and placed a hand on her forehead and said, "You don't have a fever. Here, let me help you up."

Melissa was carefully pulled up by her friend and then led toward her king-size bed. "Here, sit. I'm going to get a cold washcloth."

Alison returned holding the damp cloth and then sat on the edge of her bed and began to wipe Melissa's forehead and face. "Don't move, just rest until the dizziness passes." Alison then offered, "I'll call Quinton."

Melissa rose up quickly. "No! He has an important breakfast meeting."

She replied, "How important can it be? You're moving out tomorrow!"

Sitting up in bed, Melissa said, "I know. But it is, just don't call."

Alison agreed and then asked, "What do you want me to do?"

Melissa closed her eyes and lay back down and said quietly, "Go to the pharmacy and buy me a pregnancy test."

"What? You think you're pregnant!"

Opening her eyes up, she said, "Just go. There is no point in wasting time talking about it."

Alison got up and said, "Okay. I'll tell the movers I'll be right back and not to disturb you."

When Alison reached the doorway, Melissa called out, "Buy two just to be on the safe side, different brands."

Alison smiled and then turned around and left.

Melissa closed her eyes and drifted back to sleep. Thirty minutes later, Alison walked in and gently nudged her friend. "Sorry to wake you, but I'm back."

Melissa slowly got up from the bed and looked at the bag in Alison's outstretched hand. Taking the bag, she walked into the bathroom and shut the door as Alison took a seat on the bed and patiently waited.

Ten minutes passed before Melissa walked out of the bathroom holding two plastic sticks. Alison jumped up and ran toward her, saying, "And? What do they say?"

Melissa looked into Alison's green eyes and said, "I'm oh for two."

"What? What does that mean?"

Melissa held them up for her friend to read. "I'm pregnant!"

Alison jumped up and down and then hugged Melissa. "Oh, Melissa, it's going to be wonderful. Don't worry, you will see. Sometimes our well-thought-out plans are just not meant to be."

Melissa pulled away. "Remember that country song? If you want to hear God laugh, tell him your plans." Melissa walked back into the bathroom and discarded the sticks in the paper bag and said, "Go throw these away. I don't want them lying around."

Alison narrowed her eyes. "You're not thinking of keeping this from Quinton, are you?"

"Of course not, it's just the timing is all wrong. Too much going on today. I'll wait and tell him after we get to Birmingham. Plus, I want to be able to see a doctor first to confirm."

Alison said, "You know the sooner the better. He would wonder why you kept this from him."

"Just throw them away, please. I'll think about this tomorrow, but for now, I feel better. That nap must have helped."

"Fine. I will respect your wishes, but don't be lifting anything heavy today, or I will scream at you."

Melissa walked over and hugged her best friend. "It will be all right. You are always right, so why would you be wrong about this?"

"Exactly." Alison patted Melissa's flat belly, and both girls began to giggle as they noticed a man from the moving company walk by and look at them funny.

The day went by fast as Melissa pointed and watched as the five men packed up all her belongings that she had accumulated over the last year and a half. All her artwork was carefully wrapped and labeled and set aside for them to build a couple of crates to store them in. Melissa thought, *Thank goodness the truck is going straight to Birmingham tonight and they will unload tomorrow.*

Six o'clock finally came, and Quinton pulled into the driveway in his BMW. He got out of the car, locked up, and walked into his empty 4,300-square-foot house and found Melissa sitting on the living room floor beside two pieces of luggage.

Quinton walked toward her and said, "Hi, babe. How did it go?"

Melissa looked up with tired eyes and didn't stand to greet him. "Good. All is done. I was just waiting on you."

Quinton knelt down beside her and said in a gentle voice, "You look tired. Did you let them do all the work, or did you help?"

Melissa closed her eyes. "Yes. They did all the work."

"Good, because that is what we were paying them for."

Melissa leaned forward and got to her knees, and then quickly Quinton sprung up and helped her stand. "Thanks."

He asked, "Are we still planning on driving halfway tonight?"

Melissa shrugged her shoulders. "That's fine. They hooked up my M-Class, remember? I don't have to drive, just ride."

Quinton watched as she pulled up the luggage bar and began to move forward, rolling the pink-and-black bag behind her. "Wait! Let me get that."

Melissa turned to face him. "I got sick this morning after Alison brought me breakfast."

"What? Why didn't you call me?"

Placing a hand on her hip, she said, "You told me last night to not disturb you, something about a very important business meeting."

"Yes, well, you were sick. You should have called."

Glancing away toward the empty house, she continued, "Anyway, I sent her to the pharmacy for me."

"What did you take?"

"Two pregnancy tests. I failed both. I'm pregnant!"

Quinton stood there in the empty living room and looked at his beautiful blue-eyed blonde wife and broke out into a big grin. He walked over in two large steps, picked up Melissa, and spun her around before gently placing her back down and shouting, "Thank you, God!"

Chapter 10

Melissa was running around the house and inspecting all her Christmas lights and decorations while the catering company was still bringing food in and setting up. Quinton rounded the corner wearing his suit and Christmas tie, looking handsome as ever. Melissa took one look at him and smiled.

Quinton made his way over to his wife and touched her bare shoulder and said, "You look beautiful. You don't even look pregnant in that dress."

For weeks, she and Quinton had searched for the perfect dress for her ever-changing body. Melissa slowly turned toward the large hanging mirror in the hallway and stared at the woman looking back at her. Her floor-length red satin dress was strapless and had an Empire waist that perfectly minimized her condition. Her long blonde hair was worn down with small curls hanging around her face. Her arms looked good, without an ounce of fat, thanks to the local gym. Truly, the only things that gave a hint to her condition were her round stomach and her chest increasing to a double D. It was still the one feature that caught most people's attention when they glanced her way.

Turning back toward Quinton, she said, "Thank you. Hard to believe we only have a little over two months to go."

Quinton placed his large hands on her stomach and said, "I can't wait. I'm so happy, Melissa."

She looked up into his big brown eyes and saw love. Ever since moving to Birmingham, Quinton had been so affectionate and gentle with her. Never once had he laid another hand on her. She thought, *This move has been good for our marriage*, and she was genuinely happy when she leaned toward his mouth and kissed him.

Quinton kissed back and then leaned away and said, "What is the final count for the party?"

Melissa took a deep breath. "One hundred and sixteen."

Since moving to Birmingham, Melissa had jumped right into the thriving social circles when she joined the Junior League, the country club, and the local gym. In three short months, Melissa was voted in president of the Junior League with her financial background, and had taken up golf at the local country club. The golf and the country club were Quinton's idea. It was extremely pricey just to join, and then another fifteen hundred a month. Which didn't include golf carts!

On weekends, Melissa and Quinton would play golf with various couples and have lunch. Two more nights a week were spent there having dinner with clients and other members. It didn't take long for Melissa to feel at home, and she soon had five really close girlfriends. All of them already had children, and the fact that Melissa was about to have her first child made her even more appealing to the other women.

The doorbell rang, and Quinton held out his hand and said, "Shall we, Mrs. Pierson?"

Melissa looked at her dashing husband and smiled, showing her perfect white teeth. Taking his hand, they walked toward the oak double front doors right as a gentleman employed for the night opened the door to their first guest.

Melissa said, "Julie, Mark, Merry Christmas, please come in."

The guests seemed to keep coming over the next hour, and by eight thirty, there were over one hundred people standing around drinking wine, eating bites of appetizers, and sharing stories. For the most part,

Melissa was pleased and enjoyed herself during the party. So far, her only complaint had been her aching feet and lower back.

Quinton walked up to her and placed his long arms around her. "How do you feel, my love?"

Melissa looked up and met his eyes. "Just fine, a little tired, but all is good."

Quinton said, "You should have taken that nap today like I suggested."

Melissa thought to herself, *Like that was going to happen with the nonstop of the catering company setting up all day.* Instead she replied, "I know, you're right."

Meredith Jenkins rounded the corner and interrupted. "Melissa, you must come explain this piece of art. No one gets it."

Walking toward her, she smiled. "I know exactly which one you are talking about. That is why I bought it."

Quinton stepped away with his glass of wine, toward the direction of a couple of men, as Melissa followed Meredith over toward the foyer. When Melissa was leaving the living room, she saw Rebecca standing in the corner with a smile on her face and looking across the room, watching someone intently. She turned to see who she was looking at and found her husband staring back at Rebecca. The two didn't see her watching, and she quickly turned away from them and shrugged her shoulders. It wouldn't be the first time Quinton had caught the eye of a beautiful woman.

"Melissa, are you coming?"

"Yes." She left the room in search of her guest inquiring about her painting.

Rebecca stood five-eight with green eyes and long brown hair. Tonight she was wearing a long white gown that had a plunging neckline down to her stomach. The satin halter style dress was attached at the back of her neck with two long strings that hung over her bare back. The dress reached the floor, but had a side slit to her midthigh. She had caught a lot of attention tonight from many of the men, as well as women. Rebecca seemed to look good on any day, whether all dolled up for a party or wearing old jeans, going to the supermarket with her hair pulled back.

Despite her warm, friendly nature, many women stayed at arm's length due to jealousy. Not Melissa. Melissa embraced her right away, and the two of them had become really good friends. Mitch, Rebecca's husband, played golf a lot with Quinton, and they had become close friends as well. Countless nights had been spent at each other's house, just five doors down, since September.

Mitch and Rebecca had one child, a daughter, age two. Tonight she was with the local neighborhood babysitter and, in Melissa's mind, in good hands. She had already inquired about her several weeks ago to use when her own baby boy would finally arrive.

Melissa answered some questions about the artwork and soon found herself all alone. Taking advantage of the opportunity, she slipped away and headed toward her master bedroom to use the restroom. Opening her bedroom door, Melissa stopped dead in her tracks when she spotted Rebecca sitting on her bed, smiling back at her.

"Rebecca?"

Rebecca stood up and walked toward her friend with a phone clutched in her hands. "Sorry, I just needed somewhere quiet to call and check on Remi."

Melissa looked down at the phone and smiled. "Of course, please don't apologize. I just came in to use the bathroom. I won't be long."

Rebecca watched as Melissa walked away and entered the master bath and then closed the door behind her. Melissa used the facilities and then touched up her lips with her signature red shade before finally opening the bathroom door just in time to see the master bedroom door open with Quinton walking in.

Quinton looked over at Rebecca, and then toward Melissa. "What are you girls up to?" With a boyish grin, he asked, "Avoiding the party?"

Melissa thought all of this odd, all three in the bedroom at the same time, but quickly dismissed it and walked over to her husband and said, "Absolutely not. It is going really good." She turned toward Rebecca. "Do you think so?"

Rebecca stepped toward the bedroom door and said, "It is perfect. Just like we both knew it would be. Now, we better all get back out there before we are missed."

Quinton gestured for Rebecca to leave first and then took Melissa by the arm and followed out.

The Christmas party was a hit and would be the one social event people talked about for the next several weeks to come. Quinton had already announced that it was the first of many, and Melissa just stood by his side and smiled. Later that night, when the final wineglasses were washed and the catering company was packing the last crate, Melissa took off her shoes and slumped down on a barstool.

A young lady wearing a black-and-white uniform, with the name tag "Paige," appeared by her side and handed her a glass of water. "You look tired, Mrs. Pierson. Why don't you go on to bed? We are almost done here."

Melissa looked around for her husband, but didn't see him. Instead she saw her housekeeper, Constantine, sweeping and remembered she was going to stay the night. Realizing she was tired, too tired, she nodded her head. "Thanks, Paige, Constantine can see you out. Good night."

Melissa carefully stepped down from the stool and then grabbed her shoes and left the kitchen. Walking down the hallway that led to their bedroom, she stopped at the door to Quinton's study to see what he was possibly working on at eleven forty-five at night. Slowing down, she popped her head inside the door and saw that Quinton was seated in his leather chair, talking on the phone with his back toward her.

Melissa was about to interrupt, but stopped when she heard the tone of his voice and decided against it. *He sounds angry. Who could he possibly be talking to this late?*

Melissa turned away and continued on to their bedroom. *It can wait till tomorrow, and I'll ask then.*

Quinton turned around in his chair just in time to see Melissa's hand slide off the doorframe and away. Quickly he ended his call and then hung up the phone. He left the study and entered the bedroom just as Melissa's dress hit the floor. He watched as she stepped out of it and bent over to retrieve it.

Melissa didn't look pregnant from behind because she had faithfully kept going to the gym all through her pregnancy and had even taken up yoga. Quinton shut the door behind him and then smiled as Melissa turned around startled.

"Quinton, don't do that! You're going to scare me into labor" she said as she walked over toward a chair and draped her satin dress across it.

He laughed aloud. "I'm sorry, it's just you scare so easy."

Walking toward her, he bent his head down for a kiss and then wrapped his arms around her. He knew she was tired, but she had never denied him. Kicking his shoes off as he went, he led her over to the bed and then climbed in.

Chapter 11

Dillon Robert Pierson was born at 2:25 a.m. early on a Friday morning, February 22. The birth had gone smoothly, and now Melissa was holding her firstborn for the first time. She felt joy and completeness all at the same time. Dillon's skin was soft to the touch, and he had her blue eyes and blond hair. He truly was a beautiful baby as he rested snug as a bug in her arms.

Quinton stood by her side, snapping pictures, and then handed the camera to the nurse and said, "Take one of all of us, please."

Melissa watched as Quinton came around the side of the bed and carefully sat down on the edge beside her with a big smile upon his face. A few pictures were taken, and then he got back up and said, "Thank you very much!"

Nurse Kathy said, "My pleasure. I will give you three a few moments, and then I'll be back to check on you."

Melissa watched as she left and closed the door behind her. It was now three o'clock, and all her close friends who had been waiting in the waiting room had finally gone home with the promise to visit tomorrow afternoon.

Quinton touched her cheek softly with his hand and asked, "How are you doing? Are you in pain?"

Melissa looked in Dillon's face and replied, "I only feel bliss right now."

"I know what you mean. Who would have thought a year ago we would have our first child and be happily living in another state?"

She met his brown eyes. "Yes, a lot can happen in one year." Then she smiled.

Several minutes passed as they talked and cuddled their little boy. Soon the nurse came back in and suggested, "It is probably best now if I take him and let you get some rest. You've been up a long time."

Melissa thought about how she and Quinton had set the alarm for 4:35 on Thursday morning to go to the hospital. Melissa was four days late, and the doctor had decided to induce her due to Dillon' projected weight of eight pounds. Now, almost twenty-three hours later, she was beyond tired, so she nodded in agreement.

Quinton offered, "Why don't we let him sleep in here in case he wakes up and needs to eat?"

The nurse looked at Quinton and said, "Your wife needs some deep sleep. Remember, she goes home with him, and none of us to help her."

Quinton frowned, but agreed. "Okay, but come get me if he wakes up."

The nurse smiled and continued forward with outstretched hands. "We can do that."

Melissa leaned down and kissed Dillon on his head and then allowed the nurse to pick him up and carry him away. Quinton held the door open and then continued to watch as she held him and walked down the hall.

"Come here, Quinton, you are making her nervous."

Quinton stepped back into the room and then closed the door with a sheepish grin. "Sorry. I'll just take this chair over here, and you get some rest."

Melissa hit the recline button and then fluffed her pillow and closed her eyes. Within a matter of a few short minutes, she fell asleep. When Quinton was assured she was asleep soundly, he carefully eased out of his chair and quietly opened the door and left.

Thirty minutes later, Quinton pulled into his driveway and hit the button for the garage door to open. There, standing in the garage, was Rebecca patiently waiting on him to arrive. Quinton immediately looked into his rearview mirror and then pulled forward beside Melissa's M-Class and pressed the garage button again.

Angrily, Quinton got out of his new Mercedes sports car, slammed the door, and growled, "What are you doing here? Someone could have seen you!"

Rebecca walked forward and placed her hands on his chest, then began to quickly unbutton his designer shirt. Quinton placed his hands on hers and thought to himself, *Just once more, and then it ends, tonight.*

Melissa woke up at nine the next morning when a new nurse walked in with Dillon. She stated, "Good morning, someone misses you and is hungry."

Melissa sat up and stretched out her arms for her precious newborn.

Walking toward Melissa, she continued, "I'm Mary Katherine and will be on duty till three." The nurse motioned over toward Quinton, who was lying back in a recliner. "Looks like he needed his sleep as well."

Melissa asked, "No one came and got him last night?"

The nurse shook her head. Dillon let out a squeal, and Quinton shot up from the recliner as if a gunshot had sounded. Mary Katherine laughed, "It's amazing how little tiny things can be so loud."

Quinton got to his feet, walked over, and leaned against the bed. He touched Dillon on the forehead. "How did he do last night?"

Mary Katherine stated, "Very well. Slept a lot."

Melissa caressed his cheek as he fed from her breast, and smiled. Moments seemed to stand still as all were mesmerized by this special moment. Mary Katherine finally interrupted when she spoke softly. "You have some visitors this morning. What would you like me to tell them?"

Melissa opened her mouth to speak, but stopped when Quinton replied, "Tell them I'll be out shortly."

Mary Katherine said, "All right, I will leave you three. Just call if you need anything."

Melissa watched as she left and closed the door behind her quietly. Turning toward her husband, she said, "I don't think Nana would be here so soon. It was so late last night when she and Papa left."

"No. I think you're right. It is probably some of our friends."

"Quinton, I really wish you could talk Nana into staying with us. I don't understand why she insisted on going to a hotel last night."

Quinton smirked, "Like I can talk Virginia Leigh into anything. But, for you, I will ask again."

Melissa took a closer look at Quinton. He looked tired with dark circles under his eyes. Looking at his shirt, she noticed it was missing a button. "Did I do that?"

Quinton looked confused as Melissa pointed a finger at his chest.

Then she added, "Oh my God, you have bruises on your arms! I'm sorry, I didn't realize I was squeezing you that hard."

Quinton looked at his arms and noticed some small blue spots from Rebecca's fingers when she had panicked and grabbed him last night. Next, he noticed his shirt was missing the second button as a flash of memory went through his mind of Rebecca removing his shirt too quickly and tossing it to the ground as she pushed him back onto his sports car and got down on her knees.

Pushing all the thoughts away, the good with the bad, Quinton forced a smile and then walked away toward the bathroom to see if there were any other war wounds. Satisfied nothing else was noticeable, he walked back into the room and simply replied, "All is fair in love and childbirth!"

Melissa looked up from Dillon to face Quinton. "I guess, but sorry. I don't even remember—"

Quinton interrupted. "Stop. Don't apologize, it's okay. Remember everything we read? All the pain and discomfort goes away once the baby is born."

"Well, not exactly, I'm still pretty darn sore, and you've got some nice reminders on your arm."

Quinton was thinking about a way to change the subject when she announced, "I think he is done. Why don't you go on out and see who it is?"

"You don't want to freshen up first?"

Melissa pondered his question and finally said, "Okay, hold Dillon, and I'll just go see what repairs I can make."

Quinton took Dillon into his arms and watched her intently as she eased out of bed slowly. Making her way into the bathroom, she took one look in the mirror and immediately was thankful Quinton had made the suggestion. Ten minutes passed, and Melissa opened up the door to see her husband and son rocking in the recliner. A smile spread across her face, and she thought, *He looks so happy. I wonder what kind of father he is going to make.*

Quinton broke up her thoughts when he said, "Melissa, you're glowing!"

Smiling, she stepped carefully and got back into bed wearing her designer gown and robe. With her long blonde hair brushed out, and a fresh coat of lipstick, she did look like a woman who was blissfully happy.

Quinton stood up and walked over and carefully placed their sleeping infant in her waiting arms. "I'll go see who is here."

"We'll be right here."

Quinton smiled and left the room, then walked down the hallway that led to the visitor area. There, around the groups of people, stood their next-door neighbors, Butch and Darlene. Making his way over, he said, "Good morning, guys. We are so glad you could stop by."

"Congratulations, Daddy! I can't wait to see him!" replied Darlene.

Butch added, "You're a lucky man, Quinton."

Darlene nudged Butch and slightly frowned. Quinton, the keen lawyer, quickly picked up on it and asked his good neighbors, "What's up?"

Darlene shook her head and reached out for Butch's hand.

Quinton continued to observe their body language and asked, "Butch?"

With a heavy sigh, Butch stated, "It appears there has been a horrible accident in the neighborhood."

Quinton narrowed his eyes and asked, "Accident?"

Darlene spoke in a cracked voice, "Rebecca Dunning, she...she's dead."

Quinton's brown eyes softened as a frown spread across his face. In a sincere voice, he asked, "How?"

Butch answered him. "She was found dead this morning in her garage." Then he leaned closer and whispered quietly, "It appears suicide."

In a shocked voice, Quinton asked, "Are you sure?"

Darlene nodded, and Butch said, "That is what the authorities are saying. Poor Mitch, he is so broken up. He is beside himself with grief."

Darlene added, "I don't believe it, though. She was too self-confident and happy. No way she could have done that to herself and left Remi. She adored that child!"

Butch replied, "Darlene! Don't say that. The last thing Mitch needs to hear is idle gossip."

Quinton turned toward Darlene and touched her arm in a caring gesture. "Butch is right. Mitch needs our support right now." Removing his hands, he then lifted them to his face and then through his sandy brown hair and thought, for the first time, out loud, "How the hell am I gonna break this to Melissa?"

Chapter 12

Three days later, Quinton was driving Melissa's M-Class through their neighborhood with Melissa and Dillon riding in the backseat. Dillon had been carefully strapped into his car seat, and Melissa had refused to ride anywhere else except right beside him.

"What if he starts crying?" she explained.

They had driven straight from the hospital after the two were released, and both of the happy couple were on pins and needles as they drove their little bundle of joy in an automobile for the first time.

Quinton commented, "I can't believe how fast people fly through this neighborhood!"

Melissa thought back to her husband rushing out some mornings a little behind schedule and smiled. As they continued on, she was deeply saddened when she spotted Mitch and Rebecca's house. The funeral had been held this morning, and there were several cars parked along the street up and down from their house.

In a somber voice, she asked Quinton, "You never said anything about the funeral this morning. How was it?"

Melissa continued to stare at the people gathered around the front porch. Finally he said, "Awful. That is why I didn't want to bring it up."

Reaching the edge of their driveway, Melissa spoke. "I would like to see Mitch and Remi. Maybe I can go over there after I feed Dillon and get him settled in his bassinet.

Quinton didn't respond as he pulled into their driveway, moving past Virginia Leigh's white town car. As soon as the garage door was fully extended, Nana and Papa opened the door that led to the garage and walked out with big smiles on their faces.

Quinton suggested, "Let's just see how things go here. You might have to wait till tomorrow."

"Maybe. I don't know, it's just so heartbreaking."

Quinton turned off the ignition and then stepped out and greeted the happy great-grandparents. He helped Melissa step down and then leaned in and unhooked the car seat from the base and carefully carried his little man into the house.

"Wow, something smells amazing!" exclaimed Melissa.

Virginia Leigh replied, "I've got a homemade chicken casserole in the oven. It will be ready in about twenty minutes."

Quinton looked over at Melissa and raised his eyebrows. Melissa thought, *He is right. Mitch and Remi would have to wait till tomorrow.*

Tuesday morning, Melissa and Quinton were wide awake at 3:00 a.m. for Dillon's feeding. All three were cuddled together in their king-size bed as Melissa caressed Dillon's cheek with her free hand. After much thought, she said, "Quinton?"

"Hmm?"

"I don't understand why Rebecca committed suicide. Why would she do that?"

"I don't know. Maybe she suffered from depression and was never treated for it."

Melissa looked over at Quinton with a blank stare. "What? I can't remember one event over the last year where Rebecca was unhappy or depressed about anything."

"Yeah, but, you weren't around her every day. She must have hid it pretty good."

Melissa shook her head. "Not every day, but we saw each other at least three to four times a week. And, think of all the nights we grilled out between their home and ours. No, this does not make sense."

"Melissa, we will probably never know the truth."

Silence followed as she thought about his response.

Finally, she sighed, "You are probably right, but in the garage? I mean, surely she must have thought Remi could accidentally find her."

"No, Mitch was always the first to get up every morning. He would have looked for her and then opened the garage to see if her car was still there."

"God, that is probably how it happened. Poor man. How is he going to move on from this?" Shaking her head side to side, she continued, "He worshipped the ground she walked on."

Quinton didn't respond, and Melissa stopped all chatter about the horrific event. Picking up Dillon, she leaned his head up against her shoulder, and immediately a loud burp sounded. Smiling, she said, "Someone is happy. I think you can put him back in his bassinet now."

Quinton lifted Dillon up and kissed his forehead and then carefully got out of bed and laid him in his little bed that was two feet away from their bed. After a little pat on the bottom, he climbed back in bed and lay down, thankful Melissa had done the same with no more questions about Rebecca.

Later on at eight o'clock, breakfast was served by Virginia Leigh, and all four of them were sitting around a large wooden table as Papa said grace.

"This looks wonderful, Nana, thank you very much."

Virginia Leigh smiled back and said, "You are welcome. And I agree with you, it was much easier staying here last night. Thank you for having us."

Quinton said, "Anytime, you know both of you are welcome in our home. Now that we switched our master bedroom upstairs by Dillon's room, you don't have to climb those stairs anymore."

Melissa thought how this was Nana's second visit to their house since they moved. The last time she came, it was in October, and she stayed only two nights. Melissa had been the one to do most of the traveling back to Jackson from Birmingham. She didn't mind, though. Papa and Nana were in their midseventies now and didn't travel by car a lot. When they did fly, it was far away, for some vacation at one of their time-shares.

As homemade biscuits, grits, and eggs were devoured by all, Dillon never woke up and slept peacefully in their bedroom. Melissa had placed the baby monitor right beside her so all would hear as soon as her little man woke up.

Feeling a little less sore, Melissa insisted on helping Nana in the kitchen. After some squabbling, she got her way. Nana wasn't the only one hardheaded in this family. It was a little after nine o'clock when Melissa dried the last plate and the doorbell sounded.

"Little early for company, especially since it's your first morning home."

Melissa walked past Nana, and an image of Mitch holding Remi passed through her mind. "I'll go get it. Quinton has already left, and Papa is on the back porch reading the paper."

Reaching the hallway, Melissa could make out a tall man in his forties, wearing a suit with a gold badge displayed on the pocket of his jacket, standing to the side of the double doors through the tall glass window.

Dressed in a casual sundress that had an Empire waist, Melissa ran a hand through her long blonde hair and then patted down her dress. Hesitating only briefly, she unlocked the door and slowly opened it.

"Hello, can I help you?"

Detective Craig was patiently waiting on the other side for the door to be opened. "Yes. My name is Detective Walter Craig." He extended his hand toward her.

Melissa looked at his outstretched hand and then quickly shook it as he continued, "I wanted to ask you some questions about Rebecca Dunning. May I come in?"

Melissa twisted her lips and contemplated what he had said. Finally she opened the door wider and stepped to the side. "Yes, please, come on in."

Virginia Leigh was standing behind her and asked curiously, "What is going on, Officer?"

Melissa didn't give him an opportunity to respond. "Nana, the detective is here because of Rebecca. She was a dear friend and neighbor."

Virginia Leigh frowned. "Well, go on into the living room and get off your feet." Looking over at the detective, she continued, "She was just released yesterday from the hospital and has a newborn upstairs sleeping."

Melissa couldn't help but smile. "I will, Nana. Can we get you some coffee, Detective Craig?"

"If it would be no trouble, that would be lovely, thank you."

Without saying another word, Virginia Leigh left in the direction of the kitchen, and Melissa motioned for him to follow her into the formal living room, where they rarely entertained.

Melissa took a seat across from the detective and watched as he looked around her home inspecting his surroundings. Relieved her house was clean and well presented; she waited for him to reveal the true reason for his visit. "Mrs. Pierson, I'm really sorry about your friend."

Melissa started to speak, but couldn't get the words out, so she just nodded.

"I will get to the point. I'm investigating her death and interviewing all her neighbors and friends."

Melissa quietly said, "I was both. Rebecca and I became good friends a month after we moved here. I don't know how I'm going to be able to look at Remi and Mitch again without breaking down to cry."

Just then, tears began to flow down Melissa's face. With everything going on in her life, she really hadn't allowed herself to properly grieve. She had missed everything, the funeral visitation of her body and her graveside burial. She didn't get to say her good-byes. Now, it was as if it was all just a bad dream and she just needed to wake up.

Virginia Leigh entered with a tray of coffee and set it down gently on the small coffee table in front of Melissa. Standing back up, Nana placed a hand over her heart and said, "Oh, Melissa dear, let me get you some tissue," and she was off again.

Walter Craig said, "I'm sorry, and I know this is difficult..." He paused when Nana reentered the room once again, this time with a box of tissues.

"Thank you, Nana. I will be fine. Go and keep Papa company. This won't take long."

Virginia Leigh gave the detective a hard look and then left the room.

He continued, "I would like for you to think about the last time you saw Rebecca. Was there any hint to a troubled mind, or did she give you any impression that life had become so unbearable?"

Melissa silently thought about eating at Mitch and Rebecca's house on Sunday afternoon. Rebecca had insisted on cooking and all of them staying home instead of going to the usual Sunday meal at the club. After all, Melissa was technically due on Monday, the following day.

Rebecca had prepared a special vegetable soup and baked a new bread recipe. The meal was delicious, and everything was perfect and normal. The usual talk about politics, the weather, Melissa's unborn baby, and golf was shared among the four, and lots of laughter and smiles were shared as well. It was a beautiful afternoon amongst friends without a care in the world, except for the fact that Melissa was about to give birth.

Finally she answered, "I didn't see any signs. And I don't get it. I mean, could I've been so caught up in my own pregnancy to have missed something?" She asked herself more than answering the detective's question.

More thoughts of Rebecca holding on to her adorable daughter and running around playing hide-and-seek in the backyard with everyone watching and cheering them on filled her mind. "She loved her little girl so much, I...she..." Meeting the detective's eyes, she continued, "She couldn't have ended her own life. She would have never left her daughter willingly. This is all wrong."

Detective Craig placed his coffee back down on the table and said, "You think she was murdered?"

Melissa opened her mouth to respond, but quickly closed it when she heard Quinton's voice from behind her. "Melissa? Everything okay in here?"

Startled that Quinton was still home, she spun around.

The detective stood up and walked over to Quinton and quickly introduced himself. Quinton was short with words as the detective took his seat once more. "Your wife was just explaining to me that—"

A piercing scream sounded from the baby monitor on Melissa's lap, and she instantly jumped up. "I'm sorry. Quinton, you stay and I'll be back down shortly."

Virginia Leigh rounded the corner as well, and both ladies climbed the stairs as Quinton reached down and turned off the baby monitor and took a seat in Melissa's now-empty chair.

Quinton leaned back in the tall upright chair and spoke in a professional voice. "How may I help you, Detective?"

Walter Craig asked, "Were you at home Thursday night when Rebecca died?"

Quinton shook his head and said, "My wife and I left before five a.m. on Thursday morning, and she didn't give birth until two in the morning on Friday. I didn't return home until late Friday evening."

"I see. What about houseguests? Was anyone here Thursday night?"

"No. Melissa's grandparents stayed at a hotel. They only arrived here yesterday afternoon."

"What can you tell me about Rebecca's state of mind? Do you remember seeing her unhappy over the last few weeks?"

Quinton had no idea what Melissa had already shared with the man, so he treaded carefully. "I don't remember seeing Rebecca sad or angry. Mitch and I are good friends, and we play golf a lot. He never divulged anything that gave me the impression that his wife was unhappy. I'm sorry, I'm at a complete loss, as well as my wife, why this happened."

Nodding his head, Walter stated, "You are not the first couple to give me these answers, and I'm going to keep the investigation open for a little while longer and see if I can shed some light on her death."

Quinton stood up. "I see. Well, if there is anything Melissa and I can do to help, please don't hesitate to contact us. We are both very saddened by this news. Now, if you will excuse me, I'm going to go and check on our son."

Walter Craig extended his hand and said, "No, not at all. I will be back in touch later."

Quinton quickly escorted him to the front door and once again exchanged good-byes and then closed the door. As he reached the staircase, he felt his heart pounding madly and hoped like hell the detective hadn't noticed.

Chapter 13

Quinton was standing in front of his floor-length window, staring at the downtown Birmingham skyline, pondering the course his life had taken over the last couple of months. He and Melissa had been finally on the right track, a baby on the way, Melissa behaving like a dutiful wife, and then Rebecca entered their life. At first, it was just some innocent flirting. *Why did Mitch want to share his wife so much? I mean, suggesting we switch partners in golf and pairing her up with me in cards.*

No, he thought, *this is just as much your fault, Mitch, as mine. I would never make those suggestions about Melissa.* Immediately he thought back to the Christmas party and Rebecca's white dress. It was so hot and revealing. Every man in the room was wet and hard with desire. Surely Mitch should have seen what was coming when his wife chose such a daring and sexy dress? Who did he think she was wearing it for, because it sure wasn't for her husband.

Rebecca was a mistake, no doubt about it, but no one would ever believe him. Turning around, he gazed over his large office with expensive furniture and thought it was time to move on. An entire month had gone by since Rebecca's death, and Mitch had finally confirmed his suspicion yesterday, while out on the golf course, that Detective Walter Craig had finally closed Rebecca's case. The news was uplifting, and Quinton had his best game of golf since moving here last July.

Quinton turned around and looked at the clock. Walking over to his desk he stopped and pressed a button and said to his secretary, "Irene, you can send in my next appointment now."

"Yes, sir, right away."

Quinton continued standing and waited till the door opened. It didn't take long, and Irene opened up his door and announced, "Mr. Pierson, this is Ms. Mallory Jane Hawthorne." She stepped to the side, and a lovely, stylish five-seven blonde walked inside his office and smiled.

"Thank you, Irene. Ms. Hawthorne, it's nice to finally meet you. Please come in and take a seat."

Mallory Jane smiled and walked over in a beige silk dress and shook his hand. "It's nice to meet you as well. Melissa has told me so much I feel like I already know you."

Quinton smiled into her green eyes and was completely smitten. Mallory Jane went ahead and took the offered leather couch that he was gesturing to and took a seat and crossed her long, shapely legs. Quinton watched as she made herself comfortable and then took a seat directly across from her.

"You are at an advantage. I don't know much about you."

Mallory Jane tilted her head and smiled. "That will soon change, because if you are as good as a lawyer as Melissa says, then we will be spending lots of time together."

Quinton's heart beat a little faster, and he returned her smile.

Melissa was home alone with Dillon when she got his call. After carefully placing her one-month-old in his bassinet, she then picked up the phone.

"Hello?"

"Hi, Melissa, how are things going there?"

"Good, dinner is in the oven, and we are having roast tonight. What time are you coming home?"

Silence.

"Um, I'm going to be a little late tonight. I have an important client flying in from Houston, and he won't get here to the office until six."

Melissa frowned into the phone and then said, "Okay, do you want me to wait for you?"

"No, no, go ahead and eat and just fix me a plate for later."

Melissa thought about Mitch and Remi home alone and said, "Sure. I will see you when you get here. Love you."

"Love you too, babe."

Melissa pressed the end button and quickly dialed Mitch's house.

On the fourth ring, Mitch said, "Hello?"

"Hi, Mitch, it's Melissa. Would you and Remi like to join Dillon and I for dinner tonight? I have a roast."

"That would be great. What time?"

"Is one hour okay?"

"We will be there. Thanks, Melissa, you've been a true friend."

Melissa's eyes went a little moist, and she said, "Great, bye now."

Quinton opened up his office door and found Mallory Jane sitting on a leather chair, flipping through a *People* magazine waiting for him. When she heard the door, she looked up and smiled when Quinton nodded and closed the door behind him with his briefcase.

Mallory Jane had declined a ride and decided to follow Quinton in her red convertible Beemer. They had chosen Harry's Restaurant to discuss her business over drinks. At first she was hesitant to take up his offer, being Melissa's friend and all, but just couldn't seem to find the words "no thank you" when it came to the dashing Quinton Pierson. As she continued to drive down Main Street, she slowly convinced herself she wasn't doing anything wrong. *This is just business, right?*

Pulling her Beemer to the curve, Mallory Jane stopped in front of Harry's and handed her keys to a parking attendant. The young guy took the keys from the good-looking twenty-eight-year-old blonde as she stepped out of her shiny vehicle.

Gracefully, Mallory Jane entered the restaurant and immediately saw Quinton at the bar, patting a chair beside him. Smiling, she stepped forward and said, "You beat me. You must drive as reckless as me."

Grinning, he replied, "You have no idea."

A bartender walked up and said, "What can I get you folks?"

Mallory Jane glanced above his head at the board showing the house specials and decided. "I'll have a chocolate martini."

Quinton added, "Make it two."

Melissa opened up her front door carrying Dillon in her arms. With a big smile, she said, "Remi! Sweetie, it is so good to see you."

Mitch pushed his daughter inside the house and then said, "Thanks so much for having us, Melissa. I'm afraid I'm still pretty lousy with the cooking, and we are both getting tired of take-out."

"Anytime. It's been a while, and I'm sorry." Looking down at Dillon, she continued, "This little man keeps me pretty busy."

Mitch smiled. "I enjoyed golf yesterday with Quinton. He kicked my ass."

She smiled and with her free hand reached out and held Remi's hand and led her to the kitchen. "What is new? Quinton always wins at golf."

"Yeah, well, this time it was seriously ugly."

Taking a few more steps, they all made it into the kitchen, and Mitch exclaimed, "Oh, Melissa, this smells divine. I can't believe Quinton is missing this!"

"Don't worry, I will warm him a plate when he gets in."

Melissa walked over to the mechanical swing, placed Dillon inside, then buckled him in and pressed a button.

She headed over to the kitchen cabinet, pulled down two glasses, and said, "Would you like a glass of wine with dinner?"

"Of course."

Looking at Remi, she stated, "I have milk for you. Does that sound good?"

Remi nodded her head, and Melissa smiled back at her and grabbed a smaller glass out of the cabinet.

Mitch said, "Here, let me get the wine."

Melissa slid the unopened bottle of wine toward Mitch with the corkscrew and said, "Thanks, I'm still terrible at that."

Mitch smiled and winked. "I know, that's why I offered."

Soon, all were seated and sharing a fine meal. Remi was talking a lot, and Mitch seemed to be really relaxed for the first time since Rebecca's death. The night continued with such ease as the conversation flowed without any awkwardness.

After dinner, Remi and Mitch helped in the kitchen, and then finally, at seven thirty, Mitch said, "Melissa, this has been wonderful. Thank you."

Melissa nodded and said, "You two should come over more. Let's make this a weekly thing. Next time I will try to plan a little better, where Quinton is home."

"Sounds like a plan." Leaning over, he picked up his little angel and said, "Someone is getting tired. I better get her home. It has been quite an adjustment with her going to day care so early."

Melissa glanced at Remi and then smoothed her hair back from her eyes. "Yeah, I can imagine. Is she settling in well there at Park Academy?"

"Yes, we both like it very much, and it's close to my office."

"Good, I'll walk you two out, and we will talk again soon."

Mitch followed Melissa to the front door and said, "Thanks again, bye now."

Melissa reached out and gave Remi a kiss on the forehead. "Bye, take care, you two."

She bolted the door, quickly made her way back into the kitchen, and picked up Dillon. "You were so good tonight. Are you always going to be like this when we have company?"

He let out a little scream when the swing stopped, but quickly settled into her arms and turned toward Melissa's breast for another feeding. "Hold on, little man. Let's get upstairs first, and then off to bed you go."

Melissa fed Dillon in a white cushioned rocking chair in his room. When he was done, she carefully stood up and eased him into his bed and then turned off the light and shut the door. Glancing at her watch, it was now eight o'clock, and still no Quinton. Realizing his plate was made and sitting on the stove, covered, she went ahead and headed toward her bedroom to change for bed.

Melissa's plan was to watch TV for a little while, and by then she hoped Quinton would be home. Unfortunately, it didn't work out that way, and she fell asleep during the first five minutes of watching a sitcom.

Melissa continued to sleep and never woke up until Dillon started crying at twelve thirty, early the next morning. Slowly she raised her head and was immediately met with kisses.

"Quinton, you're home."

"Yes, you were sleeping so peacefully I didn't want to wake you. I'll go get Dillon. You stay put."

Melissa watched as he flipped the light switch by the bed and got up and left the bedroom. She slowly leaned up on her elbows and readjusted the pillows to help her get comfortable for Dillon's nighttime feeding.

Soon Quinton came back in with a wailing baby and said, "There are just some things a daddy can't do."

Melissa smiled and held out her hands for her precious little darling. Instantly Dillon began feeding, and Quinton snuggled up close to her and watched.

Melissa looked over at her husband and asked, "What time did you get in?"

"Not too late, I don't even remember the time."

"You look tired. Do you have a busy day tomorrow?"

Quinton thought back to his conversation with Mallory Jane and then said. "Yeah, I'm afraid I do."

Chapter 14

Melissa was sitting on the floor in the nursery getting Dillon changed for the day when Quinton popped around the corner and said, "What time tonight?"

Melissa thought about the work that lay ahead of her and mentally calculated what time she needed to be home to get ready, and then how early to get there before the big event began. "Be home by four thirty. We will leave here no later than five fifteen."

"Five fifteen? You're kidding me. The event doesn't get started till seven."

Melissa gave her "look," and Quinton frowned.

"Okay, dear, I will be home and ready by five fifteen. What about Dillon? Were you able to get another babysitter?"

A week ago, Bethany Rose, Dillon's usual babysitter, had canceled and left her in a terrible bind. The Junior League annual ball had been in the plans for months, and all the good babysitters had been yanked up weeks ago. It wasn't Bethany Rose's fault, though. She couldn't help that her grandmother had slipped and fallen and her parents made the decision to take her with them to Tennessee since school was out for the summer.

"Yes, after calling everyone I knew and repeatedly getting turned down or laughed at, I called a nanny service."

"Oh, who has used them before?"

Immediately Melissa's head was full of innuendos that Quinton had made over the last year about her decisions on child rearing. Frustrated from the lack of attention he had shown her, and their son, for too many months to count, she exploded. "Quinton, he is my son too. Don't you think I did my homework? Look, I'm stressed enough. Don't start on me with this."

Melissa watched as he threw his hands up and left the room without another word spoken.

Quinton entered the garage and stepped into his sports car. Immediately he stopped frowning and smiled as an image of Mallory Jane filled his thoughts and he couldn't wait to see her all dolled up. For weeks, she had only hinted at her dress but never showed him no matter how he pleaded or tickled her in bed. *Yes,* he thought, *I will be home and ready on time.* Mallory Jane was sure to be there just as early.

At eight o'clock, Melissa dropped Dillon off at a local day care and then was on her way to the Grand Hamilton. She was schedule to arrive at eight thirty, and along with her team, she was going to work the next several hours overseeing everything. For over a year now, she had served as president of the Junior League, and after this event, she was thinking about turning the role over to someone else. It was just too hard with Dillon, especially since he was showing early signs of the terrible twos. Pulling into the front to valet park, Melissa spotted Julie and Mallory Jane stepping out of their vehicles and handing over the keys to a young attendant. Julie waved and smiled, and Mallory Jane followed suit.

Melissa said thank you to the attendant and then opened up the back door to her M-Class and retrieved some more baskets for the silent auction. Julie stepped over and grabbed two, and Melissa grabbed the remaining two and said, "Can you believe this? I had people ringing my doorbell as late as nine thirty last night dropping these off. I thought Quinton was going to strangle me."

Mallory Jane lost her smile and held out her hand and grabbed a silver bow basket from Melissa and commented, "There's nothing like waiting till the last possible moment, is there?"

Melissa shrugged her shoulders. "Well, at least we have them, I think this brings the total to three hundred and twenty-seven, the most ever at this event."

Julie laughed, "And you think they are going to let you give up this job at September elections."

Mallory Jane chimed in, "Julie is right. You're perfect for this job."

Melissa sternly replied, "Oh no, I'm going to give it up. I promise to sign up to help with the fundraising next year for this ball, but that is it!"

All three ladies made their way inside and spoke briefly with the front desk and then quickly were escorted to the enormous ballroom. Looking around, Melissa was shocked at all the people helping out with decorations. There were probably already twenty-five women scurrying around like busy bees. She thought to herself, *Thank you, God, no way I could get this place ready for over eighteen hundred people by myself.*

"That sign-up sheet was an excellent idea. Everyone has their directions and knows their job. We might even wrap this up by two," Julie remarked confidently.

Melissa was too afraid to say anything. She didn't want to jinx it. She walked over to the tables with the baskets, made some more room, and placed the pink-and-yellow one down that contained a week's vacation package to Miami.

The two ladies followed her over with their baskets, and Julie asked Melissa, "Which one has your eye tonight?"

Melissa thought about the hundreds of items up for bid and answered, "Something about a vacation. Quinton and I haven't had a real vacation since our honeymoon, and trust me, we are due!"

Julie laughed, and Mallory Jane remained quiet. "Don't worry, things will turn around. It's always like that with your first child. At night, everyone just wants to sleep." Julie spoke with an encouraging smile.

Mallory Jane said, "I had no idea."

Melissa looked toward Mallory Jane. "Don't worry, a husband and children are in your future. You'll know what we are talking about one day."

Mallory Jane was married, but it hadn't lasted longer than a year. Now, she ran her own successful company and gave the appearance to all that she just didn't have time for dating now.

Melissa heard her name called from across the room and looked around until she saw Evelyn, a petite brunette, waving her hands in the air. "I think she needs some help with the balloon bridge. Can y'all get bid sheets for these baskets and make some more room?"

Mallory Jane agreed. "Absolutely, go, all is good here."

Julie turned to face Mallory Jane and asked, "Who are you bringing tonight?"

Mallory Jane thought about the agonizing decision she had had to make several weeks ago. Finally, she'd asked an old college friend she used to date. Jared lived in Mobile and was recently divorced. It scared her how he had jumped at the opportunity to come up and attend the ball. She secretly hoped Quinton would understand. She hadn't told him yet, and she was unsure how he was going to act. For weeks, their relationship had intensified thanks to Melissa being so consumed with planning the charity ball.

"Jared McMilligan. He is from Mobile."

"Oh, has he arrived in town yet?"

"Not yet, sometime after five."

Julie raised her eyebrows and asked coyly, "Is he staying the night?" Mallory Jane just smiled and replied, "Yes, what choice does he have? We probably won't be done here till after midnight."

Julie smiled and looked over the baskets. "I like this one. I would love a trip to Gatlinburg, especially during the fall, when all the leaves are changing colors."

Mallory instantly thought of Quinton and their one weekend getaway that they were able to plan three months ago. It took forever to plan. Funny, it had been to Miami, at the same resort that had made the donation that Melissa was carrying in earlier.

Julie interrupted her thoughts when she said, "I'm going over to help Marianne with the flowers."

Mallory Jane nodded her head and continued to inspect the baskets and make sure all were correctly labeled for tonight.

Melissa was still helping Evelyn when she got a text on her phone. Pulling it out of her designer jeans, she pressed a button and read: *Dress is ready to be picked up.*

"Thank God!"

Evelyn looked over. "What?"

"Oh, just that my dress is ready to be picked up."

"You mean the one you're wearing tonight?"

"Yes, I bought it over two months ago, and when I went to try it on a week ago, it was too big."

"You have lost weight. You look real good, Melissa. I can't tell at all you've had a baby."

"Thanks, I am just now down to my before-pregnancy weight."

"No! You lost that a long time ago. I think you are smaller now than before you were pregnant."

Melissa smiled back and replied, "Evelyn, I met you when I was four months pregnant. Trust me, I am now just back to my old weight."

Melissa continued to work and thought about the battle over the last two months to lose that last five pounds. Her weight had been a struggle for several months after having Dillon. For some reason, she just couldn't get motivated with the complacency of staying at home. It also didn't help that Rebecca had been her workout buddy. Going to the gym without her just seemed wrong.

Melissa remembered Quinton's comment after their annual Christmas party: *"When is my beautiful wife gonna be a size two again?"*

She thought, *He had too much to drink, and it was cruel, but at the same time, he must have really meant it, and it took being drunk to say it.*

After New Year's Eve, Melissa started going to the gym three times a week, and that is when she found the local day care for Dillon. Finally, after five hard months, she went from a size eight to a two. Since Dillon was born, this was the first time she looked in the mirror and felt really good about herself. Now she just hoped Quinton would notice and say something nice. For weeks she had waited for some kind of response, but nothing.

Closing her eyes, she asked, *Why is there always something that seems to be holding us apart?* Quinton still hadn't touched her since that last awful fight, but still, was it normal to have sex with your spouse only once every two weeks, if you were lucky?

Thinking back, she thought about all the long hours he put in at the office. Just when she was at her breaking point, he seemed to always pull her back in and assure her all was right with their marriage. Maybe Julie was right. Things were different that first year with a new baby. Melissa let go of the balloon pressed between her fingers, *Yeah, but he is closer to two than a newborn now.* Frowning, she saw the balloon sailing off around the room.

"I'll get the balloon, Melissa. You look deep in thought."

Getting her head out of a fog, Melissa laughed, "Oh, sorry."

From across the room, someone yelled her name, and once again she was off to help with more questions. All day went on like this, and by one o'clock, she was exhausted.

Julie asked loudly, "Melissa, is this it? The place looks fantastic!"

Melissa picked up a sheet of paper and looked over the printed list of items to do, all checked off. "I think you're right. We're done." Looking around at all the women, she shouted out, "Well done, ladies!"

Cheers rang out around the room as people clapped and looked around the ballroom at all their hard work.

Julie picked up a small piece of streamer on the floor and added, "Let's get out of here and go kick up our feet and relax. We're gonna need it before tonight."

Melissa looked around and asked, "Where is Mallory Jane?"

Julie replied, "Her date arrived early and surprised her. She has already left."

"Who is her date?"

"Some handsome man from Mobile, I haven't met him yet."

"Really?" She stretched the word for effect. "I didn't know she had a boyfriend from out of town. That would explain a lot."

"Yes, it does. Maybe she will share more about how they met tonight."

Melissa looked down at the seating chart. The round decorative tables were set up for parties of ten, and Mallory Jane and Julie were both seated at her table. Smiling, she thought tonight was going to be fun.

Chapter 15

Melissa was standing in front of her bathroom mirror wearing a sheer white robe and nothing else. Picking up her brush she continued fixing her long blonde hair when she heard the bedroom door open and close. Looking in the mirror, Quinton appeared and came to a complete stop. With a grin upon his face, she watched him move closer and soon felt his muscular arms wrap around her waist.

Smiling in the mirror, Melissa said, "Hi, babe, glad you're home. Your tux is hanging in the closet."

Quinton didn't let go and started kissing her neck. Melissa, still holding the brush, said, "Quinton, now is not the time. I'm trying to get ready here."

He didn't listen and carefully undid her robe and stepped back as it hit the floor. Melissa placed her brush down and looked intently in the mirror back at her husband and thought, *You have got to be kidding, now he is interested? He works late all the time, and the one night I have the biggest event of the year planned, he finally takes notice of me!*

Slowly Quinton placed his hands on the small of her back and then ran them around the front, over her flat stomach. Taking a step closer, he looked into the mirror and watched as his hands ran over her tone, fit body. In a sexy whisper, he said, "You're turning me on, you look so hot, Melissa."

Melissa watched in the mirror as he continued to caress her. She closed her painted eyes and tried to breathe. She had been waiting to hear those words for so long, too long. Soon her desire met his, and she quickly spun around, and Quinton lifted her up and placed her on the bathroom vanity. Slowly he worked his fingers over her sexy, fit body and then knelt down on his knees. Melissa arched her back and moaned. She grabbed Quinton's head and raked her fingers through his hair. When her mind was about to explode from his touch, he stood back up and quickly carried her to the bed.

Twenty- five minutes had passed before Melissa jumped up and screamed, "Quinton, we have got to hurry!"

Quinton pulled her back down and said, "One more kiss and then you can get up."

Melissa held him tight and kissed him back, but it was much too fast. Quickly, she pulled away from his grasp and ran into the bathroom. She picked up her makeup brush and went back to work.

When Quinton stepped out of the shower, the doorbell sounded and he said, "I'll get that. It's probably the service."

Melissa only nodded, then went into the deep walk-in-closet and found her blue dress. She carefully stepped into it and pulled it up. Since Quinton wasn't around, she had to struggle with the zipper, but finally got it. Looking at the clock, she said aloud, "Shit, I'm gonna be late for my own damn shindig."

At 5:35, Melissa kissed Dillon good-bye and then rushed out the door. Traffic was moving well, so that was a plus. Quinton drove a little faster than normal and was doing his best to make up some time.

He placed his free hand on top of her thigh that was exposed from the slit and said, "You take my breath away in that dress. How am I gonna be able to concentrate tonight?"

Melissa smiled and thought, *I do look good. I'm proud of myself.*

Quinton casually asked, "Who are we sitting by tonight?"

"Julie and Mark, Cassandra and Johnny, Mitch and Reb—" She stopped, and a hand went over her mouth. "I mean, Joshlyn, that is Mitch's date."

Quinton looked over, and their eyes met.

She quickly added, "I know, it's been over a year, but—"

"I know. Just try not to call her Rebecca tonight."

Silence followed over the next several minutes as both were deep in thought.

Finally breaking the silence, Quinton asked, "Anyone else at our table?"

"Mallory Jane and her date."

Quinton removed his hand from her thigh and placed it on the wheel. "Who is her date? Do we know him?"

"No, Julie said he was from out of town. This must be the guy she has been seeing for a while now, which would explain a lot."

"What do you mean?"

"Well, you know how gossip gets started between a bunch of ladies that don't work."

"Yeah, I do. So what are they saying?"

"Nothing really. It's just that she has been so evasive and secretive lately."

"Oh. I haven't noticed anything different in our meetings."

Melissa laughed, "You wouldn't, you're a guy. Anyway, some of the ladies suspected she was having an affair with a married man."

Quinton kept his eyes on the road. "I see. That will end tonight after everyone meets him." Taking his free hand off the wheel, he touched her thigh once more and then continued, "Now what are all the ladies gonna talk about next?"

Melissa laughed. "Oh, they will find something else or make up something!"

Quinton shifted his weight behind the wheel and sped up. Soon he was coming to a quick halt in front of the downtown Grand Hamilton, and then he tossed his keys to the attendant.

Quickly they got out and made their way down the long hallway that led to the gigantic ballroom. The balloons, candles and table decorations had been strategically placed and the ice sculptures glistened under the dimmed lights setting the mood for an evening of romance.

Melissa turned to Quinton and proudly asked, "Well, my handsome husband, what do you think?"

Quinton looked around until his eyes found Mallory Jane. Her back was turned to him, and she was wearing a sheer white backless gown with silver sequins resting just above her perfectly sculpted tight ass. Immediately all thought of another man left his mind, and he said, "Stunning!"

Melissa grabbed his hand and said, "Good, I'm glad you think so. Come on, it's time for you to be the dashing host with me."

Quinton slowly peeled his eyes off Mallory Jane and looked at his wife's face. He tried to block all thoughts of Mallory Jane out of his mind and concentrate on Melissa. She was just as beautiful and stunning tonight. Thinking to himself, *Lord, what have I gotten myself into this time,* slowly a smile formed on his face. "Okay, let's do this. Tonight I'm yours." And in the first time in a long time, he actually meant it.

The night went on without any hiccups or flaws. Melissa was congratulated on the success when she finally announced at the end of the night that they had raised $392,250 from the baskets at the silent auction. Cheers went up as Quinton placed his loving arms around his wife and kissed her.

Jared saw Mallory Jane frown. "What is wrong, babe? Isn't this good news?"

Mallory Jane looked at Jared, standing six-two, and one of the most handsome men in the room, and replied, "Yes, it is." She finally smiled. "She broke my record, that's all."

Jared laughed aloud and wrapped his arms around her. "You Southern women crack me up sometimes."

The next morning, Melissa slept in with the help of the overnight child-care service. It was Saturday morning, and she was in no hurry to go anywhere. Finally, Melissa rolled out of bed at ten o'clock and looked for Quinton, who had already gotten up.

Slowly she got dressed and made her way downstairs to find her little family. Instead of Quinton, she found Anna holding Dillon in the kitchen. "Dillon, come see Mama!"

Dillon turned around and smiled and giggled. Anna put him on the floor, and he ran to Melissa.

"Good morning, sunshine, how did everything go last night?"

"I fun," exclaimed Dillon as he gave his mommy a big hug.

Knowing he wouldn't expand further, Anna explained. "All went very well. He ate everything and went to bed by seven thirty. This morning he got up at six thirty, ate all his breakfast, and I was just cutting him up an apple for snack."

"Thanks, Anna, I really appreciate it, and I will request you again in the future."

Anna smiled. "Anytime, he was so easy, and you have such a nice home for an overnight stay."

Melissa's eyes scanned around, and she asked, "Where is my husband?"

"Oh, he left this for you. He already paid me till noon and told me to let you sleep in."

Melissa took the note from her outstretched hand and replied, "Thanks." Kissing Dillon, she placed him back down. "I'm going to take advantage of you and go get a shower." Then she left the room with his note in her hand. As soon as she hit the stairwell, she began reading.

> *Melissa,*
>
> *Client left a message in middle of night and I had to go. Hope to be home before you wake up.*
>
> *Love,*
>
> *Quinton*

Melissa crumpled up the note and threw it in her bathroom wastebasket without given it another thought.

Quinton woke up in Mallory Jane's arms. The first thoughts that entered his mind were, *What the hell am I gonna do? She is pregnant! I can't possibly father another child outside of my marriage. I can't give up Dillon, I won't.*

Mallory Jane opened her eyes and looked at Quinton. "What are you thinking?"

Quinton looked into her green eyes and said, "That as much as I love my son, I can't lose you."

She smiled, and Quinton embraced her. His mind went to work.

Chapter 16

Melissa bent over and kissed Dillon on the forehead and said, "Mommy will pick you up after lunch, okay?"

Dillon clapped his hands, and grits splattered on Melissa's knit dress and all over Quinton, who was sitting on the other side of the high chair. She laughed, "Oops, my man," and grabbed a napkin and quickly cleaned herself off and then grabbed her purse. "Bye, guys."

Quinton grabbed her arm and pulled her to him, and then he stood up. "What about my kiss?"

Melissa smiled and said, "Yes, dear, I thought you had your fill this morning," and winked. He lowered his mouth to hers and kissed her tenderly and continued to hold on as Melissa tried to pull away.

Finally, he let go and said, "I love you, Melissa."

She tilted her head and replied, "I love you, Quinton."

She waved good-bye and blew her men a kiss and walked out of the kitchen and into the garage to get into her M-Class.

Pulling out of the driveway, her mind began to float toward this weekend. Tomorrow she and Quinton were heading to Gatlinburg without Dillon for a long weekend. It was going to be their first trip together since having Dillon. Doing the math in her head, she realized it had been over two years! *Way overdue!*

She smiled as she thought how great things had been between them lately. First, he surprised her with the trip, and then he started spending more time at home. Melissa slightly blushed at the thought of their lovemaking this morning. There was something about it that seemed different—no, special, she thought. *Oh, how gently and slowly he took me, and then he held me in his arms afterward for such a long time, running his hands through my hair and over my body as he continued to kiss my neck and back until it led to more lovemaking.* She smirked. *Normally he is always in such a hurry, but not today.*

Just then, all happy thoughts left as Melissa saw Mitch flagging her down, and she pressed the brakes. Mitch ran over toward her, and Melissa lowered her window and looked around for Remi. "Hi, Mitch. Everything okay?"

Mitch's eyes looked a little glazed as he spoke. "I…I got a call from a jewelry store on Fifth Street."

Melissa waited patiently for him to finish, and finally he did after looking down and staring at his feet for a while.

"Apparently, Rebecca ordered something or had some of her jewelry repaired. I…I…" He closed his eyes. "Can you go by there and take care of it?"

Melissa reached out and grabbed his hand and looked at him with her tender blue eyes. "Of course I will. But why haven't they called earlier? It's been a long time."

"That is the thing. She already paid for it, so they put it to the side and didn't really pursue it until they stumbled on it today."

"What is the name of the store?"

"David's Fine Jewelry, and I…I don't know, maybe I should go, but I feel like I'm finally moving on with Joshlyn, and I—"

"Stop, don't say more. I understand. I'll take care of it and will let you know if it is something important, okay?"

"Thanks, Melissa."

She nodded and placed her hand back on the wheel and slowly moved forward as Mitch turned around and headed back to his own vehicle with Remi waiting inside.

Pulling out of the neighborhood and onto Highway 31, Melissa began to reminisce about Rebecca. As if it were last weekend, she could see and hear Rebecca laughing and picking up her wineglass for a toast. Soon thoughts led to the many gym sessions that they had shared together followed by coffee at the club. Slowing down for a red light up ahead, Melissa started tearing up with emotions for her dear old friend. Staring straight ahead, waiting for the light to turn green, she wondered once again, why?

Slightly shaking her head, she asked aloud, "Why did you do it, Rebecca?"

Soon the light turned green, and she tried her best to push the thoughts away. These days, whenever she thought about Rebecca, she felt a sense of guilt. If she hadn't been so caught up in her own pregnancy, maybe, just maybe, she would have seen it coming.

Up ahead, Melissa saw the entrance to the interstate and quickly maneuvered into the right lane. Since traffic was moving so well and she was making good time for her morning meeting with the Junior League, she decided to go to the jewelry store first. It definitely would be easier now, without Dillon in the car, than with him after lunch, she thought.

Knowing the store was on the way, but not real sure which street it was located on, she pressed her OnStar button. Responding to a voice, she spoke the words "David's Fine Jewelry Store" and then the word "directions." A voice responded to her command, and soon a route was planned on her GPS screen.

Within the next ten minutes, Melissa found the jewelry store, and a parking spot. She quickly looked both ways and crossed the street.

As she entered the store, a bell sounded, and immediately she was greeted by a young lady in a nice navy suit. Melissa looked around and noticed this was indeed a "fine" jewelry store.

Melissa smiled and walked over and said, "I'm here to pick up a package for Rebecca Dunning."

The lady smiled and said, "Just one moment."

Soon the manager came out with a small gold paper bag and said, "I'm so sorry to hear about Rebecca. I felt terrible about letting this package go unnoticed for so long. The order was engraved. I hope this can bring some closure."

Melissa nodded and said, "Thanks, maybe it can." Awkwardly, she reached out and took the fine quality paper bag and then turned around and left.

Forgetting to check the traffic, a horn blew, and Melissa jumped back, shattering her nerves even more. Taking a deep breath, she waited for the car to pass and then sprinted across the street to her parked M-Class. She unlocked the door, climbed in, and closed the door, but didn't start the engine. She looked at the gold paper and then timidly pulled out a velvet box. Slowly she opened it to reveal a beautiful gold watch for a man. Closing her eyes, a tear slid down her cheek, and she shook her head. No way she was reading the message now. Carefully she closed the box and placed it back into the paper and lifted her console and placed it inside.

Inserting the key, she cranked up her M-Class and checked the traffic and then pulled back out onto the street. When Melissa was about a half mile away from the store, she had to brake for an upcoming light. Slowly she pressed down on the brake pedal—and nothing. Melissa tightened her grip on the wheel and frantically started pumping the brake pedal.

Nothing!

Panic was beginning to take over as everything began to slow down in her mind. At the last minute before nailing the car in front of her, she pulled up on the emergency brake just as the light turned green and the car began moving in front of her.

Tires squealed, and Melissa skidded into a sidespin, but stopped safely before hitting anyone or them hitting her.

"What the hell!"

Melissa didn't move, and she was shaking. A man driving behind her got out of his car and ran over toward her, yelling, "Are you okay?"

Melissa lowered her window and in a quivering voice said, "My brakes didn't work. I-I pulled the emergency brake and—"

The man looked at her with a strange look. "What do you mean they didn't work?"

In an exasperated voice, she said, "I don't know anything about cars."

Horns were beginning to blow, and then suddenly she realized all traffic had stopped and she was blocking a four-way intersection with her vehicle.

The man said, "Okay, here, slide over and let me drive it over to the curb. I'll go slow and use the emergency brake like you did. One thing is for sure, you have got to move your vehicle."

Melissa rose up and quickly moved over the console and into the passenger seat. She watched as the man guided her vehicle over to the side and used the brake once again to stop it. Turning off the engine, he said, "Look, I have to go, I've got an important meeting, but there is a body shop about a block away." He pointed left, and Melissa looked that way and saw the sign.

The man got out of her car, and she yelled, "Thanks," as he jogged back over and got into his vehicle, which was now blocking traffic as well.

The man quickly waved and started up his engine and took off.

Melissa just watched as the next few moments went by. All the traffic picked back up, and people stared at her out the window. Melissa reached over, grabbed her purse, and stepped out of the SUV, then locked up and started walking. It wasn't far at all, and the place looked nice as well.

Taking the last few steps, Melissa thought about calling Quinton, but decided to take care of this herself and then call him and let him know what the man said about the car. Melissa was dressed in a purple knit dress with a belt tied loosely around her waist. Her long blonde hair was blowing in the breeze, and you could hear her heels tapping along the sidewalk as she walked. Looking at her watch, she thought, *Now I'm going to be late.*

Opening the door to the service center, Melissa was instantly greeted by a middle-aged mechanic working behind the desk.

"Hi, may I help you?"

Melissa smiled her glorious smile and said, "Yes, my brakes just went out at that intersection," and she pointed in the direction to her left. "I have a two thousand nine M-Class, black, and it is pulled over along the side of the road."

The mechanic walked out from behind the desk and peered through his glass door. He saw her SUV and said, "Nice car. Don't understand why your brakes would go out like that. But yeah, I can take a look at it right now."

Again she smiled and then said, "Great. Um, I'm late for a meeting that is ten minutes down the road. Do you have a pickup service, or another vehicle I could drive?"

The man said, "I'll take you. Just fill out this paperwork first, and then I will need your keys."

In no time at all, Melissa was on her way to her Junior League meeting with Arnie as her chauffer. Melissa didn't talk much, nor did he. She thought he was nice, but wanted to keep this as professional as possible.

Arnie pulled up along the curb of a business complex that held their office and said, "You should hear back from me in the next two hours."

Melissa stepped out of the car and then said, "Thanks, I will get a lift back over." She shut the door and walked down the sidewalk and didn't look back.

Surprisingly, Melissa was only twenty minutes late, and the girls didn't seem to mind, as they were all sitting around and chatting with coffee cups in their hands.

Melissa stated, "Sorry, guys, car trouble. Are we missing anyone?"

Evelyn said, "Just Mallory Jane, she called to say she will be late."

Melissa nodded. "Okay, let's go ahead and get started. I have a list a mile long!"

The meeting went on, but was briefly paused as Mallory Jane walked in around 10:25 and quietly mouthed, "Sorry," and took a seat. No one really questioned her due to the fact that she ran a very successful business and was always on the go. Mallory Jane didn't serve an official title, but she had so many connections that she was vital to the nonprofit organization. Melissa was just happy she could make a meeting at all.

Melissa studied Mallory Jane's face for a few moments before continuing. She looked tired. Making a mental note to talk with her later, she glanced back at her list and then carried on with the next topic.

For the next hour and a half, plans were made, questions asked and answered, and candidates reviewed for this year's senior scholarship. Satisfied that the golf tournament was planned and they had narrowed the scholarship award down to three deserving students, Melissa said, "Okay, guys! This looks like a great place to stop. We will plan on same time next week, and don't forget to e-mail me any topics you want on the agenda."

Chairs were slid back, papers were quickly gathered up, and everyone started breaking away from the conference table. Melissa looked down at her phone and saw that she had three messages. She hit a few keys and placed the phone to her ear to listen.

The second message stated: "Arnie here, got your SUV fixed and would like to talk to you about it as soon as possible. It's important."

Melissa was happy to hear that she could pick it up, but was a little perplexed about the other part of the message. Closing her phone and sliding it back in her purse, she called out to Julie, "Hey, can you give me a ride? My car is fixed now."

Julie answered, "Sure, no problem."

Good-byes were said around the room, and soon both ladies were walking out and headed toward Julie's car. Suddenly Melissa stopped and looked around for Mallory Jane.

"Forget something?"

"Yes, I mean no. Has Mallory Jane already left?"

"Yeah. She ran out as soon as you said your last words. Didn't talk to anyone. Just left."

Melissa looked toward Julie and asked, "Did she look tired to you?"

Julie thought about the question as she opened the door and got in behind the wheel. When Melissa was buckled up, she finally replied, "I-I really didn't notice. Is that bad?"

Melissa offered, "No. It is just, well, Rebecca was on my mind this morning, and I was thinking how I missed something and I just need to be more observant with my friends."

"We all missed something with Rebecca."

"Yeah, we did."

Traffic was a little slower due to lunch hour, but it was nice to get fifteen minutes in with just Julie and no one else. Julie soon suggested, "I'll see Mallory Jane again on Sunday. I'll talk to her."

"Thanks, just don't mention the looking tired part."

Julie laughed, "Oh, I won't, don't worry about that. Now, enough about Mallory Jane, are you excited about your Gatlinburg trip this weekend?"

"Yes, I've been packed now for three days! It has been so long since we have taken a real vacation, just the two of us."

"Are you worried about leaving Dillon?"

"Yes, that is the hard part. But I'm very confident in Anna. She was a real godsend to find her the night of the ball. I've used her so many times since."

"Dillon will be fine. Besides, we will be close by, so just give Anna our number."

Melissa smiled. "Already have a contact list, and yes, yours is at the top."

Julie looked over and smiled back.

Melissa stated, "I'm not sure Quinton and I are going to know how to act without work and Dillon."

"Oh, everything will come flooding back. You guys will have an amazing time."

"Yes, I'm still shocked at the planning, though. I mean, yes, Quinton had the highest bid, and I knew we won this package, but the fact that he booked the trip and then only told me about it last week was a huge surprise."

"Surprises are good. It's what keeps a marriage fresh."

"You're right, I shouldn't question anything and just be happy that he planned it all by himself."

Julie sighed, "I wish Mark would do something like that. I told him about your trip, but I don't think he got the hint."

Melissa laughed and then said, "There it is, the next left at the light."

Julie turned on her turn signal and waited at the intersection for the light to turn green.

"This is where it happened. The brakes just started to go out. Look! You can still see my skid marks."

"That is so scary. You could have been really hurt."

"Oh, I know. I haven't even told anybody about it but you. Quinton is in meetings all day, and I won't hear from him till later tonight."

"You didn't call him?"

"It wouldn't have done any good to worry him. Besides, there happened to be a repair shop right here, so I just took care of it."

Julie slowly pulled to the curb and then Melissa got out. "Thanks, Julie. I will call you before I leave town."

"Do you want me to wait?"

Melissa just shook her head. "That's okay, talk soon." Then she turned around and walked up the sidewalk to the front door.

Opening the door, a bell chimed, and Melissa was immediately greeted by Arnie. He looked at another mechanic and commanded, "Man the desk till I get back."

He walked over and said, "Follow me. I want to show you something."

Melissa looked around at the establishment and saw the side door that led to some kind of office and watched as he headed in that direction. She fell in behind and entered the small office and watched as he closed the door behind them and gestured toward a chair. "Please have a seat."

Melissa slyly inspected the seat for grease as she placed her briefcase and purse down on the vinyl floor. Happy it looked clean, she gracefully sat down and crossed her legs.

Arnie had already walked around his desk and pulled out an old, faded, and stained fabric chair and quickly got to the point. Picking up a small rubber hose, he said, "This here is a brand new brake line."

Melissa looked at his outstretched hand and hesitated briefly before reaching out and taking it. She said, "Okay, but I really have no clue about cars."

Arnie didn't smile. Instead he looked down, pulled out his desk drawer, and removed the brake line that came off her car. "This is the one I removed from your M-Class." Seeing her hesitation, he offered, "It's not dirty. Take it and tell me the difference between the two."

Melissa did as she was told and began to inspect both pieces. With a dumbfounded look on her face, she said, "I give up. I don't see anything," and she tried to hand the pieces back.

"Look closer, it's there."

Instantly Melissa thought of Dillon and how she was ready just to go and get him and be on her way home. She really didn't care about the mechanism of her vehicle, she just wanted it fixed where she could drive it again. Looking up at him, she tried not to be rude when she politely asked, "Arnie, please just show me. I have a little boy waiting on me."

Arnie's face turned hard, and then he pointed to the one on the left and said, "There is a small hole in the middle. A puncture."

Melissa placed the new one back down and began to rub both hands back over the length of the piece until she discovered it. She looked up quizzically and said, "This little hole caused my brakes to go out?"

Arnie sat back and said, "It leads to another problem, but yes."

Melissa looked back down at the puncture and tilted her head. "What caused this, a rock?"

Arnie sat back up in his chair and looked straight into her blue eyes and shook his head.

Melissa started to grow uneasy, and she turned around behind her to see the closed door to the office. Turning her head back toward him, she just asked, "Well, is it fixed now? I mean, can I drive it out of here safely?"

Arnie reached out with his stained fingers and placed them on one of her hands and remarked in a serious tone, "Mrs. Pierson, this was done intentionally. It was very hard to find."

The color drained from her face, and she yanked her hand back, dropping the rubber hose onto his desk, and then watched as it rolled off and hit the ground.

Arnie stood up and walked over and then leaned down and picked the hose back up. "I'm sorry to frighten you, but I think we need to call the police."

She tried to speak to answer, but couldn't form the words. *Is this man saying someone purposely cut my line and wanted me to wreck? Oh, he is nuts! No one would want to hurt me. I don't even have any enemies.*

Melissa pushed back her chair, stood up, and then grabbed her purse and briefcase and stated in a voice she hoped sounded steady and confident, "Look, Arnie, this is some kind of mistake. I have no enemies. I live a very peaceful life with very few dramas."

"Mrs. Pierson—"

"No, please, Arnie, there has to be some mistake. Really, now I must go. My son is waiting on me at the day care." She turned and walked over to the door, twisted the handle, and pulled it open. "You have my credit card details, so just charge your price for fixing it."

Arnie looked back at her with an uncomfortable expression.

She continued, "Is the car ready? Can I drive it now?"

Arnie handed her the keys and said, "Yes. It is out front."

Melissa grabbed the keys from his hand and then turned to leave with her belongings.

When she made it two steps, he called out, "Mrs. Pierson?"

Melissa sighed and took a big breath, then spun around to face the mechanic and waited.

"Look, I'm sorry, just do me one favor, please?"

She didn't answer, and he continued anyway.

"Don't tell anyone about this, and sleep on it overnight. If you change your mind, and I hope you do, I'll keep the brake line."

Melissa looked at his dark brown eyes, and she could see that he was truly sincere. Not knowing what to say, she just nodded her head and turned around and walked out of the building.

On the drive over to the day care, Melissa couldn't get Dillon out of her mind. *What if he was in the car with me?* Images kept flashing through her mind of her crashing head-on into another car and then getting nailed in the side by another car as she spun around.

Melissa blinked her eyes a couple of times and then tried to relax her grip on the steering wheel. She was holding on too tight, and her fingers were starting to throb. With one of her hands, she hit the CD button, and one of her favorite country singers belted out a tune. Listening to the song for a few minutes, Melissa just couldn't get into the rhythm of the "Old Blue Chair" and then hit the off button and drove the rest of the way to the day care in silence.

Soon Melissa arrived at the child-care center and parked her car and quickly got out. Slamming the car door, she hurried to the entrance and was instantly greeted by Marguerite, who passed her the papers to sign out Dillon. Taking the pen, she looked at the clock and then wrote "12:42" and signed her name.

"Is he asleep?"

Marguerite nodded her head and said, "We just couldn't keep him awake. He fell asleep ten minutes ago."

Soon another young girl opened up a half door and handed a sleeping Dillon to Melissa. Carefully the transfer was made without him waking up, and then somehow she was able to grab his bag and was back outside and walking toward her car.

Gently Melissa eased Dillon into his car seat and buckled him up. She picked up the bag that had fallen on the concrete, quickly tossed it on the floorboard, then closed the door as silently as she could.

Settling in, Melissa fired up the engine and then left the small parking lot and headed toward home. With each mile that passed, Melissa kept a vigil on her rearview mirror for any signs of Dillon waking up. She thought, *He's not. Once he is down for a nap, he is very hard to wake up for the next two hours.*

Dillon had always been a deep sleeper. Melissa contributed it to the fact that he played so hard and his little body was just given slap out by the time naptime came around. Melissa thought of other children and how some just couldn't conform to any kind of routine. *Not my Dillon, he is like clockwork. Twelve thirty comes around, and he is done.*

Melissa made it home without any mishaps and continued to push out of her head all doubts that Arnie had created with his wild ideas. Soon she pulled Dillon's bedroom door shut and then started toward her own bedroom to change. When she pulled off her watch, she immediately froze.

"Oh shit, I forgot about the watch! Damn, I hope it is still there. Oh, why didn't I take it with me to my meeting?"

Quickly she made her way downstairs and then out the door to the garage. She hurried over to open the door. When she leaned over and opened the console up, instant relief washed over her when she saw it. She picked it up, closed everything, and made her way back into the house and up the staircase again.

Sitting on her bed, she removed the box from the gold paper and opened it up to make sure the watch was actually still in the box. Satisfied, she ran her fingers over the fine gold and then over the glass. Twisting her lips, she closed it and then stood up and wandered over to her closet to change.

Taking off her shoes, she thought, *Should I look and see what it says, or should I just go ahead and give it to Mitch?*

She really didn't want to pry into their personal affairs. *It could say anything, and he might not want me to read it.*

Trying to push the thoughts out of her mind, she placed her shoes on the shelf, untied her belt, and then pulled her purple dress up and over her head. Standing there in her underwear, she finally blurted out loud, "Oh, for God's sake, Melissa, just read it!"

She spun around, waltzed back over to her bed, picked up the box, and removed the watch. Gently she turned it around in her hands and then brought the watch closer to her eyes and began to read.

Quinton,

All my heart and all my love.

R

Instantly Melissa dropped the gold piece and watched as it fell onto the bed and her hands shook profusely in front of her eyes. She instantly felt cold and sick as her stomach did a flip, and she ran to the toilet to relieve herself.

Sitting there, shaking, and wrapping her arms around her stomach, she began to cry, "No! No, this isn't right."

Images began to flood her mind: Rebecca and Quinton sitting side by side and looking into each other's eyes. The look she gave him at the Christmas party. *Why was she in my room again?* Rebecca and Quinton driving together in the golf cart when they were playing a competitive round with Mitch on her side. Quinton reaching to touch Rebecca's shoulder in Remi's backyard swing. And there was more.

Minutes passed by as Melissa was in shock, realizing for the first time all the things that didn't add up. How could she have been so stupid? How had she missed it? Yes, she had been pregnant, but still?

Several more minutes passed by, and then finally Melissa was able to get up and leave the bathroom. Making her way back over toward the bed, she sat down and picked the watch back up and read the message again as tears continued to still fall slowly. She grasped the watch in her hands, then threw it across the room. She fell back onto her bed, wrapped her arms around herself, and closed her eyes.

An hour passed, and the only movement came from Melissa's chest as she continued to hold on to life and concentrate on breathing.

Another twenty minutes passed, until Melissa sprung up out of bed at the sound of Dillon's voice. Somehow she moved forward, but didn't actually feel anything she touched. Opening the door, she saw Dillon standing up in his bed with a big grin on his face. With a breaking heart, she ran toward him and picked him up and squeezed him in her arms. She just wanted to hold him and feel his unwavering love forever. Of course, Dillon wasn't going to have any of that, and he quickly started squirming, and Melissa was forced to place him back down on the floor.

Without a care in the world, Dillon made his way over toward his toy box and began to pull out his trucks one by one and never looked back as his mommy fell onto his twin bed, not able to move once again.

With squinted eyes, Melissa stared at Dillon as he sat on the floor and played with all his various trucks of different sizes and shapes. He was so happy, oblivious to the pain and heartbreak that surrounded him.

Thirty more minutes passed, and then Dillon said, "Yuise."

With every ounce of willpower, Melissa pulled herself up into a sitting position and got up to tend to her child. Realizing she was still not dressed, she picked him up and walked back into her bedroom and quickly pulled out some jeans and a T-shirt. By the time she was dressed, Dillon was bouncing all over her bed, and most of the pillows had fallen to the floor. The gold paper bag had been crushed and had fallen to the floor along with the empty watch box.

Melissa forced herself to turn toward the opposite side of the room and locate the watch. Hoping it wasn't still there and this had all been a bad dream, her hope was soon shattered as she found it lying there beside the window half hidden behind her long drapes. Forcing her mind to make her body move, she soon retrieved the watch and then quickly made her way over to the box and placed it all inside the crumpled paper.

Now what?

Dillon continued to bounce and giggle as if there weren't a care in the world, oblivious, once again, to the fact that his mommy was broken and not enough hugs and giggles could ever put her back together again.

Chapter 17

Friday morning, Melissa got up slowly, dressed, and then hugged Dillon tight before releasing him to Anna. Blowing a kiss with her hands, she added, "Good-bye, my little angel, I love you!"

Quinton placed an arm around Melissa and said, "Honey, he is going to be fine."

Melissa peeled her eyes off Dillon and looked into her husband's face and began to play the role of her life, literally. "I know, darling. Let's go." She took his hand and followed him out to the garage and watched as he opened the trunk to his car and placed their luggage inside.

She didn't dare question when Quinton announced, "I've changed my mind. Let's go in my sports car."

Both got in, and Melissa quickly buckled up and concentrated once again on just breathing. The thought of being in a carport alone with her husband scared her shitless. For hours and hours last night, she couldn't get Rebecca out of her mind. What she had done was the ultimate betrayal, but she knew in her heart that she would never leave her daughter and take her own life.

Slowly she looked over at Quinton as he raised the garage door and started the engine. *How did he do it, and why? Did Rebecca threaten to tell me, and then he snapped?* For hours Quinton was by her side in the delivery room. Did he decide to end it once he saw their precious son?

Closing her eyes, she concentrated again on breathing. Her mind and heart knew this man sitting beside her had ended Rebecca's life and was dead set on ending hers. Why else would he insist on taking Dillon to child care for the first time ever? Why else did he have an odd expression on his face when he saw her last night? Why would he get up in the middle of the night and pace back and forth, unknownst to him that she was wide awake, listening in the dark?

Again, she concentrated on breathing and inhaled sharply when she felt his hand touch hers. "Melissa, are you okay? You almost look as if you're about to have a panic attack."

Opening her eyes and placing her other hand on top of his, she stated clearly, "I am! We're leaving our son for a four-night trip for the first time."

Quinton then smiled and said, "I know, darling. All will be fine, just wait and see."

Melissa looked over at his profile as he continued to shift gears and get the car up to full speed, and replied, "You're right. It will. We are going to have the trip of our lives. Just like Costa Rica, only shorter."

Quinton thought of Costa Rica, but his images weren't the same as hers. He couldn't get past the young Brazilian nineteen-year-old he had met at the bar—and later had to smash to pieces after he realized she stole his wallet while in her apartment. Quinton had left Melissa asleep in the small hut over the water without ever being the wiser. Quinton was barely able to get Melissa off of the Osa Peninsula and back to San Jose safely before questions were asked and the young woman's body was discovered.

"Quinton?"

He quickly cleared his thoughts and turned to his wife. "Yes?"

"How was your dinner meeting last night?"

Suddenly, the faces of his partners in his law firm came to mind. He had purposely set up a dinner meeting with his close associates

126

in preparation for the call to come in. Everything had been set in motion to end this conflict between his marriage and Mallory Jane. Unfortunately, no one had to witness his shock and grief at the news that would come that a car accident had claimed his wife's life. Somehow, the brakes had held, and now she was sitting beside him, none the wiser, looking forward to their perfect little getaway.

"Quinton?"

He looked back at Melissa and smiled. "The meeting went great. You are looking at the most productive lawyer at the firm."

"Oh, wow! That is great news. We should be celebrating. That is quite an accomplishment in just two years."

Quinton looked into her blue eyes, but didn't see the sincerity. "Are you sure? I mean, I have spent a lot of time away from you and Dillon."

Melissa broke eye contact and looked straight ahead. She was going to speak again, but felt her lower lip quivering. *Damn it! I have got to get a hold of myself.* Slowly she closed her eyes and took a deep breath and then turned back to face her husband. Looking at his side profile, she tried to see the monster disguised behind those soft brown eyes.

Finally she said, "I understand everything. You have worked very hard and diligently at your new life in Birmingham."

Quinton looked toward Melissa and then placed his hand on top of hers. "I work hard so you and Dillon can have everything you ever dreamed of."

She narrowed her eyes and spoke softly, "We don't need more money, Quinton. We have done very well for ourselves over the last few years. No need to work harder."

Quinton removed his hand and stated, "I will always work harder, Melissa. There's no stopping that. It is who I am. You know that."

Melissa didn't want to go down this path, so she said, "You are right. Besides, there will be more kids, private schools, college, and so on."

Quinton felt his throat tighten at the thought of Mallory Jane carrying his child. She was four months along now, and she was starting to show. This was all wrong, he thought. Was he making the right choice? Was Melissa sitting beside his side, alive, a sign that he had made the wrong decision? Thoughts of Mallory Jane flashed through his mind, and he could clearly see her laughing and smiling. They were so much alike, and the two of them had made such a great team at work. He loved the way she tilted her head as her hair fell across her face. Her touches sent waves of lightning bolts through his body that he couldn't deny. Even now the thought of her sent chills down his arms. Last week, she had given him an ultimatum: leave Melissa now, or she would walk out his door and never see him again. Finally, after two days of agony of not seeing or hearing from her, he finally agreed and promised to end things with Melissa.

"Quinton?"

He looked over to Melissa and replied, "Yes?"

"What are you thinking about?"

A smile crept across his face, and he answered, "Oh, just the plans I have for you this weekend."

"Oh, surprises like Costa Rica?"

Quinton had to break away from her inquiring blue eyes. He wasn't sure he could pull this off completely. This was going to be harder than he thought. He remembered how upset he was all last night that the accident had failed, but at the same time, when he climbed back into bed at 3:00 a.m., he was immediately filled with a sense of relief as his wife lay by his side, sleeping soundly.

"Yes. Just like Costa Rica, Melissa."

Chapter 18

After climbing in Quinton's sports car uphill for the last several miles, Melissa and Quinton finally arrived at their private chalet overlooking the Smoky Mountains in Gatlinburg, Tennessee. The sun would be setting within an hour, and Melissa stepped out onto the balcony and looked at the sight before her. Fall was Melissa's favorite season, and she took in the magnificent sight to give her strength for what lay ahead. The last rays of the day were shining through small cracks of the golden- and orange-leafed trees. A soft wind was blowing. Melissa continued forward until she reached the edge of the balcony and then placed her hands on the rail. She looked down to what appeared to be an endless drop-off. Suddenly, hands wrapped around her and pushed her up against the railing, and Melissa suddenly felt faint. Quinton was holding her tight and leaning on her with only the railing to save her from the depths below.

Finding her voice, she carefully turned around while her hands remained firmly on the railing. "It is beautiful, don't you think?"

Quinton's eyes left hers, and he slowly released his strong hold on her and relaxed in a stance to take in the scenery. "Yes. It is quite beautiful." He looked toward her and saw the light reflecting on her golden locks and her soft golden skin against her black cashmere dress. Her blue eyes were wild with a fire he couldn't describe as he felt an urgency and need for her that he hadn't experienced since the night of the Junior League ball. Quickly he stepped into her and picked her up and carried her over to the hot tub that overlooked the mountains and began stripping her down.

Melissa felt his hard, muscular body surround her, and she went limp. Suddenly she realized he had other plans for her besides her body being flung over the railing to her death. As he pulled off her last leather boot, she fell backward, only to be caught up against the side of the hot tub. Time began to stand still as he took off his clothing and then picked her back up and submerged her naked body in the water. Melissa tensed at his touch, and Quinton paused briefly to look into her eyes, but then continued on with his plans. Melissa placed her chin on his shoulder, closed her eyes, and willed herself to play a role that would allow her to live just long enough to save herself.

Melissa stepped out of the hot tub thirty minutes later and said, "I'm going to get that bottle of wine I saw in the kitchen. I'll be right back."

Quinton released hold of her arm and watched as she stood up and water dripped from her hard, toned body. He couldn't keep his eyes off of her. Thoughts surrounded his mind once again of how beautiful his wife was. As she finally rounded the corner with a towel wrapped around her and disappeared, Quinton submerged his entire body into the water. Time began to stand still, this time for Quinton, as he tried to push past the demons fighting in his head. Soon, the pain in his lungs began to pass the violence in his mind, and he rose up out of the hot tub in a standing position and looked out into the distance at the last rays of the setting sun.

Melissa glanced behind her and found that she was still alone in the kitchen after she poured both glasses of wine. Quickly she ran to her purse and removed two small plastic bags and tore a slit in each. Next, she glanced once more and then turned her back to the balcony as she poured the sleeping aids into a glass of wine. With her finger, she swirled the wine, until all remnants of the powder were gone, and then picked up the glasses and headed back outside.

Quinton was lying back and had his eyes closed as his head rested on the edge of the tub. Carefully she placed a glass beside him and then stepped in with her own, drug-free, drink.

Feeling water rise up his chest, Quinton opened his eyes, peered at his loving wife, and reached for his glass. "Thank you, my dear. Now come and sit beside me, and let's enjoy these last few moments of this amazing sunset."

Melissa forced her winning smile and slid over beside him. She snuggled her body up against his and took a sip of wine as he did the same.

As they each drank from their glasses, neither talked. Both were caught up in their own emotions of this game of cat and mouse with high stakes.

When Melissa finished her wine, she offered, "I won't be long. Give me twenty minutes, and I will be ready for dinner."

Quinton looked at her as she pulled away and asked, "Are we going back down the mountain or eating here?"

Melissa said, "Well, it is almost seven thirty, and I'm not sure what is in the fridge here."

Quinton leaned forward and yawned. "No, no, that is fine. Go on and get dressed. I will be out shortly."

Melissa smiled, then reached out and placed her hand on his cheek. She held his stare briefly before turning away and getting out once more.

At eight fifteen, Quinton was behind the wheel of his sports car and was driving back down the mountain toward the Stone Grill restaurant. It had taken a few calls, but they were finally able to get in for an eight-thirty dinner reservation. Most places were booked, but they got lucky.

Dinner went well, and their steaks were served to their liking. Melissa had so far only taken two sips of her wine and hoped like hell Quinton wouldn't notice and ask questions. So far, he was on his third glass, and his yawning had increased to the point that he was now apologizing.

"Don't be silly. You have been working hard lately. Why don't we skip dessert, and I will drive us back?"

Quinton looked over the dessert menu and then placed it down. "Okay, but how about we get some of that pecan pie to go? Who knows, I might get a second wind later."

Melissa smiled and thought, *Doubtful*, but agreed with him anyway. "Absolutely."

The waiter came over, and soon their bill was settled up, and they left the restaurant with Quinton holding a plastic bag and Melissa holding the car keys.

With shaking hands, Melissa hit the unlock button and quickly got in before he changed his mind about her driving. When Melissa buckled up her seat belt, she noticed Quinton missed a step as he bent over and climbed into the passenger seat. Turning her focus back to the wheel, she turned the ignition switch, and the sports car fired to life.

When Melissa eased away from the curb, she looked in her rearview mirror and then pulled out onto the highway. She tightly held the wheel and continued to look straight ahead and into her rearview mirror for any cars following them up the mountain. Casually she glanced toward Quinton and found him leaning his head back with his eyes closed. He had placed the pecan pies on the floor, and she looked at his waist and found that he had also buckled his seat belt as well.

Patiently, she drove slow and waited until she could hear Quinton snoring before making her move. Finally, when they were about three miles away from their chalet, she heard the sound emerge from his lips that she had been dying to hear.

Quietly she spoke. "Quinton, are you awake?"

Time stopped as she waited for some movement, or a voice to emerge from his lips, but nothing. Slowly, Melissa pulled into a driveway at a sign that read: Holly Hills Chalet #3. Gently she leaned over and unbuckled Quinton's seat belt and cringed at the sound of the release button. Again, she waited for him to stir and wake up, but nothing.

Silently she said a prayer and then carefully removed his seat belt away from his body. Looking away from him, she quickly checked to make sure her belt was secured tightly and then eased back onto the main highway and up the mountain, once again surrounded by darkness.

Over the next minute, doubts crept into Melissa's head, and she was beginning to lose her nerve as she glanced Quinton's way. He was sleeping so peacefully. Suddenly, the sight of the mechanic, holding the brake line and frowning, filled her thoughts. Then, another image of Rebecca appeared, happy and running free with Remi. Melissa closed her eyes and shook her head briefly.

When she opened her eyes back up, she saw the yellow sign that showed the curves up ahead. Feeling slightly faint, her hands began to sweat as she held tight the steering wheel, and then slowly, a tear began to roll down her cheek. Pressing harder on the gas pedal, she began to climb upward and took the oncoming turn fast and then jerked the wheel hard toward her right, and suddenly the car left the highway, into the unknown. At the sound of metal bending and glass breaking, the last thought that went through Melissa's mind before losing consciousness was Dillon. She was holding him in her arms as he slept soundly, holding his favorite stuffed animal. Oddly, she felt at peace.

Chapter 19

Melissa carried Dillon down her staircase and was greeted by Nana at the foot of the stairs.

"Are you ready to go?"

"Yes, I don't want to stay long today. It is flu season, and the less Dillon is in the hospital the better."

"I agree. Are you sure you don't want me to stay home with him while you go alone?"

Melissa thought about the question, but didn't change her mind. "No, Quinton has been asking for Dillon nonstop for three days."

"Well, I understand, but he is going to be released tomorrow. One more day won't kill him."

Melissa looked hard into Nana's eyes and tried to read her. Finally she said, "Nana, what is bothering you?"

Nana placed her hands on her hips and said frankly, "You. Something is not right with you. You are different since the accident. More distant."

Melissa felt tears in her eyes, and she instantly held up her free hand and pulled her grandmother in close for a tight embrace.

"I'm so sorry, Nana. You are right. I'm not myself."

Nana pulled back and looked into her granddaughter's eyes. "Melissa, you have got to forgive yourself. You are not to blame yourself for the accident. It could have happened to anyone. You were not intoxicated. The lab reports show that."

Melissa took a deep breath and said, "Thanks, Nana, I think I just need to hear that sometimes."

"Well, has your husband implied differently?"

Melissa quickly reflected back to a previous conversation with Quinton. Never had he once questioned her or accused her of anything. Since his fifth and final operation, Quinton had only been protective and loving toward Melissa and Dillon. For weeks, Melissa doubted herself and the decision she had made over a month ago. Now she was struggling with what had to be done now that Quinton was to be released tomorrow and coming back home.

"No. He just talks of how thankful he is to be alive and that he looks forward to coming home and being a family again."

"Well, see? What has got you so worried?"

Melissa looked away to face Dillon and lied, "Nothing. You're right."

Nana turned around and headed toward the kitchen, which led to the garage, and Melissa followed her with Dillon.

It took thirty minutes to get to the hospital in downtown Birmingham. Soon, both ladies were stepping out of an elevator on Quinton's floor, when Melissa caught a glimpse of someone stepping into the other elevator as she moved forward pushing Dillon's stroller. When Melissa turned to see who the familiar person was, the elevator door closed.

Realizing Melissa had stopped, Nana turned around and asked, "What is it?"

"Nothing, I just thought I recognized someone."

"Who?"

"I think it was Mallory Jane from Junior League."

"Well, could have been. It is a big hospital."

Melissa didn't feel like explaining that Mallory Jane was also a business associate of Quinton's, so she shrugged her shoulders and began pushing Dillon again.

As Melissa rounded the corner, a nurse waved to her from behind the desk and said, "Good morning, ladies."

"Hi, Donna. How is my husband today?"

"Good. But he is getting restless now that he knows he is going home tomorrow."

Melissa nodded and continued on down the hall. After taking a few more steps, she paused and then turned around and asked, "Did he have any visitors this morning?"

Donna placed a pen under her chin and thought for a moment, "Yes, one of his colleagues from work stopped by. Gave him a stack of files."

Melissa smiled. "Thanks"

Slowly, Melissa pushed the door to room 326 open and poked her head in. Quinton was sitting up and looking over some paperwork with open files around his feet. Noticing the door opening, he stopped reading and placed the paper down in one of the open files and closed it. Quickly he stacked all the files together and placed them on the table beside him.

Melissa held the door wider as Nana pushed Dillon's stroller in.

He shouted out, "There is my little man!"

Dillon squealed at the sight of his daddy and immediately started getting out.

Nana helped him catch his balance and then said to Melissa, "You should buckle him in."

Melissa tried not to roll her eyes when she said, "It doesn't do any good, Nana. He knows how to unhook it."

Both ladies turned their attention back to Quinton as he reached down and then pulled Dillon onto his bed.

Melissa stepped forward to help and said, "Hey, take it easy. You pull something, and they will not let you come home tomorrow."

"Wild horses won't keep me from leaving tomorrow. I'm going home!"

Dillon clapped his hands and said, "Daddy coming home!"

Quinton wrapped him into his big arms and playfully ruffled his blond hair. Nana took a seat and smiled at the events that unfolded. Melissa did her best to watch and smile and not get sick.

Twenty minutes had come and gone, and Dillon was no longer content sitting in Quinton's bed and wanted down to roam around.

"We need to go. He doesn't need to get down and start touching everything."

Thankfully, Nana stood up and agreed, and even Quinton knew better than to argue with Virginia Leigh.

"Okay, so what time are you coming by tomorrow?"

Melissa bent over to buckle Dillon in and gave him his juice. "I don't know, I guess around noon. If you are going to be released earlier, just call."

Quinton nodded and asked, "Virginia Leigh, do you mind stepping out with Dillon for a moment?"

Nana looked quizzically at the couple, but replied, "We will be at the nurses' station."

Both watched as Nana left with Dillon, and then Melissa turned around to face her husband.

Quinton sat up some more in the bed and then asked, "What car are you driving now?"

And just like that, it all started all over again. Melissa chose her answer carefully. "Well, as you know, your sports car was totaled."

"And I ordered another one, a newer one."

"Yes, it arrived last week. It is parked in the garage."

"So, have you driven it yet?"

Melissa ran a hand through her hair and sighed.

"Melissa?"

"Yes. I drove it to the grocery store the other day. I wanted to see how it would feel being back in such a small vehicle after the wreck."

"And?"

She shook her head. "I didn't like it. I drive my M-Class."

"Any problems with it?"

Melissa felt the color drain from her face, so she looked down, opened up her purse, grabbed some ChapStick, and applied it to her

139

lips to buy some time. Soon she felt she had recovered enough and finally replied with what she hoped was a good enough answer.

"Actually, since the accident, I have been a little wary and more careful driving. I decided to take the M-Class in for routine maintenance, just to be on the safe side."

This time it was Quinton's turn to look away briefly.

Melissa let the awkward moment pass and then stated, "They replaced a few parts that were worn. I don't know what they were, but I paid the bill."

"Good, that was smart to do."

Melissa forced a smile and then turned to walk toward the door. When she had her hand on the knob, she turned and said, "I don't need to keep them waiting. I'll see you tomorrow."

Quinton tilted his head and then moved his finger in a motion to call her over to his bedside. Melissa let go of the doorknob and walked over timidly. When she was only inches away, he reached out and grabbed her and pulled her into his strong arms and held her tight against his chest, too tight in Melissa's mind.

"I love you, Melissa, and I can't wait to come home to my family."

Melissa pulled back enough to look into his eyes and responded, "Dillon has missed you."

"And what about his mother?"

Melissa's lips slightly trembled as she forced a smile, "I have missed you as well."

Slowly, Quinton released his tight embrace but held on to her hand as he kissed her gently on the lips.

Melissa kissed him back and then slowly backed away and said, "Tomorrow, Quinton," as she left his side and quickly left the room.

Shutting the door behind her, Melissa's knees started to give, and she braced the wall next to her for a moment to collect her thoughts. Nana saw her from down the hall and gave a worried expression. Carefully Melissa straightened back up and tried to act calm and normal as to not alarm Nana. The last thing she wanted was to play twenty questions with Virginia Leigh, because she knew she would eventually lose.

Chapter 20

The next day Quinton took a shower and shaved around ten o'clock after his nurse left. It was official. He was to be released today at noon. He wasn't 100 percent yet, but Dr. Michaels had said he should be in another month or two. That was good enough for Quinton, and most importantly, he could start back to work immediately. The doctor did recommend him to cut back on his hours for the first week and take it slow. Quinton had promised, but doubted he would listen. He would agree to just about anything as long as the doctor agreed to sign the release papers.

Quinton looked at the clock on the wall, and it was now eleven o'clock. Time seemed to stand still as he patiently waited for another hour to pass by. Picking up his remote to the TV, he pressed the top button and began to flip through the channels, searching for a golf game. After cycling through twice, he finally found a game that had just started back up after a commercial. Settling back in his bed, he made himself comfortable.

An hour passed by quicker watching TV, and it was now 12:05. After getting out of bed, Quinton opened his door and looked down the hallway to search for Melissa. *Where is she? She knows how excited I am to leave.*

Quinton left his room and walked to the nurses' station and found Betty, one of his nurses. "Have you seen Melissa?"

Betty looked at the elevator and then back to Quinton and said, "No, sorry. She will be here soon. She probably just got stuck in traffic."

"Is everything ready here? I can go ahead and sign."

Betty pulled his chart and without looking up commented, "Dr. Michaels is with a patient now, but you are next."

Quinton tapped his fingers along the counter and said, "Okay, I'll go back and wait in my room."

"I know it's hard waiting, Mr. Pierson, but I'm sure you will be on your way in the next thirty minutes."

One hour later, Dr. Michaels left Quinton's room, and he was left standing with his release papers and no Melissa. He got out of bed, walked over to the window, and peered outside to look at the traffic on the freeway. All lanes had steady traffic, but all vehicles were moving at a good pace. He took out his cell phone and dialed home.

"Pierson residence."

"Hi, Virginia Leigh, has Melissa left yet? I'm officially released."

Silence.

"Virginia Leigh?"

"Um, Melissa left at ten o'clock. She's not there?" She sounded panicked.

"Ten o'clock? It should only take thirty minutes to get here at that time of day."

"Well, she was going to stop off first at her Junior League headquarters and then be on her way."

"So Dillon is not with her?"

"No, Dillon is with her, so she wouldn't have stayed long at the office. You know how restless he can get. I don't understand, Quinton, where she is. Have you called her?"

"Three times in the last hour."

"Well, Quinton, that doesn't make sense. It wouldn't have taken her that long to get there. It has been..." She looked at the clock and then continued, "Over three hours!"

"Let's not jump to conclusions. Look, I'm going to make some calls, and if she is not here in the next thirty minutes, I'm gonna take a cab."

"Well I am jumping to conclusions. Birmingham is a dangerous place, and she has to go through a rough area to get to the hospital. So yes! I am jumping to conclusions, and I'm going to go ahead and call the police."

Quinton decided she was right and not to argue. "Okay, you do that, and I will start calling her friends. Call me if you hear anything, and if not, I'll be there in about an hour."

Hours went by, but no word from Melissa.

Finally, at nine o'clock that evening, two officers knocked on the Piersons' door.

In a matter of a few seconds, Virginia Leigh opened the door with a worried expression on her face. "Have you found Melissa?"

Quinton and Papa appeared behind her, and Quinton asked, "Did you find them?"

The officers removed their hats. The older one said, "Can we come in?"

Virginia Leigh placed a hand over her chest, and Quinton said, "Yes, please."

Quinton motioned for everyone to step into the formal living room, and then he closed the door and eagerly met up with them. "Please just tell us, what did you find out?"

The younger officer looked at Quinton and then to Virginia Leigh and held her stare as he stated, "We found the M-Class that is registered in her name."

Virginia Leigh gasped, "Oh, thank God! Where?"

The officer hesitated and then finally replied, "The M-Class registered in her name was found on a dirt road outside of a small town called Brookwood."

Quinton asked, "A dirt road?"

The older officer moved forward and placed a hand on Virginia Leigh's arm. "It was stripped and burned. I'm sorry. We are still looking, but there is no sign of Melissa and her son."

For the first time in Quinton Pierson's life, the earth stopped moving, and darkness filled his mind, as he swayed side to side at the news of his missing wife and child.

New Beginnings

Chapter 21

Melissa was sitting on a beach in southeast Queensland wearing a purple two-piece swimsuit, and her long blonde hair was pulled up into a ponytail under a very large hat. Dillon was also sporting a swimsuit, with a long-sleeve sun shirt to protect his precious skin. Together, they had spent the last hour building sandcastles as waves continued to crash to shore and knock them down. Dillon had thought it was the funniest thing ever to witness, and he giggled and clapped his hands. Melissa smiled back at him and hurriedly built another sandcastle before another wave came.

It all felt a little strange. It was two weeks before Christmas, and here she was sitting on a beach, and it was summertime. Australia was so different from the States, but not too different that she couldn't adjust and start a new life. Back in October, she had chosen Australia because they spoke English and it happened to be on the other side of the world, someplace, she hoped, she would never be found.

The first few weeks were unbearable as she constantly thought about deceiving her grandparents. *Oh, what must they be thinking?* she thought. Reflecting back on it all, she wished the private investigator had given her more details of what was happening after she and Dillon were whisked away and given a new identity. But he refused, and she had to ask no further questions, or the deal was off.

Dillon clapped his hands once more and knocked her mind back into reality. As she watched him play, he suddenly jumped up and chased after a wave. Melissa got to her feet quickly and ran to him. She held his hand as he playfully bounced in the water.

Watching Dillon play, she knew that he was happy. This week, Dillon had asked only once for his daddy, but she knew memories would soon fade, and he would eventually forget about Quinton. Melissa just hoped dearly that she could do the same.

"Excuse me, but I believe this belongs to you."

Melissa cleared her mind and turned to the strange voice from behind. Immediately she caught her breath. It was a man holding a shovel in one hand and a surfboard in the other. Melissa tried to peel her eyes away from his hard, muscular exposed body and look into his face to respond.

"Oh yes, thank you." She reached out and grabbed the blue shovel and then bent over to pick up Dillon.

"Do you live here, or are you on holiday?"

"Holiday, but I moved here...well, both."

The surfer smiled and then looked down at Dillon and responded politely, "Cute kid."

Melissa beamed with pride. "Thanks."

"So you are from America, right?"

Melissa felt her throat tighten and treaded carefully. "Yes."

"I thought so, somewhere from the southern part, right?"

Melissa was finding it hard to remember her well-concocted story. Looking into his blue eyes, she finally responded, "Yes."

He smiled at her answer, and she immediately saw that he had a dimple on his left cheek. Dillon began to squirm in her arms. She leaned over and released him, then watched as he took the shovel, ran back to their toys and what was left of their sandcastles, and took a seat in the sand.

Realizing Dillon wasn't going to bolt and run down the beach, she returned her gaze back to the surfer and smiled.

"Well, I'm going to hit the waves. They are nice today."

Melissa placed her hand over her forehead to block the sun and looked out to sea. There were several surfers catching the waves, probably his friends. She turned back toward him. "Thanks for the shovel."

"No worries. Hey, I live right over there. Maybe I will see you around."

Melissa turned toward where he was pointing and saw a small blue beach house standing on poles. Turning back around, she saw his extended hand.

"I'm Carey."

Melissa looked back at Dillon to buy some time to collect her thoughts. He hadn't moved from his spot. Slowly tilting her head upward, she said, "I'm Teresa, and that is my son, David, but he goes by Dillon."

"Nice to meet you." He shook her hand and then quickly released his hold and started backing away toward the water. "Put more sunscreen on. The sun can be brutal here."

She nodded and watched him turn around, run into the waves, and start paddling out to sea.

Dillon called out, "Mommy, I'm firsty!"

Melissa headed over his way and took a seat beside him. She opened up a small cooler and found his juice. "Here you go."

As Dillon drank, Melissa stared out to sea and watched as Carey and the others surfed along the top of the waves with such ease. "What a beautiful day it is, Dillon!" She reached into her pink beach bag and removed the sunscreen to reapply.

Dillon saw what was coming and instantly squirmed and shouted, "No!"

Melissa handed him his favorite little blue boat and said, "Here, play with this in the water puddle, and I will be done in a flash!"

Several minutes later, the sunscreen was put away, and Melissa sat back on her elbows and looked around at all the families who had gathered for a family day at the beach. People were smiling and laughing and having a good time. A sudden jolt of homesickness overtook Melissa, and her eyes moistened.

"Mommy, go in vaves!"

Relieved by the distraction, Melissa stood up and held Dillon's hand and walked toward the water with him carrying his little boat. When Dillon's feet hit the water, he jumped up with joy and squealed. Melissa just smiled and told herself all was going to be just fine.

Chapter 22

Melissa closed Dillon's bedroom door and walked toward the front of the small two-bedroom beach cottage to check the door to make sure it was securely locked. Satisfied, she returned to the kitchen and removed a beer from the refrigerator and headed out to her balcony to listen to the waves. Taking a seat in the hammock, she sipped on her favorite Aussie beer, XXXX Summer.

Calculating in her head the rent, bills, and the high price of food, Melissa realized it was time to get a job. She had brought twenty thousand in cash, but unfortunately, she lost 10 percent with the exchange rate on day one. She picked up her laptop from the coffee table, pulled up her résumé, and glanced over it one more time to check for errors. It was strange to see the name Teresa B. Smith, with a degree in finance from the University of Florida. The name and university were all wrong, but the degree was genuine, though unfortunately, she couldn't produce the real one.

Frowning at the job experiences, she had no choice but to leave them and try to win over her new employer with her bubbly personality. Yesterday, Melissa had searched and found four jobs along the Sunshine Coast, where she lived, that fit her qualifications. With the child care all lined up for tomorrow, it was now up to her to make her new life work.

After saving the open document, Melissa placed her laptop back down and looked out toward the beach. It was a full moon tonight, and many people were walking on the beach with their families. School was out for the summer break, and most locals and vacationers were making the most of the beautiful night. Melissa stood up with her beer and walked closer to the balcony and leaned over to her left to see if she could see Carey's place. Making out the palms and the fence line, she concluded that the place two houses down she was looking at was his. There was a light on, and there appeared to be a few people hanging out on the back porch. Leaning forward more, she tried to listen for voices, but heard none over the sound of the breaking waves.

The house between them was set back some, which was nice because it opened up the view to where one could see the entire coastline to the left. The real estate agent had stated the house was a vacation home and she would probably see the owners the week of Christmas. Looking toward her right, she had a view of a thick reserve, which she liked because it gave her more privacy.

Melissa heard voices and looked down toward the coastal sidewalk that ran between her house and the sand. Spotting a family walking, she smiled. She could hear the young boy asking about Santa and his Christmas presents. Immediately she thought of Dillon and his anticipation of opening gifts. At his age, he was just starting to get the idea of presents and the joy of opening them. Yesterday, Melissa had bought a small artificial tree, and together they put it up in the corner of the living room. Glancing through the glass doors, she could see the blue lights blinking and smiled. Dillon had chosen the blue lights since blue was his favorite color. Nothing else was bought; it was just too hard to get into the Christmas spirit with ninety-five-degree weather.

So far, Melissa had met three of her neighbors, four if she counted Carey. The street she lived on was a small cul-de-sac and had four houses that were oceanfront, like hers, and three that were on the opposite side of the street, with limited views of the ocean. Directly across the street lived Bob and Kim, a retired couple from Brisbane. Beside them were a young couple, Riley and Katherine, who had three children, the youngest being just one year older than Dillon. She had already become good friends with Katherine, and Dillon enjoyed playing with her little girl, Cheryl. The house beside them was another retired couple, whom she had only waved at on her way in and out in her "so far, so good" used vehicle.

"Do you want some company?"

Startled, Melissa looked down toward the bottom of the stairs and found Carey smiling up at her.

"Um, my son is asleep."

Climbing the stairs, he said, "I'll be quiet."

Melissa was a little taken aback by his forwardness, but tried not to read too much into it. So far, everyone she had encountered over the last month was so friendly and went out of their way to be helpful. She tried to convince herself it was only normal for her neighbor to drop by and chat.

Stepping to the side, she said, "Okay."

"Nice night."

"Yes, it is."

Carey looked around the back porch. "This is a nice house. My good mate Pete used to rent this place. He moved to the bush with work."

Again she answered, "Yes, it is." Realizing she was being repetitive, she added, "I was lucky to find a furnished place. They are harder to find."

"Yeah, especially this time of year. So, do you have a partner that is coming up for the holidays?"

Melissa met his gaze and shook her head. "No husband. I've never been married."

"Oh, okay. But there must have been someone. I mean, you have a nipper."

"A nipper?"

He grinned. "A kid." Melissa broke eye contact, and he quickly added, "Sorry, I didn't mean to pry."

Facing him once again, she smiled and said, "It's okay."

"So what do you think of our beer?"

She smiled. "I like it. A lot!"

"Yeah, the Summer is new. It hasn't been around long."

Awkward silence followed, and then Melissa shouted out, "Oh, where are my manners? Would you like a drink?" "Nah, I'm good. Another night, though. I got to work early."

"Oh, what do you do?"

"I'm a professional surfer."

"Really?"

He laughed, "No. I wish. I own my own business. I build houses."

"Really?" Again she realized she was being repetitive and instantly laughed out loud.

He laughed as well and said, "You're funny. So, do you work?"

"Give me a few days and ask me again."

"I will. Well, it's been nice, and hopefully I'll see you around again."

"Yeah, I'm sure you will."

Waving his hand in the air, he turned around and left back down the stairs. Melissa watched as he took a few steps, and then he turned back around and asked, "Do you want to barbecue sometime?"

Melissa felt her throat tighten at the thought of a date and opened her mouth to respond, but no words formed.

Sensing her hesitation, he continued, "Just the barbecue down along the pathway."

Melissa knew what he was referring to and finally spoke. "Yeah, that sounds nice." She watched him walk along the sidewalk back down to his place.

Looking past him, she could see the grill he was referring to. One thing Melissa had noticed right away were the public grills set up all over the coastline, free to use. They were regularly cleaned, and many Australians loved to barbecue. She and Dillon and had used that grill at least a half a dozen times already. In fact, picnics became something that Dillon requested frequently.

Hearing a sound to her right, Melissa quickly looked over to the reserve to determine the noise. Suddenly a bird swooped down across the balcony and then flew into her house.

"No! Get back out!"

Desperately, Melissa pulled the balcony door open to the fullest extent and then ran to her pantry and got the broom and started shooing the bird out. Finally, after a two-minute comedy show, the black-and-white magpie left the house and then landed on the corner of the balcony and stared back at Melissa.

Walking over, she stepped out onto the porch and then pulled the screen back and said, "Don't you do that again!"

The bird tilted his head and then flew away.

Chapter 23

Monday morning seemed to come earlier than normal. It had been nice living a life with no alarm clocks or set schedule. Usually she woke up when she heard Dillon talking over the monitor, but not today! Hitting the alarm button on her phone, she rolled out of bed at six o'clock.

When Dillon woke up at seven, she was already dressed for her job interviews and making breakfast. Sitting in his chair with a booster seat, Dillon asked, "Where we go?"

Melissa placed the omelet on his plastic plate and replied, "I'm going to grown-up meetings, and you are going to Katherine's house to play with Cheryl."

Clapping his hands with excitement, Dillon screamed out, "Cheryl!"

"So, my little man, you need to eat first, and then we will get you dressed and go."

Quickly Dillon picked up his fork, and Melissa took a seat beside him and finished the last few sips of her coffee.

By seven thirty, Melissa was waving bye to Katherine and Dillon and pulling out toward the direction of Mooloolaba, a beachside town fifteen minutes south of where she lived.

Traffic was going good, and Melissa arrived ten minutes early for her eight o'clock interview. She parked her car and stepped out in her black skirt and white silk blouse, carrying a small folder containing her résumé. It didn't take long to locate the building of Morrison Advertising and then climb the stairs that led to the entrance. Like most places, there was an open parking garage on the bottom floor and then a set of stairs that took her up to the main level. She opened the glass door, then looked at the business directory, found Morrison located on the fourth floor, and took the elevator.

When the elevator door opened up, Melissa was in the atrium of Morrison Advertising. Confidently she stepped forward and walked straight to the reception desk to check in. Melissa was asked to wait in the small waiting room and was offered coffee, which she politely declined. She thought, *Coffee and white blouse don't mix when one is nervous as hell!*

It didn't take long before a middle-aged man appeared and called out, "Teresa Smith."

Melissa stood and walked over and shook his hand with a firm shake. "I'm Teresa."

The man smiled. "I'm Andrew Morrison." Then he gestured down the hallway and said, "Please follow me."

As they walked, he asked, "Have any problem finding the place?"

Melissa shook her head. "None, the directions were good."

Opening a door, Andrew stood to the side, "Please come on in and take a seat."

Melissa stepped into the room and found six other people sitting around a large conference table, waiting for her. Taking a deep breath, she walked over to the vacant chair for her and took a seat.

Andrew spoke. "Melissa, this is my team, and I hope you don't mind the large group for your interview."

Melissa forced a smile. "Not at all, I look forward to meeting people that I will work with."

Andrew quickly made introductions and then took his seat and fired away. "So, first of all, tell us why you came to Australia."

Melissa thought, *Here we go! It is time now to deliver my well-rehearsed speech.*

Smiling back, she started, "I moved to the Sunshine Coast a month ago looking for something new and fresh. I'm at a stage in my life where I wanted something different that presented a challenge and change of scenery, so here I am."

A redheaded lady on the far end asked, "So what do you think of our country?"

"Beautiful. People have been so friendly and made me feel truly welcome. After a month of living here, I have questioned when and if I'll ever go back to Florida."

A few laughs and smiles were shared, and then it was straight down to business.

Andrew asked, "You have worked for the last five years as a manager of a dry-cleaning business, correct?"

Melissa straightened her shoulders and responded, "Yes. It was a family business. Once I graduated from Florida, I returned home to help my father since my mom had died the previous year. A few months ago, my father was killed in a car accident, and I decided to sell the business and start over fresh somewhere else."

The room got real quiet, and an awkward moment passed before Andrew replied, "I'm sorry to hear that."

Melissa nodded. "Well, as you can see with the financial statements, the business was a success the entire time I managed it, and we grew our operation to include many chain hotels."

"Yes, I see that." Pausing briefly to look over her résumé, he then added, "Tell me something more that we can't see with these papers."

Melissa smiled her winning smile and continued to talk about experiences from her last job in Jackson with Guin and Williams. Of course, she had to twist and turn the facts some, but it came across wonderfully presented.

Another hour passed with more questions and, in Melissa's mind, good answers. Finally Andrew Morrison stated, "Thank you, Teresa, I don't believe we have any more questions at this time." Melissa saw an older man nod toward him, and then Andrew said, "If you wouldn't mind waiting outside in the waiting room, someone will be out shortly."

This was unexpected. Melissa hadn't anticipated waiting. She just thought someone would call her in a few days to let her know if she got the job. Standing up, she said clearly and loudly enough for all to hear, "Certainly."

Andrew smiled, then opened the door for her. He closed it once she made a few steps.

Melissa waited in the waiting room for twenty minutes, and then one of the ladies came out from behind the doors and made her way over to her.

"Teresa, I am pleased to inform you that we would love to have you as a part of our team here at Morrison Advertising."

Melissa beamed with pride and shook her outstretched hand. "Thank you so much!"

"Now as you know, this is a temporary position, but if all works out well, we could be looking at offering you full-time work."

Melissa smiled. "That would be great!"

The lady returned her smile. "My name is Karen, and we will be working very closely together over the next several weeks."

"I look forward to it."

"Me too. Now, if you have the time, I would like to walk you down to the HR department and get the ball rolling on your work visa and the rest of your paperwork."

"No problem, I have the time."

"Great, follow me."

Katherine opened the door to an exuberant Teresa. "You're back early. How did it go?"

Waving her hands, Melissa shouted out, "So good, I had to cancel my remaining interviews!"

"Good on you! Let's celebrate!" She motioned Melissa inside her home.

As they made their way into the living room, Melissa immediately saw Dillon and Cheryl playing with trucks on the floor.

Taking a seat on the couch, Katherine asked, "When do you start?"

Melissa clapped her hands and smiled. "In three days!"

"Wow, that is fast. I'm so excited for you, but also bummed! Who am I going to have coffee with at the park?"

"We will still find time to get together, I promise you that!"

Katherine frowned a few seconds and then replied, "Okay. But I am going to hold you to that promise, starting now."

Melissa smiled. "Let me go home and change and grab Dillon's pram, and I will be back in a jiffy."

"Well look at you! We are going to make an Aussie out of you yet!"

Melissa returned her gaze with a confused expression on her face.

"You used the word 'pram,' not 'stroller'!"

Melissa got up and smiled back at her dear friend. "Well, you might be right then." Then she hurried out the front door.

It was two o'clock in the afternoon as Melissa sipped on a cappuccino while Dillon and Cheryl played on the park playground. Sitting on the bench, she gazed out to sea and admired the beautiful day. The play equipment was strategically placed beneath a very large tree, which was perfect for shade, and several benches surrounded the park that gave nice views of the beach below the small, sloped beachfront.

"You are going to miss this!"

"Oh, I know, but I should be home by four thirty at the latest, and that is Dillon's favorite time at the beach, as well as mine."

"How early do you have to be there?"

"Eight forty-five."

"Oh, that is not too early. Hey, I got a friend I can call to give a recommendation on day care."

"Good, I need to start that today."

"You might even find someone to come to your house."

Melissa frowned. "That would be too expensive."

Katherine shrugged. "You're probably right."

"I have been so careful with the money I received from my family business, and I don't want to start being frivolous now. Besides, Dillon will start school in a few more years."

"You will be fine. After all, you did major in finance."

Melissa looked away and thought, *You have no idea.* This job would be a breeze compared to her role that she held in Jackson as a top executive. Moments went by as she continued to stare out to sea and reminisce about her last job at Guin and Williams. She loved her job very much and missed everyone there a lot. Shrugging the thoughts out of her mind, she was determined to start her new job with optimism and a fresh start.

"Teresa?"

"Huh?"

"Where did you go?"

"Another place."

"Well jump out of it because there is a hot guy waving at you from the water."

Perplexed, Melissa looked away from Katherine and out to sea, and sure enough, someone was waving at them.

"Do you know him?"

She hesitated briefly. "Yeah, I think that is Carey, you know, the guy that lives on our street."

Katherine placed a hand against her forehead to block the sun and stared intently. "I think you are right. When did you meet him?"

"Just the other day, at the beach."

"Well, you obviously made an impression because here he comes!"

Chapter 24

Melissa struggled to regulate her breathing as Carey slowly approached wearing lime green swim trunks and holding his surfboard easily. When he was a few feet away, he set his board down and then ran his hands through his wet blond hair, slicking it back off his forehead.

"Good afternoon, ladies. Enjoying the day?"

Katherine replied first, "Yes, very much."

Melissa glanced over at Cheryl and Dillon, who where sliding down the slide together. They were playing without any care to the adults assembled together at the bench.

Carey followed her eyes and saw the kids playing and then asked, "How are you today, Teresa?"

Glancing up into his gorgeous blue eyes, she timidly announced, "Good. I thought you had to work today?"

Katherine turned to face Melissa with a quizzical expression on her face, but Melissa ignored it.

"I did. I started early. I like to surf in the early afternoon, you know, less likely to be shark bait."

Melissa changed her expression. "Is that really true?"

With such ease, he shook his head. "Nah, you just got to stay away from murky water. That is my rule of thumb."

Melissa forced a smile.

"So, do you want to give it a go?"

Melissa glanced over her attire. She was wearing her Australian name-brand Lorna Jane workout shorts and tank top. "I'm really not dressed. Besides, Dillon is playing on the slide." She pointed toward him just as he and Cheryl flew down the slide for the hundredth time.

Katherine interrupted quickly. "I will keep an eye on them. Go give it a try while you have a pro to show you."

Melissa shot her friend a look. "I'm not wearing my swimsuit."

"Who cares? You are in Australia now!" exclaimed Katherine.

"She is right, come on!"

Before Melissa could respond, Carey reached out and grabbed her coffee and gave it to Katherine, and with another quick move, he pulled her forward on her feet and tugged her toward his board.

"Wait, my flip-flops!" She kicked off her shoes toward Katherine and couldn't help but smile back at her friend, who was beaming with the thought of seeing Melissa surf for the first time.

"They are called thongs, remember?" yelled Katherine with a smile.

Carey picked up his surfboard and began a slow jog down to the sand and placed his board down by the waters' edge. "Just a few pointers first."

Melissa watched as he lay down on the board and then positioned himself upward in one swift move to demonstrate how to properly place her feet for balance.

After two more demonstrations, he said, "You try it now."

Melissa felt a little goofy lying on the surfboard in the sand, but did as she was told. The first try was a little off the mark, and after sharing a good laugh together, she tried again.

"Better! Now let's hit the water!"

Timidly, Melissa watched as he high-stepped a few waves with the board and didn't start moving till he shouted, "Come on!"

Looking back up at the grassy park area, Melissa could see Katherine motioning her forward, laughing. Turning back around, she finally followed Carey into the water. The water felt good with the ninety-degree weather with no clouds to block the sun. She slowly met up with Carey, and instantly he picked her up and gently placed her down on the board.

"Lay down, and I'm gonna be right here beside you. When I say paddle with your arms, paddle! And when I say jump up, jump!"

Melissa forced a look up into his face with the sun beaming behind him, hurting her eyes, so she squinted and faced ahead and downward at her board. It seemed like minutes passed by until Carey found the perfect wave and began shouting, "Paddle!"

Scared but excited, Melissa began looking ahead and paddling with all her might. Soon, after a few strokes, she heard him scream behind her, "Jump!"

Doing as he instructed, she pushed up with her hands and knees and landed her feet on the board in a squatting position and then took a leap of faith and stood up, catching her balance. Just as she was standing, she caught a ripple, and with the unexpected force, she went sailing to her left and into the water. Feeling a tug on her ankle, she knew the surfboard was still attached, and she reached out for it and grabbed hold. Just as she was climbing on, another wave caught her and sent her spiraling round and round as water crashed all around her.

After what seemed like a minute surrounded by waves, suddenly she was pulled up into Carey's strong arms and brought back to shore. Coughing slightly, she heard Carey laughing, "Oi mate, are you okay?"

Releasing herself from his arms, she ran a hand over her face and then smoothed her hair back off her face and eyes. Looking down at her body, she saw how her workout clothing was clinging to every curve. Embarrassed, she stammered, "I'm...I'm okay. Was that supposed to be fun?"

Carey's leaned his head back as he laughed out loud. "You did good on your first try. You got up! Most people don't get up."

Somehow Melissa didn't feel encouraged, but finally cracked a smile. "That was refreshing."

He grinned and grabbed her arm and began dragging her back into the water. "Got to get back in before you think too much and give up."

"Wait! Wait!" But her cries were not persuasive enough as she continued to be dragged back farther out to sea.

Once again, she was picked up and placed back on the board and told, "Lay down, and paddle when I say paddle!"

"And jump when you say jump! Right?" she responded, smiling.

He winked at her, then jerked his head back toward the ocean and said, "Oh, oh, this is gonna be a big one! Hold on!"

Quickly he jumped on top of her and started to paddle farther out to sea. Just when it appeared they were gonna be swamped by an oversized wave, they tipped the top just in time.

Carey looked at her frightened face and calmly said, "You're not ready for the big ones yet."

Safely beyond the wave, he eased back into the water, taking her with him. As their bodies floated close to one another, bobbing up and down with each ripple of the water, she was caught in a moment of peace and warmth. Somehow she felt safe in his care.

Several moments passed as he looked into her eyes without breaking eye contact. Finally he remarked, "I like you. I want to get to know you better."

Opening her mouth to speak, he interrupted. "Oh, not now, here comes a nice gentle one. Up you go!"

Before she could register it all, she was lying back on the board and paddling as commanded. Feeling the tug on the board, she jumped as instructed and landed nicely on her feet. Feeling the board shift over the wave, she relaxed and caught her balance long enough for a short ride.

Crashing back into the water, she heard from a distance, "Whoo hoo! You did it, mate!"

Finding the bottom of the ocean, she stood up and grabbed on to the board and held tight as it continued to carry her to shore. Within seconds, she was back on shore and placing the board down. As Carey made himself to shore, she bent over and peeled the velcro strap away from her ankle before she was forced to try it again.

"You done?"

Melissa smiled and then looked toward the park until she found Dillon. On the bench, Dillon was sitting beside Cheryl and Katherine, clapping his hands as he stared toward her. Instantly, Melissa waved back with pride and then spun around to face Carey. "Thank you, that was a lot of fun! I'm glad you pushed me into doing this."

Carey reached out and touched her hair and pulled it back off her forehead. "Good, you will ride longer next time, you'll see."

She stammered, "Ne-Next time?"

He laughed as he bent over and picked up his board and then stood back up in a relaxed stance. She couldn't help it, she looked over his hard chest and his lean waist, and then her eyes worked back up toward his face. He was smiling a mischievous grin, and she instantly blushed.

"S-Sorry."

"For what?"

Looking away, she said, "Let's go back up."

As she moved forward, he grabbed hold of her arm and pulled her back around to face him. He didn't embrace her, but slowly released her. "I had fun. Barbecue with me tonight."

Slowly she peeled her eyes off his hands and looked up into his face. A moment passed, and neither said anything as they searched each other's faces for clues to what this might be. Finally she nodded and then smiled slightly.

He returned her gesture. "I'll see you at the barbecue at six." With his free hand, he waved up toward the park to Katherine and the kids, then turned away with his board and started paddling back out to sea.

Melissa stood mesmerized as she watched him make it to the other side of the breaking waves with such ease. He gracefully sat up and waved back to her and then looked away toward the upcoming waves. Finding one he liked, he began paddling and within seconds jumped up and maneuvered side to side through the long, breaking wave. Finally, when it ended, he jumped off the board and into the water once more. Catching his eye, she gave him the thumbs-up and then turned away to make her way back up to the park.

When Melissa reached the park bench, Dillon was shouting, "Yeah, Mom! You wode the vaves!"

"Yes, I did! When I get better, I will have to teach you!" She placed her hand over his blond head of hair and gave it a friendly jostle.

"Sooo, that went well. I think there is more to tell," Katherine replied coyly.

"Well, we will see." Looking toward Dillon, she asked, "Dillon, do you remember Carey? He found your shovel."

Dillon placed his hands on his head to lay his hair back down. "Um-huh."

"Well, we are going to meet him later tonight at the barbecue. He is gonna cook for us."

Holding her breath for his reply, she was relieved when he responded, "Yummy! A picnic!"

Smiling, she looked away toward Katherine, who had clasped her hands under her chin and nodded her approval. "Well, I hate to break up this party, but I have to get back and start preparing dinner as well."

Katherine stood up and guided Cheryl toward her pram and then bent over and buckled her up. Melissa, noticing the time, got up as well and pulled Dillon's pram over to the bench.

When Dillon saw the gesture, he pouted. "No! I want to watch Carey in the vaves!"

Melissa turned away from him just in time to see Carey sailing over another wave effortlessly. "Okay, buddy, we will stay and watch Carey a little longer."

Chapter 25

At five forty-five, Melissa began to get nervous. It had been a long time since she had gone on a date that wasn't with her husband. She rattled off in her head subjects that were safe to talk about and tried to think of things that might be of interest to him. Struggling with what to wear, Melissa stood in her closet clothed in only her underwear. So far, she had changed four times.

"Ugh! What am I doing?" she shouted.

From in the living room of their small cottage, Dillon yelled back, "What?"

Frustrated, she yanked down a sundress and hollered back, "Nothing!"

"Otay!" he responded, and she could hear him now making zooming noises with his trucks.

Stepping into the orange sundress, she began the process of pulling it up over her shapely hips and then up over her full chest. Next she zipped it up and then tied the strings behind her neck. Walking over to her floor-length mirror stand, she closely examined herself. Turning a little to the side, she smoothed it out over her flat stomach. *Is this too dressy? After all, it is just a barbecue on the beach.* The sundress revealed her bare bronzed back, and the length fell just above her knees, showing her long, sexy legs. Just when she decided it was too dressy, she heard a knock on the back door.

"Mommy, Mommy! Carey!"

With wide eyes, Melissa looked at her watch and saw that it was now six o'clock. She rushed over to her dresser, quickly sprayed some perfume on her wrist, then wrapped her long blonde tresses up into a quick twist and clasped them with a clip. She applied her bronze lipstick and then rushed toward the living room to find Carey waiting with a grin.

"You look nice. Here, have a beer."

Melissa reached out and grabbed it, noticing he had chosen to buy the XXXX Summer, her favorite. "Thank you."

"Are you ready?"

Melissa looked down at Dillon as he jumped up and down shouting, "Weady!"

"I guess that is a yes!" he said.

"Do I need to bring anything?"

"Nope, all taken care of, let's go."

Walking out the back door, she slid the screen closed and then locked it with a key. Carey noticed her movements and commented, "We can see the house from the barbecue."

"I know. Old habits die slow."

"Yeah, I guess it is a lot to get used to here."

Carey reached down and grabbed Dillon's hand as they made their way down the stairs. Melissa watched as both walked hand in hand, both wearing khaki shorts, T-shirts, and baseball caps. The only difference in their attire was that Dillon had chosen his cowboy boots, and Carey, logically, had chosen his flip-flops. Melissa couldn't help but smile as Carey looked down and laughed as Dillon clambered down the sidewalk in boots.

At the barbecue, he had already set up a place to sit at the nearby picnic table and had steaks and vegetables all laid to the side of a hot plate, ready to cook.

"This looks great."

"Good, I forgot to ask you if you ate steak."

"I do, and so does Dillon. Actually, he eats everything."

"That is also good to hear because I also brought some roo kebabs for you two to try."

Melissa's eyes widened. "You mean as in kangaroo?"

"Awesome," chimed in Dillon. "I wanna see!"

Carey bent down and picked up Dillon high enough where he could see the four wooden sticks with small pieces of meat on each one. "You are gonna like it. You will see." Placing Dillon back down, he glanced over toward Melissa and said, "You will too."

Forcing a smile, she said nothing.

Dillon wandered off toward the picnic table and sat down with his small backpack and began pulling out toys. Since they barbecued often together, Melissa kept a small bag of toys just for this purpose, to entertain him while she cooked. This time, though, she was getting waited on, and that brought her much satisfaction.

Walking over closer to Carey with her beer in hand, she casually asked, "So how long have you lived here?"

Carey began unwrapping the meat and placed it on the hot solid steel surface and replied, "My whole life. I grew up here."

"Really?"

Placing the last stick on the barbecue and picking up his beer for another swig, he then replied, "Really. I was born in Coolum. Business is good here, and I've always had a steady amount of work flowing in."

"Does your work ever allow you to travel?"

"Absolutely, since I'm the boss, I can take on jobs to suit my own schedule."

"So where all have you been? In Australia?"

"Just about everywhere. I try somewhere new every year. My favorite is the Northern Territory. It's beautiful. You will have to see it while living here."

"And your next favorite place?"

Turning the meat over, he answered, "North Queensland, up where the Barrier Reef is."

"I would love to take Dillon to see the Great Barrier Reef."

"Yeah, he would like it, but I would wait till he gets a little older."

"How old?"

He looked back at her with a serious expression. "Maybe five or six. Why? How long are you going to be living here?"

Melissa thought, *There it is. The question I didn't want to get.* She had asked herself that a dozen or more times since living here the last month. Could she stay indefinitely, or would she one day go home and try to reclaim her life back on her terms?

"Not an easy answer, is it?"

Melissa found his soft blue eyes and honestly answered, "No, it's not."

"I would imagine it was hard to leave your family and friends behind. Will anyone visit?"

Melissa looked toward Dillon and tried to picture her Nana here with them and playing on the beach and building sandcastles. She would probably have a dog by then, and she could picture Dillon throwing a tennis ball and watching a little Jack Russell run after it on the beach as she and Nana watched with such happiness.

He nudged her arm. "Hey, you gonna be okay over the holidays?"

She smiled. "Yes, I plan to spend the day with Katherine and her family at the beach."

"Good. I'm sure we will run into each other. My parents will come up from their house, along with my sister and her hubby and nippers."

"Sounds nice." Changing the subject, she quickly stated, "I start a job after the holidays."

"Well, congratulations. Where at?"

"In Mooloolaba, with an advertising firm."

"Good, it is close by. Got plans for him yet?"

"Made a few calls today, and plan to check out a few tomorrow."

Melissa took the last sip from her beer, and he said, "There is plenty more in the cooler. Help yourself."

"Thanks, I'll grab you another one as well."

Walking over to the picnic table, Melissa noticed that Dillon had decided to draw in his *Blue's Clues* notebook. Just as she stuck her hand in the cooler, she froze when she saw a family picture with the names Mommy, Daddy, and Dillon written in her old babysitter's handwriting. *Damn! Why didn't I rip out the old pages!* Melissa pulled two XXXX Summers out of the cooler and walked back over toward

Carey, praying Dillon wouldn't come running with his artwork for show-and-tell.

Taking the beer from her hands, he asked, "Since Dillon is probably too young to go to the Reef, why don't you let me take the both of you to Moreton Island?"

Melissa looked out to sea and pointed. "That is Moreton Island, correct?"

"Yep."

Hesitating a moment to ponder the significance of his question and if she wanted to carry on this relationship, she asked herself, *Is this healthy for Dillon? After all, he is over there drawing Mommy and Daddy photos!* Finally thinking it was the right thing to do, move on—after all, she did get a job, and she wasn't running—she said, "How do we get there?"

A pleased expression formed over Carey's face. "We have a couple of options. There is a barge that you can drive your four-by-four on, and it takes you to the island. Once there, you can drive on the beach all over the place."

"That sounds fun. I've done four-wheeling before, and it was a lot fun!"

Just like that, a memory of her and Quinton holding on for dear life as they climbed a washed-out road that would take them to their rafting adventure came flooding back to haunt her. The day had been a good one, and she remembered instantly the rock pool and waterfall. A frown formed on her face as she began to question why she hadn't been enough for him. Why did he seek out Rebecca? Why did he kill her?

Quickly realizing she was elsewhere, she tuned back into reality and turned around to face Carey as he continued.

"Another option is a passenger ferry, and you stay at the resort on the island."

"There is a resort there?"

"Yeah, only one, there are a few beach homes, though, you could rent." Realizing her thoughts about renting a room, he quickly added, "Or the best option, to take a day trip on my boat."

With a look of surprise she asked, "You have a boat?"

"I do. A fishing boat."

Melissa looked toward his house, but didn't see where he would keep it.

Reading her thoughts, he clarified. "I keep it at a marina in Mooloolaba."

"Okay, I know where that is. Dillon and I walked along the walkway that is between the marina and the beach."

"Yep, that is the one. It's nice there, isn't it?"

"Beautiful!"

"Mommy, Mommy! Look what I drew!"

Melissa spun around to face her son, and to her displeasure, she saw the drawing on the opposite page as he ran toward the both of them. Melissa turned around to face Carey with a ghostly expression on her face.

Noticing her face, he looked closer at the book that Dillon was proudly holding. "Nice picture, Dillon. Now go put that away with all the toys because the food is ready."

Dillon turned back around and began packing his toys away off the table. Carey looked indifferent as he began piling the steaks, vegetables, and roo kebabs on a platter. When he was finished, he turned to face her with the food in one hand and a beer in the other and said, "When you're ready, not before, now let's eat!"

Melissa stepped to the side as he made his way to the picnic table and then slowly followed him.

Chapter 26

Quinton sat in his study holding a picture of Melissa with Dillon in her arms. God, she was beautiful, he thought. With his finger, he traced the outline of her face. For this photo, her hair was worn down, just as he liked it. She was wearing a teal blue strapless dress that made her eyes seem bluer than normal. She hadn't lost all her baby weight, but still, she was truly stunning. After another moment, his eyes shifted to Dillon in her arms. Just like his mother, blond, and blue eyes that were twinkling back into the camera as he had snapped the shot.

Putting the frame back down on his desk, he pondered the day the picture was taken. Suddenly the memory came flooding back. The grape Popsicle that Dillon was holding had been purchased at the local park. Together, as a family, they had spent the day swinging on the play set and lounging on a quilt that was laid out on top of the dark green grass.

"This is nice, Quinton. We need to do this more often." Melissa's voice rang out in his head, and he felt a cold shiver run down his back. As if it were yesterday, he remembered responding, *"You're right, we should. This is nice."*

Dillon had laughed and giggled uncontrollably that day as he pushed him back and forth in the toddler swing. Melissa had joined alongside and was swinging in her cotton sundress. He could see her hair blowing in the wind as she swayed. She watched Quinton with a playful smile and flirted with her eyes. She was so alive that day, he thought.

Running his hands through his hair, he quickly sat back up and pushed the fond memories away. Grabbing the stack of bills that had been piling up, he thumbed through them and pulled out the ones that were the most pressing. After ten minutes of paying bills online and filing, he came across it.

Under his credit card statement was a letter-sized envelope from an auto repair shop. With curiosity, he opened it up knowing he hadn't charged anything lately, but wanted to make sure all bills had been paid from the accident in October. Knowing Melissa, she probably hadn't taken care of everything from the car while he was recovering in the hospital for several weeks.

Turning it to the side, he sliced it opened with the letter opener and pulled out the enclosed paper and read.

Mrs. Pierson,

Thank you for allowing our body shop to repair your vehicle on Oct. 8, 2010. We value your patronage, and if you ever need any services again, please give us a call to set up an appointment. Please find our magnet enclosed with our phone number and business hours.

Sincerely,

Arnie Banks

Owner of Arnie's Body Shop

Quinton looked at the magnet and tossed it around in his hand, then threw it in the trash bin along with the letter. Seeing that there was nothing else, he pushed back from his chair and went into the kitchen to make his lunch. Opening the refrigerator, he pulled out a pasta dish that was left over from the night before, from his dinner date with Mallory Jane.

Deciding that pasta shouldn't be eaten without wine, he uncorked a new bottle and poured a glass. As he sat at the bar eating, he began to read the wine label. Suddenly he realized it was the same brand as the one he had with Melissa up in Gatlinburg. Angrily he walked over to the pantry and stored the bottle inside, then closed the door to her haunting ghost, which seemed to be all around him today.

Just as he made his way back to the bar and took a bite of his pasta, the phone rang, and he jumped, knocking his wineglass off the counter, and it crashed onto the floor. He heard Melissa laughing behind him, and he turned around and found only empty space. Even though she wasn't there, he could hear her playful voice. *"Why, Quinton, I think you've had too much!"*

The phone continued to ring, and it slowly drowned out the thoughts of Melissa in his head. Standing up, he carefully stepped around the broken glass and answered the phone.

"Hi, baby! Did I catch you at a bad time?"

"What? Um, no, just made a mess in the kitchen."

"Oh, do you need some help?"

Quinton rolled his eyes. "No. I'm good."

"Okay, well the reason I'm calling is I need you to check some paperwork on the Brown acquisition that took place in October."

"From October, why?"

"I know, I just had some loose ends that I am tying up, and I think one of the papers got misfiled or misplaced. Oh hell, I don't know, it was such a crazy time then when you were in the hospital. I might have even—"

Quinton interrupted. "It's no problem. Send me an e-mail with the specifics, and I'll look into it."

"Thanks, already sent the e-mail just before I called."

Silence.

"Quinton?"

"Yes, I'm still here."

"What are you doing later on? I think I'd like a backrub after all the work I've been doing today."

"Busy. You might have to call a local masseuse."

Silence.

"I'm sorry, dear, that was ugly. If I get time later, I'll give you a ring. How is that?"

"Sounds better. Later." And the phone line went dead in his hands.

Placing the receiver down, he thought about the last few weeks with Mallory Jane. She had increasingly become so needy and damn moody. *I don't remember Melissa being like that while she was carrying Dillon. Oh hell, maybe she was and I just wasn't home enough to notice. Or maybe all my free time was spent thinking of Rebecca.*

Quinton grabbed a towel off the counter, and with his other hand the garbage can, and walked back over to clean up his mess. He preferred sweet tea now, so he made a glass and then picked up his pasta bowl and headed back toward his office. Settling back down in his chair, he picked up his mobile phone and saw that he had one missed call, Mallory Jane. Next, he made a few clicks with the mouse and pulled up the e-mail she had sent earlier and looked through the transactions. Scanning over the dates, he needed his calendar for a reference. Flipping through to the month of October in his leather-bound diary, he immediately saw "Gatlinburg Trip" scrawled out largely over four days. More ghost appeared clouding his mind. Pushing the unpleasant memories away, he compared his calendar to the e-mail.

Finally, after twenty minutes, he was able to respond to Mallory Jane's e-mail and close the inquiry and pack away the Brown acquisition once more. Looking at the time, he closed out of his e-mail and picked up his dirty dish and left the study. Just as he made it to the living room, the doorbell rang.

He jogged to the door and opened it to find Mitch holding a case of beer. "Kick-off time, ready to see the Colts kick some ass!"

Quinton smiled back at his old neighbor and gestured him inside.

It wasn't until nine o'clock when Mitch left to go home and Quinton locked up and headed up the stairs to bed. As he passed Dillon's room, he paused for a moment, like always. Slowly he lifted his hand to the closed door and waited. With the effects of the alcohol of the day, he was a little more somber tonight, and the death of his son was a little more difficult than normal. Gradually, he pulled his hand away and continued to his room, alone.

Quinton usually had no problems with sleeping. But tonight, something kept nagging at his brain that was unsettling. After tossing and turning for about an hour, he finally got back up to use the restroom again. Just as he lay back down and closed his eyes and sleep was beginning to take over, he jolted up and slung the sheets off his body and got out of bed. Turning on lights, he fled down the stairs and rushed into his study. He ran over to the trash bin and pulled out papers until he found the note from the auto repair shop. The date was October 8. Flipping through his dairy, he instantly saw what had kept nagging at his brain. The visit to the auto shop was all wrong! They didn't leave to go to Gatlinburg until the ninth.

Noting the time, Quinton couldn't call or do anything to confirm the date. Slowly he got back up and made his way back toward his bedroom, knowing sleep wouldn't come anytime soon.

Chapter 27

Quinton awoke with a dull headache to the sound of his alarm. He had set it for seven in the morning, which happened to be the opening time for the repair shop. Taking the magnet in his hands, he quickly dialed the number shown.

"Good morning, Arnie's Body Shop, how may we help you?"

"Yes. I received a letter in the mail concerning a repair that was made on October eighth for Melissa Pierson. Could you kindly let me know what the service was for?"

"No problem. Was it a bill?"

"No."

"Okay, what was the last name again?"

Feeling his head pound harder, he stated, "Pierson, Melissa, October the eighth."

"Okay, let me put you on hold for a minute, and I'll look that up."

Quinton allowed the receiver to fall down the side of his face and rest on his shoulder as he tilted his head backward and mouthed a load of profanity toward the ceiling.

In the course of the three minutes to reply, Quinton could feel his blood pressure rising.

"Sir, I found the invoice."

Trying not to lose his patience, he asked, "And...what was the service for?"

Time began to slowly tick. He listened as the lady read aloud as she scrolled down the invoice. Finally, she said bluntly, "Here we go. She had new brakes installed."

Feeling left Quinton's face and hands, and he quickly sat back down on the bed.

"Sir, is there anything else? It was paid for by a credit card on the same day as service, so there is no outstanding bill."

"No. I mean yes! Did she come in for a routine service?"

"Um, I can't be sure, nothing was noted, but I can talk to the head mechanic, Arnie."

Quickly he interrupted. "No. That won't be necessary."

"Are you sure? It has on the invoice that Arnie did the job. I could ask, and he might remember."

"No, that is quite all right. I just wanted to make sure the bill was paid, that's all."

Quinton thought back to when Melissa was visiting him in the hospital. *"I took my M-Class in for a service,"* he clearly remembered her saying. Now he was confused. Was this before or after the accident? Quickly, confusion began to cloud his thoughts, but he was interrupted.

"Sir, is there anything else?"

"Um, yes, are you sure the date was October the eighth instead of November the eighth?"

"Well, it has in the computer the eighth of October. I don't think that is an error. You could always check your credit card statement."

Quinton slammed his fist against his forehead and thought, *Of course, why didn't I think of that sooner?* and quickly replied with, "I will, thanks, that will be all."

"Okay then, you have a nice day."

In a quiet voice, he mumbled, "Thanks, you too," and he hung up the phone and stared at the wedding portrait that hung three feet from his bed. Looking into her blue eyes, he asked aloud, "Did you know, Melissa?"

And of course, no response. Only the presence of her ghost filled his room. Angrily, he stood up and removed the picture. He opened her closet, threw it in, and slammed the door.

Next, he took off downstairs, toward his study, and immediately searched past credit card statements from Melissa's file. As he pulled out the statement, he silently cursed how Mallory Jane was keeping him so distracted from everything. Recently, she was putting on the pressure to announce their relationship. God, how could he get through to her that the math wouldn't add up, especially with her starting her six month of pregnancy.

Finally, he found what he was looking for, and as clear as day, the date of service was for October 8, at Arnie's Body Shop, for $288.

Placing the statement down, he leaned back in his chair and said aloud, "Shit! She knew."

Chapter 28

Melissa packed away the small Christmas tree and lights as Dillon played on the floor with his new toys. Looking at the small box, she couldn't help but think about all the decorations up in the attic of her house in Birmingham. Did Quinton decorate and throw a big lavish party without her, she thought. A flood of memories of caterers, a Christmas tree so big it required two people to put up, and her and Quinton all dressed up returned. As if he was standing right beside her, she could hear him, *"Come on, Barbie, join Ken. We need to get downstairs before we are late."* Slowly, a smile crept over her face at the fond memory. But unfortunately, the bad came with the good, and a flash of Rebecca in her bedroom the night of the party brought reality crashing down once again.

"Mommy! Mommy!"

Suddenly Melissa realized she was crying and wiped her eyes and then turned around to face Dillon.

"What da noise?"

Melissa looked at where he was frantically pointing and searched the dark corner of the room with her eyes. "What noise, Dillon? I don't hear anything."

Frightened, Dillon jumped up with his truck and ran toward her. "A monster, Mommy!"

Embracing Dillon in her arms, she tried to calm his fears. "I don't see any monsters. You're safe!"

Dillon snuggled deeper into her chest and mumbled, "I don't like monsters!"

"I know, baby, but there are no monsters here." But as she said the words, she couldn't help but think of Quinton and continued to scan the small room and down the dark hallway that led toward their bedrooms. Deciding to conquer their fear head-on, Melissa slowly stood up with Dillon still latching on to her.

As she took the first step toward the hallway, Dillon began to squirm and yell. "No! No, Mommy!"

She held him tighter. "Shh now, it is all right. I'm just gonna turn on the light and let you see there are no monsters."

As she flipped the switch for the hallway, Dillon continued to squirm and refused to remove his face, which was buried in her chest. She turned on another light in Dillon's room and then their small bathroom they shared. "Dillon, look, no monsters!"

Slowly he raised his head up and looked into her eyes and quietly said, "Look under bed."

Melissa walked toward his twin bed with *Blue's Clues* bedding and carefully knelt down to lift the bed skirt as Dillon buried his face again and held tighter. Lifting the fabric, she said, "Dillon, look honey, no monsters."

Carefully he turned his head and peered over her right shoulder and immediately relaxed. Taking advantage, she gently placed him on the bed and then stood up and smiled. "Are you going to sleep with your truck?"

Dillon looked at his red truck and clutched it tighter and nodded.

"Okay, do you want some water before bed?"

Dillon shook his head and then lay down and pulled the covers over his body.

Melissa bent down and kissed his forehead. "Love you, my little man. See you in the morning."

"Wuv u too, Mommy!"

Melissa smoothed out his hair and then stood up and headed for the door.

Just as she turned out the light, Dillon bolted up and yelled, "Closet, Mommy!"

Turning the switch back on, Melissa placed a hand on her hip and frowned. "Dillon, baby, there are no monsters! Here, I will show you!" Quickly she walked across the room and swung open his closet.

Wham!

Startled, Melissa jumped back as a ball rolled off the top shelf and bounced onto her. Seeing his mommy jump back from a ball, Dillon started laughing.

"Oh, you thought that was funny, huh?"

Melissa picked up the ball and placed it in the bottom of the closet and then closed the door. Spinning around, she noticed Dillon had lain back down and was still smiling. Blowing him a kiss, she continued out of the room, pulling the door shut behind her, with only his *Blue's Clues* night-light shining in the small corner.

Melissa stood outside Dillon's door and paused to listen to the silence that drifted throughout the house. Finally, she released her hold of his doorknob and walked back into the living room, but stopped suddenly when she heard a noise coming from behind.

Quickly she spun around and stared at an empty hallway. Taking a deep breath, she ran her hands through her hair and then set off toward her bedroom to discover the source of the noise. Opening the door, she flipped on the lights and scanned the room. Immediately she found the source of the noise and sighed with relief. Walking toward the open window, she could see two birds sitting on a branch that was brushing up against her screen. In a quiet voice, so as not to disturb Dillon, she shooed the birds, and then color instantly drained from her face as she discovered the sliding screen was unlocked.

"What the hell! I know this was locked!" Doubt began to creep into her mind, and she asked aloud, "Right?"

With shaking hands, she slowly slid the screen back and leaned her head forward and then side to side. There wasn't much to see, and she immediately felt foolish as she snapped the long branch in two and then quickly slid the screen back and locked it.

Taking a deep breath again, she quickly turned around and then jumped back, startled, at the sight of Dillon at the foot of her bed two feet away. Placing her hand over her chest, she exclaimed, "Dillon, you scared me! What are you doing back up?"

"I'm scared, Mommy! Sleep with me!"

Melissa bent over, picked him up, and carried him back to his room. She laid him back down in his bed.

As Dillon let go, he pleaded, "Pease, Mommy!"

Giving in, Melissa sat down, and Dillon scooted over to make room.

"Okay, but not another word, do you hear?"

Dillon clutched his truck tighter, nodded, and then closed his eyes. Melissa lay down, wide awake, and just stared at the white ceiling. She, too, was a little freaked out, but the only difference, for her, was the fictional monster had a name.

The next day was New Year's Eve, and Melissa smiled at the thought of Carey coming over. After bumping into him on Christmas Day, they had spent a few hours together on the beach. She had thoroughly enjoyed his family, and it had really helped with her homesickness. That day, he had asked her if she had plans for New Year's Eve. She had responded that she would get back to him and had waited five days before answering. Yesterday morning, she decided to allow herself to be happy and thought it would make her a better person and parent if she was happy and fulfilled. At first, she was worried he had already made plans since it had been several days before she replied with an answer. Luckily, he hadn't changed his mind.

So now, Melissa stood in her closet, once more debating what to wear. This was officially their second date, and they were staying home due to Dillon being asleep in his bedroom. Looking at her watch, she noticed it was eight thirty, and he was scheduled to arrive in the next fifteen minutes with their dinner. She was the one who had decided for the date to start after Dillon fell asleep, so she fed him his favorite sandwich and bathed him and tucked him in for the night at eight o'clock. Now she didn't know where the last thirty minutes had gone, and she still wasn't dressed.

Scanning her clothing options once more, she settled on a long black fitted dress that she and Katherine had found in a boutique in the quaint little town of Montville, just west of Coolum. After taking it off the hanger, she carefully pulled it on and then tied the decorative strings behind her neck. Now the decision was to wear shoes or not to wear shoes. After looking at all the choices, she decided to go barefoot. Walking out of her closet, she checked that her hair was still intact after getting the dress on. Wearing it down but pulled up on the sides, she liked the way she looked. As she was splashing on some perfume, she heard a light knock on the back door and smiled.

Rounding the corner of her room, she could see Carey down the hallway at the back porch. Motioning him in with her hands, she continued forward as he stepped inside and pulled the screen door closed behind him.

"You look amazing! Happy New Year!" He placed the food down on the counter and opened his muscular arms for an embrace.

Smiling, she stepped into his waiting arms and then leaned up for a small kiss. As his lips brushed up against her cheek, she didn't pull back, and slowly she turned to face him on her tiptoes and gently kissed him on the lips. As she rested her feet back flat on the floor, he pulled her closer with one arm and then placed his other hand under her chin and leaned back down for another kiss, this one a little longer.

Immediately warmth spread through her body as she kissed him back tenderly. Pulling back slightly, she peered into his blue eyes and felt an instant chemistry forming. Slowly inhaling, she whispered, "That was nice."

Not breaking his hold, he leaned in closer and replied, "Yes, a nice start to the evening and to the New Year."

Moments went by as they stared into each other's eyes, debating the next move. Finally, Carey stepped back with a smile and said, "Hungry?"

Glancing at the take-out, she said, "Starved!"

Dinner was eaten, and conversation flowed so nicely that Melissa almost forgot she was Teresa. She wondered if he could tell she hesitated before answering a question or thought a little too long before expanding on details about Dillon. She got up from the back porch lounge and went back inside to grab some more beer. When she returned, Carey had made himself comfortable in her hammock.

He patted the cloth beside him. "Come join me."

Melissa stepped forward and gently situated herself without any mishaps with her dress or drinks.

"Now, that is better."

Suddenly a burst of flames shot into the air.

"Wow, someone is starting early." She looked down at her watch and noticed it was ten o'clock.

"Yeah, it will go on all night. It will be beautiful."

"Too bad Dillon is asleep, he would have liked this."

"Do you want to wake him?"

With no hesitation, she quickly replied, "No."

He smiled and placed his free arm around her and then took a swig of his cold beer.

Carey felt her tense beneath his arms, but it quickly subsided. He knew there was more than met the eye with her, but he was in no hurry. He liked her a lot, and he could wait, he thought. Gently he began to rub her right arm and leaned his head into her long blonde hair. Oh, how he wanted to explore every inch of her body. She was stunning, as well as beautiful within. His thoughts dug deeper as he realized she must have been in something really deep to make her run to Australia alone with a kid.

"I had a great week at work."

"Good. Do you like the people you work with?"

"Yes, there is this one lady named Karen. She is really nice, and we ended up meeting for drinks on Wednesday night."

"Oh, where at?"

"This pub along the Esplanade in Mooloolaba, called Fridays."

"I know the place. It has amazing views of the water."

"Yeah, the sunset was nice."

Carey shifted his arm and then asked, "How did Dillon do at day care?"

Melissa reflectively turned her head and kissed him on the cheek. "You are so sweet for asking. He did well. I think it is good for him to be around other children."

"You said this was temporary work, right?"

"Yes. After a few weeks, they will evaluate my work and then make a decision to pursue the work visa."

"Our country is a little harder to obtain a work permit in without a citizenship."

"So I've read. If it doesn't work out, I guess we will be moving again."

Taking a sip of his beer, he pondered what she'd said, or didn't say, with that last statement. "Well, we will just have—"

"Hey! Hey! There you are!"

Carey stopped talking at the sound of his friends' voices from down the coastal pathway. Taking another quick swig, he then rose up and removed his arm from around Melissa. "Those are my good mates."

Melissa quickly got up and then motioned for them to come on up to her back porch.

Carey introduced the guys as they climbed the last few stairs. "Teresa, this is Pete and Chris, my two mates from Dalby."

Melissa shook their extended hands and then said, "I'll get two more beers."

Pete held up his small cooler in his hand and said, "No worries, babe, I got that covered."

"So what are you guys doing in town? I thought you couldn't get away from work."

"Naw, we blew off work at five and decided to come on down to the coast for the night and head back tomorrow evening."

"How far is Dalby?" asked Melissa.

Chris replied, "About three hours."

"Oh, not far at all."

Pete took a swig of his rum-and-cola mixture and then said, "Well, it seemed like forever when you've been working in the bloody hot sun all day."

"Well, take a seat. Can I get y'all something to eat?"

"Y'all? Damn, mate, you are from the South!"

Melissa smiled and said, "Yep, from Alabama. I'll be right back."

Carey watched her walk into the house and thought about what she had just said. Earlier she stated she was from Florida.

"Bro, where did you find her? She's freaking hot!"

Carey smirked at Pete and said, "She happened to live two houses down."

Chris burst out laughing. "Did she bring a friend?"

"Nope. Just her son."

In a serious tone, Pete asked, "She got a partner or is she divorced?"

Carey looked back toward Melissa in the kitchen and then honestly answered, "Not real sure."

Chapter 29

Several weeks had gone by, and Melissa and Dillon had settled in quite nicely at work and day care. She and Karen, her coworker, had become good friends and enjoyed sharing that one drink once a week after work. With each passing day, she thought more about Carey and less about Quinton. Even though she had seen Carey only twice since New Year's Eve, she couldn't help but wonder what direction they were headed toward. He had been so busy with his latest job and had traveled a lot. She, on the other hand, was tired when she came home each day and wanted to spend as much time with Dillon as possible. The two times he was free, they had spent the day at the beach and barbecued.

As she picked up the toys in the living room, her phone rang. She placed the blue boat into a basket and walked over to grab the phone.

"Hello?"

Silence.

"Hell-o! Anyone there?"

The line went dead.

With an eerie feeling, Melissa hung up the phone and glanced around the room. It was dark outside, and Dillon was already asleep. She walked over to her back porch screen, flipped the lever, and locked it. Even though it was a warm night, she felt cold. *When will this feeling ever go away? I would have heard something by now if there was a problem back in the States or if he knew I tricked him, right?* She asked herself more questions, but found no consolation with the answers. Walking toward her bedroom to grab a new novel she had purchased earlier today, she stopped short when she heard a loud bang behind her.

Holding on to the doorframe, she spun around and faced her back porch, where the noise had come from.

Silence followed.

Time seemed to stand still as Melissa waited for the unknown to happen. Just when she thought she was going to hyperventilate, she heard a tap on the door, and Carey's voice.

Melissa let out a deep breath, tilted her head back on the doorframe for balance, and tried to steady her nerves before returning his call.

"Teresa? Hey, are you okay?"

Realizing he could see her from the living room lights, she pushed off the wall and walked toward him with uneasy steps.

She unlocked the door. "I'm sorry, you startled me!"

"Aw shit, I'm the one sorry! Come here."

Melissa allowed herself to be fully embraced in his arms.

"You're shaking. I'm really sorry." Slowly he began moving her toward the couch. "Sit down."

As he suggested, she sat. Looking up into his concerned face, she blurted, "I'm embarrassed. I feel so foolish!"

"I should have called first."

Quizzically she asked, "You didn't?"

He narrowed his eyes. "No." Then with a sly grin he asked, "Do you remember having a conversation I don't know about?"

Playfully she punched him in the chest, and he lunged forward and tackled her sideways, down onto the couch. Resting on his elbows and stretched out on top of her, he looked intently into her eyes and then lowered himself down closer and kissed her.

She kissed back.

His hands moved around her face and through her hair as he felt the passion ignite between them. Deeper he fell into her and kissed her more. Suddenly, Carey felt a presence in the room, and he quickly jerked his head upward and looked toward the hallway. There, standing in the hall, was Dillon with a worried look on his face.

Quickly, Carey sprang up in one quick motion and landed on his feet. Startled by it all, Melissa came out of the fog and sat up and faced Dillon. "Sweetie, you're up. Are you okay?"

"He is not my daddy! I want my daddy!"

Melissa's hand flew to her chest, and then she quickly stood up and ran toward Dillon, who had already turned around and run back into his room, crying. Turning around briefly, she stated, "Please stay. I'll be back soon."

Carey watched her walk away. He paced back and forth and then finally walked over to her refrigerator and grabbed a beer. Twisting the cap, he mumbled, "Damn, what the hell have I gotten into!"

Carey was working on his third beer when Melissa stepped back into the living room and announced, "He is asleep now. I'm sorry about that."

Reminding himself that he'd promised patience, he answered, "All right. Maybe I should go."

Melissa shook her head. "I don't want you to. I...I would like to explain..."

Carey held up his hand. "I get it. You are not from Florida, and you are running from something, probably your husband."

Melissa stared back and blinked a few times.

"Look, I get it. Believe it or not, it happens a lot here. People show up on the other side of the world, running. It happens. Or what do you Americans say? Shit happens?"

Melissa took a timid step toward him and paused briefly before running into his arms. Carey struggled to move his beer out of her way and then quickly embraced her.

Running a hand through her long blonde hair, he whispered, "Hey, hey, no worries. We can fix this."

Melissa pulled away and looked into his dark blue eyes and said, "No. I don't think we can," and then buried her face into his chest.

The next hour, Melissa did most of the talking. Carey rarely interrupted or asked questions. When she was done explaining her situation with Quinton, he surprised her with, "What are you doing tomorrow?"

Taken aback, she replied, "What?"

"You know, tomorrow is Australia Day, our national holiday, and I know you aren't working because nobody does."

Melissa narrowed her eyes and smiled as she tilted her head to the side. "No, I'm not working tomorrow."

"Good. I will pick you up around eight, and make sure you and Dillon bring togs and sunscreen."

"Aren't you gonna—"

Standing up, he said, "You know, I think we've done enough talking tonight. You need to get some sleep because we have a big day tomorrow."

"But, you didn't—"

"Melissa"—realizing that sounded strange, he smiled and then leaned over within one inch of her face and whispered—"if I don't leave now, you won't be sleeping alone."

He watched as her eyes slightly widened, and then he moved in for a quick kiss on her lips before standing back up and walking toward the back door. "Lock up behind me, and I'll see you at eight."

Melissa watched as he disappeared and then sank into the couch, breathless.

The next morning, Melissa woke up to noise coming from Dillon's monitor. He was awake and playing in his bed. Smiling, Melissa remained in bed and listened as he sang and talked to his *Blue's Clues* dog. Instantly she jumped up when she saw the time, seven forty-five. Throwing off the sheets, she quickly ran toward her bathroom and frantically began brushing out her hair. Just when she had her hair into a neat ponytail, Dillon walked in behind her.

"Mommy?"

Melissa spun around in her nightgown and quickly gave him a good-morning hug. "Sweetie, we are going on an adventure today. What do you think about that?"

Time stood still as she waited to hear what was going to come out of his mouth. Would he remember last night and ask more questions, or was he really half asleep when he saw her and Carey together last night?

A feeling of relief washed over her when Dillon finally broke into a big grin and asked, "What adventure? A big adventure with rocks?"

Smiling, she knew how much he enjoyed being outdoors. But suddenly she realized she didn't know how to answer because she didn't know herself. "Well, it is a surprise..." She paused and then continued, "With Carey."

Jumping up and down, he shouted, "Yippee! Yippee!"

Breathing easier, she said, "Now, I need you to go in your room and put on your swim shorts and a T-shirt. Can you do that for Mommy?"

He gave no verbal answer, but she knew he understood because he bolted out of the bathroom and back into his room. Quickly she ran toward her closet and stripped down and put on the first sundress she saw. Next, she grabbed her swimsuit and a pair of flip-flops and threw them in her bag. Seeing the sunscreen already inside, she ran to the laundry room to grab a towel and threw it inside as well.

At eight o'clock, she saw that Dillon was all dressed and ready, and she had just enough time to brush her teeth before she heard the knock on the back door.

"Coming!" she shouted. "Dillon, are you ready?"

Dillon was already running toward the door when she came out of the bathroom.

Seeing Carey swoop down and pick up Dillon, she stopped in her tracks and smiled at the sight.

Chapter 30

Dillon was sitting in his car seat in the backseat of Carey's truck, which was called a ute by Australians, eating a granola bar. With a mouthful he yelled, "Boats! A blue boat, Mommy!"

Melissa turned her head to Dillon and smiled. "Yes, there are lots of boats."

She had remained quiet over the short drive over to the Mooloolaba marina where Carey docked his boat. Doubts had crept in her head about putting Dillon on a boat. Yes, he was going to be two in another month and Carey had bought the correct size for his life jacket, but still, she had doubts.

Shutting off the engine, Carey explained, "There will be lots of boats around today due to the holiday, so you shouldn't be worried about being all alone in the ocean."

Melissa smiled back. "Good. I like lots of boats around me when I'm in the big blue sea!"

Carey grabbed a large cooler with wheels from the bed of his ute and then placed a large bag full of supplies on top. "Here, you take his life jacket and place my keys in your beach bag."

Melissa did as instructed, and they were soon making their way down the pier and onto Carey's fishing boat.

"Boat is wellow! That is a girl color!"

Carey and Melissa stopped in their tracks and laughed. Carey rubbed Dillon's hair and then hoisted him into the air and over the side of the boat. Next, Carey held Melissa's hand as she stepped safely aboard.

"Well, I like the big yellow boat!"

Carey grinned. "Thanks!"

With everything packed away for the ride, Carey untied the ropes and pushed off with his foot, then rushed back to the helm and pushed the throttle forward. Melissa checked Dillon's life jacket once more and then took a seat beside him.

"It will take a few minutes to get out to sea. Going through the canal, there is a no-wake zone."

Melissa nodded and stretched out her legs on the long cushioned seat beside Dillon and looked at the beautiful homes lined along the canal. There were so many different boats, sailboats, small yachts, skiing boats, as well as fishing boats like the one they were on. As Melissa looked forward, she realized they were in one big line going out to sea. Several people were waving as they passed each other on land and shore.

"Mommy, Mommy, look, a fish!"

Melissa looked just in time to see the splash and water ripple.

"You will see lots of fish today, Dillon, as well as dolphins and sea turtles," replied Carey.

"Wat about sharks?"

Carey looked toward Melissa, who had quickly looked into his eyes for a reassuring answer. "We shouldn't see any sharks."

"Aw man, I want to see a shark!" Dillon settled back in his seat and crossed his arms with a big frown.

Carey laughed and shook his head.

Soon, they rounded the jetty, and Carey pressed the lever forward to pick up speed. "Hold on. It will be rough for a few minutes until we get over the bar."

Melissa held one hand on Dillon's jacket and the other on a stainless steel bar as they rode the waves up and down and water sprayed along the sides of the boat, getting them wet.

Dillon screamed out, "Whoo hoo! This is *fun*!"

Carey glanced over and shouted, "You haven't seen nothing yet!" and then looked into Melissa's eyes and winked.

Just as Carey explained, the ride did get smoother as the boat planed out around twenty-five knots. Melissa began to relax a bit, and readjusted Dillon's hat with string so it wouldn't fly away, and then looked toward the shoreline. "Wow, you weren't kidding! Look at all the people!"

"The biggest beach day of the year!" shouted Carey.

A few more minutes passed by, and Carey slowed the boat down to half speed. "Dillon, do you want to come sit in my lap and drive?"

Dillon's eyes widened, and he looked up at Melissa.

"Go ahead, you can go."

Melissa helped Dillon down and held his hand until Carey grabbed him and hoisted him up into his big chair. She leaned back once more and watched as the two bonded. She smiled.

For the next five minutes, Carey explained all the gadgets and the fishing navigation system to Dillon.

Twenty minutes later, Dillon screamed out, "Fish!"

Carey looked at the fishing sonar and agreed. "Yep. I would say this is the spot."

Carey carefully stood up, placed Dillon down, and guided him back to Melissa's seat. "Let's turn around and anchor here and see what's down there."

Dillon pulled up on the bar and leaned over the boat as Melissa held on to his waist.

"Oh my gosh! A shark!" screamed Melissa.

Carey put down his fishing pole and took a step toward where Melissa was pointing. Placing a hand over his forehead to block the sun, he soon saw the fin. "No worries, little lady, it is just a dolphin!"

Dillon clapped his hands with glee and yelled, "Dolphin!"

Carry opened a small container built into his boat and pulled out a small fish. "Do you want to feed it?"

Dillon jumped down, losing his balance with the bulky life jacket, but Melissa caught him, and then he ran the two steps toward Carey and immediately grabbed the fish and threw it overboard.

Suddenly, not one, but three dolphins appeared and dove at the fish. Melissa smiled as she watched Dillon clap for joy and then stammered, "Another one! Another one!"

Again, the fish was thrown, and the dolphins dove down into the water for it.

"Let's bait our hooks now and see what we get."

Dillon watched as Carey grabbed bait, mashed it on a hook, and dropped the line down into the water. Handing him the rod, but keeping his hands firmly around the handle, he straddled Dillon and waited for the bite.

In a matter of seconds, the line gave a tug, and Carey instructed, "We got one, mate! Now help me pull it up."

With several cranks, they pulled the fish up as Melissa handed Carey the net.

Dillon screamed out, "It's blue!"

"What kind of fish is that? It looks like it belongs in an aquarium," remarked Melissa.

Carey laughed and answered, "It is a parrot fish, good eating!"

The fish was bright blue with dark yellow stripes and a touch of pink. Carey grabbed it carefully with one hand and then pulled the hook out with his other one. "Let's measure it to see if it is a keeper."

Carey asked Melissa to check the poster that was rolled up to see the minimum size. While she looked, he placed the fish on his measuring chart mounted on the side of the boat and pointed to a number for Dillon to see. Holding it in place, Carey patiently waited for Melissa to answer.

"Twenty-five centimeters, limit is six."

"All right! See, Dillon? It is twenty-eight, so it is a keeper!"

Carey threw the fish into a built-in cooler at the floor of the boat and then placed more bait on the hook and dropped another line. Turning around, he stated, "Mommy's turn."

"Oh no! Y'all go ahead. I don't know nothing about fishing!"

Not being deterred, he walked over and handed Melissa the line. "Just hold on, and crank when there—"

"I got something!" Melissa jumped up and began cranking away on the reel.

Carey watched as she struggled, and moved Dillon over to the side and whispered in his ear, "I think it is too big for her to pull up."

"It is not! I got it!" For what seemed like five minutes, but was more like thirty seconds, Melissa fought the fish. "I don't know if I can get it!"

"Yes, you can! Now don't lose it!"

Feeling the pressure, Melissa repositioned her feet and leaned into the side of the boat and turned the reel faster. Soon, a bright pink image formed below the water and swam side to side. "I see it! It is right there! Get the net!"

As she turned toward Carey, he was smiling and already holding the net, ready to swoop it up. "A few more cranks and you got it!" Struggling harder, she finally got it close enough to the boat where Carey could lean over and grab it. Pulling it up out of the water, he beamed with pride. "It's a snapper! And it is a keeper!"

As Carey took the fish off and baited the hook once more, she asked, "How many more rods do you have?"

With a grin he answered, "Plenty!"

Chapter 31

After a couple of hours of loading up with fish, Carey took Melissa and Dillon to Moreton Island, the second largest sand island in the world. There they anchored along several other boats by the shore. After making sure the anchor would hold, Carey hooked up a barbecue on the back of the boat and began cutting up two fish to cook and eat. Dillon was right by his side the whole time, watching the entire process.

Melissa turned her head away from the fish guts and toward the clear turquoise water. Down on the ocean floor, she saw hundreds of starfish. Soon, a large turtle swam by, and she yelled over to Dillon, "Look, a sea turtle!"

Dillon ran to her, peered over the side of the boat, and watched with amazement until it disappeared. When Dillon left to help Carey again, Melissa decided to join the other people who were taking a swim.

"Dillon, I'm gonna put on my swimsuit. Stay with Carey."

Reaching into her bag, she found her suit and then quickly changed in the berth below. Climbing the stairs, she was taken aback again with Carey's patience with Dillon. The two really looked like they were enjoying themselves.

Seeing her standing there, watching out of the corner of his eye, Carey looked toward Melissa and offered, "There is a snorkeling set under that seat. Pull it out and use it."

"Are you serious?"

Excited by the idea of having a mask and seeing the starfish clearer, she bounced toward the seat and pulled it up. Below, there were three different sets, and she picked each one of them up, reading the sizes. She couldn't help notice that she might not be the first girl he brought along since there was one to fit her size-seven foot. Pushing the unpleasant thoughts out of her head, she shrugged her shoulders and began to take them out of the mesh bag.

"Come sit on the edge over here and put them on. It will be easier."

Melissa did as she was instructed and couldn't hide the excitement in her eyes. As she passed them by, she gave each a kiss on the cheek and then lowered herself down to the small platform that was behind the boat. When her flippers were on tightly, she jumped in with the mask and snorkel in her hand. Soon, she was spitting into the mask and then rinsing it out and fitting it tightly around her head.

"Stay close," she heard Carey say.

Looking up with a confused look on her face, she saw him smile and wink right before he turned back around to continue preparing lunch.

Melissa eased away from the boat and began floating on top of the water. She couldn't get over the many starfish. Never in her life had she seen so many. Deciding to get a closer look, she began swimming toward shore. When she was close enough to stand and touch bottom, she took a breath and went under the water and grabbed a starfish. Rising up, she removed her mask to take a closer look. She examined it and noticed it was lighter on one side with a design when she flipped it over.

"Melissa, look over here!"

Melissa glanced over toward the boat just as Carey took a picture. When he put the camera back down, she waved at Dillon, who waved back. She dropped the starfish back into the water, then repositioned her mask around her eyes and began to swim close to shore, looking for large seashells.

After several minutes, Melissa raised her head up and looked for the boat. It was a long way off. She had floated in the current down the shoreline. Looking toward the beach, she saw several people walking around, barbecuing and playing cricket, and she was instantly relieved that she wasn't alone. She began to swim toward the shore.

Sitting in the sand, Melissa reached down and pulled off her fins and then removed her mask from her tangled hair. Finally pulling it free, she heard someone approach behind her.

"Here, let me help you up."

Startled, Melissa turned around and looked up into the hot, blazing sun and saw only a blur. Shielding her eyes, she waited for the person to come into focus. Standing in front of her was a good-looking guy with sandy brown hair. Instantly she thought of Quinton and froze.

Seeing the look on her face, he took a step back and gestured. "Hey, I'm sorry, didn't mean to scare you, mate."

Melissa forced a smile and commented, "No, I'm good, thanks."

He stepped forward, reached for her hand, and helped bring her to her feet. "You aren't Australian, are you?"

She shook her head. "No, American."

"Well hell, welcome to Australia! Want to grab a brew with my mates?"

Melissa saw the young men standing around a barbecue and a cooler waving at her. With a bashful smile, she waved back and stated, "Sorry, I'm with someone," and she pointed out to sea. From a distance, she could see Carey looking her way and waving.

"No worries! Enjoy the day!" He turned around and walked over to his mates, shrugging his shoulders, stating loudly, "I tried!"

Melissa started walking down the sandy beach and could feel all eyes on her. Seeing all the groups of people, mostly men, she began to question the size of her swimsuit. She picked up the pace and began jogging. When she was directly in front of the boat, she waved at Carey and then froze as she stepped one foot into the water. She turned around and scanned the area behind her after a feeling washed over her that she was being watched. There along the beach, were two groups of families hanging around their tents and barbecues. She studied the brush and green weeds along the tall sand dunes behind them. Nothing. For some reason though, she couldn't shake the sensation that someone was indeed watching. Just as she started to turn back around, she saw someone move in the bushes. Instantly, a chill ran down her back, and she started backing into the water.

"Hey, are you okay?"

Hearing Carey's voice, she turned around to face him and Dillon, then back around once more. Seeing no one, she slowly turned back around and then walked into the water. As she balanced to fit her fins on securely, she couldn't shake the feeling she wasn't alone. Turning around once more and finding no one, she carefully pulled her hair back and then placed her mask back on and began swimming toward the boat.

When Melissa reached the platform, Carey lowered the stairs and then grabbed her fins and mask from her outstretched hand. "Just in time, lunch is ready!" As she climbed up with his help, he said coyly, "I saw that local try to pick you up, poor mate!"

Melissa looked into his soft eyes and smiled. "Oh, you did? Worried?"

She watched as Carey's eyes scanned the length of her body, then moved slowly back up and stopped at her eyes. "I was trying to figure out how I was gonna watch Dillon and swim to shore to kick his bloody ass."

218

Melissa felt her face turn a soft shade of pink as she smiled back and responded, "He didn't hold a candle to you," and then she leaned in for a soft kiss on his lips.

Carey placed his hand on the small of her back and pulled her in for a hug. After a brief moment, he slowly pulled away and squeezed her arm. "Let's eat. Come see what your little man made you."

Melissa took another step up onto the back of the boat and walked over to the table that Carey had somehow attached to the floor and sat down beside it. Dillon was already seated and eating his fish with his hands.

With a full mouth, he stated, "Um, um, good!"

Melissa grinned and was happy to see asparagus and rice along with the fish. "You have a rice cooker?"

"Down below, there is a small kitchen on the other side of the toilet."

"Nice." She took a bite of the fish and then exclaimed, "Very nice, Chef Tell!"

"Why, thank you! Here, let me grab you a beer."

Since she was closer, she responded, "I'll get it," and she jumped up and walked over to the cooler and bent over and lifted the lid. When she stood back up, she immediately felt a chill down her back as she saw the brush swaying side to side on the near-empty beach.

"What is it?"

Shaking the feeling, she turned around and walked back over, handed him a beer, replied, "Nothing," and then sat back down beside him as he placed an arm around her.

Together, the three of them ate and relaxed over the next few hours. With Carey's help, they were able to lower Dillon into the water on a board for him to float around on. When Dillon started nodding off, they laughed at the thought of how tired he was.

"He had a good time today."

"And his mom?"

"The best!"

Getting settled back on the boat, Carey hit the switch to raise the anchor, and they were soon off. As they cruised along the shore back to the marina, Melissa leaned back on the long seat with Dillon asleep in her arms and took in the beautiful sunset over the Glass House Mountains that lined the coastline.

Every now and again, Carey would glance her way and smile.

Returning his smile, she had no more thoughts of Quinton. As Carey turned back around, she studied his bronzed body as he stood behind the wheel. He was wearing only his swim shorts, which sat low on his hips, showing off his amazing physique. As she continued to stare, her heart missed a beat as he turned back around and met her eyes. She blushed.

Moments went by, and Melissa was filled with an emotion she could no longer control. The next time he turned around, she motioned for him to come to her. Seeing the look in her eyes, he slowed the boat. Looking around and seeing no one near them, he put the boat in neutral and walked over to her.

"Could you put Dillon on that bed below?"

Carey looked into her eyes and hesitated only briefly before lowering down to pick up a sleeping Dillon. Once in his arms, Dillon barely stirred as he carried him away.

Melissa stood up and walked over to the edge of the boat and looked out to shore at the setting sun. Soon she felt his strong arms wrap around her body, and she melted with his touch. Slowly he pulled her hair back and lowered his lips to her neck. A warm chill ran down her back as he continued working around her body with his hands and mouth. Soon, he was standing between her and the edge of the boat with his hands tangled in her hair and his mouth pressed tightly against hers.

Melissa rested her palms on his bare chest as she kissed him back. Slowly, she moved her hands down until she found his waist. Pausing briefly, she moved her hands lower, to the top of his swim shorts, and gave them a gentle tug.

Carey pulled back and looked into her eyes intently and then dove quickly back to her mouth. He untied her top and slowly pulled it away, exposing her hard nipples. Lowering his mouth, he played with his tongue until she arched her back and slightly moaned. Next, he untied the strings at the sides of her bottoms, and he stepped to the side and watched as they fell to her feet. His hands worked their way down her stomach, and he watched as they explored her beautiful, sensual body. After pleasuring her more, he worked his hands back up over her chest and then found her open mouth.

Lowering his mouth to hers, he whispered, "I want you, now."

After Melissa reassured him with her hands, and her mouth on his, he carefully lifted her up. Feeling an awakening in her body she hadn't felt in so long, Melissa quickly wrapped her long legs around his waist and pulled herself closer until he was inside of her. Soon, Melissa felt the earth move as the boat slowly rocked back and forth under the setting sun.

Hours later, Carey helped put Dillon to bed and together they walked into the small living room. As he turned around toward her, she was once again filled with lust. Reaching out for him, he grabbed her and wrapped her up tight in his arms. "I don't want to go," he whispered.

Melissa smiled as her face rested on his chest. "I know, don't."

Slowly pulling away, he kissed her forehead as his hands gently ran down the side of her body. "Four more days at work and then I'll be back."

Taking a step toward him, she rested a finger on his chest and pouted. "Four more days."

Picking up her hand, he kissed and then released it. He stepped backward toward the back porch and opened the door and stepped out. Winking, he said, "Saturday, nine o'clock" and he closed the screen.

"We will be ready," she said and then watched as he turned around and left.

Melissa walked forward and locked the screen and then turned around quickly as a cold chill ran down her back. Feeling the hairs on her arms tingle, she rubbed them and shuddered. She went to her bedroom and checked out her closet and then walked over to the screen to her open window and noticed that, once again, she had left for the day with it unlocked.

What the hell, Melissa, are you trying to scare yourself into insanity? she thought. Quickly she locked the screen and then left her bedroom for a warm shower to help settle her nerves.

Chapter 32

In downtown Birmingham, on Fourth Street, a man walked through the back doors of his establishment and greeted his longtime girlfriend, Frieda. Joey, a private investigator, had been away on an assignment down in New Orleans for the last several weeks.

Frieda jumped up and ran toward him. "Oh, I missed you! Don't stay gone so long next time!"

"I'm sorry, babe, next time you come with me."

Joey wrapped her in his arms and gave her a kiss. Soon, the front door chimed, and Frieda moaned, "Damn, I should have turned the sign off."

Joey grinned and then said, "You go. I want to get a shower and shave."

"I will, and I'll come wash your back," she said with a mischievous grin.

Joey smiled and headed to the small one-bedroom that was off the back office. Looking around, he was impressed how clean the place looked. Having Frieda move in two years ago was one of the smartest decisions he had made in the last five years. He walked into the bathroom, leaned into the shower, turned on the water, and then

223

began undressing. Soon, he was under the water when he heard a loud crash coming from the other side of the wall.

"What the hell?"

He heard another noise as he turned off the water. This one sounded like glass breaking. Quickly Joey pulled on his dirty jeans and grabbed his gun that was lying on the sink counter. Quietly he left the bedroom and worked his way down the small hallway that led to the front of the house that held his office, which was open to the public.

Frieda was shouting hysterically, "What do you want? I don't have any money! Please don't!"

Joey made his way to the edge of the door and carefully tilted his head forward until he could see the events unfolding through the crack. The glass door was smashed, and papers and books were scattered all along the floor. A large black man wearing a Chicago Bulls hat on backward had his back toward Joey. Instantly, he recognized the colors and knew this was a gang robbery.

Frieda was pressed against the wall, and the young teenager was holding a knife to her throat. Scanning the room, he looked for others. Toward the far left, he saw another gang member. This kid was white and looked younger. He was wearing the same colors, but he was much smaller and skinner. Taking another peek at Frieda, he could see he didn't have much time. He had to make a decision, and fast.

The white kid yelled, "Give me the code, or he is gonna cut out your tongue and shove it down your throat!"

Joey glanced back and didn't see the white kid's gun, so he went for the black kid first. Aiming his gun toward the center of his jacket, he pulled the trigger.

Frieda screamed as his knife scraped her throat and then fell to the ground beside the dead kid. With no time to waste, Joey spun around toward the white kid just as he pulled his gun, but it was too late. He had fired first, and now the kid was crumpled against the safe with a bullet pierced through his heart.

Adrenaline pumping, Joey ignored Frieda's screams and ran toward the front door and looked for more gang members. No one else was there except curious bystanders who were carefully standing behind parked cars, and other shop owners peeping their heads out of their own establishments.

From his right, he heard Lou, his neighbor who owned a pawnshop next door. "Joey, I already called nine-one-one! Are you hurt?"

"No, but Frieda"—he turned around and looked at her and saw that she was bleeding pretty badly—"she needs an ambulance!"

Joey didn't wait for a response. He turned back around and ran toward Frieda and placed his large hands around her neck to stop the bleeding. With wild eyes, she looked back at him and tried to talk.

"Don't talk. Just breathe and hang on! The ambulance is on the way."

For twenty-five minutes, Joey pressed his hand against Frieda's neck until help finally arrived. First, cops came in with guns raised and yelled, "Get up and put your hands upon your head!"

Joey turned his head to face the young cop and screamed, "I can't! She will bleed to death!"

With his free hand, the cop held the radio up from his shoulder and talked into thin air.

"Damn it, do something! She is dying!"

The cop continued to stand there with his gun raised until other policeman arrived and checked the gang members. With his gun still pointed at Joey, the cop yelled out, "Put your gun on the floor where I can see it, now!"

Joey kicked the gun out from under him and screamed, "I'm not armed now! Do something!"

Twelve hours had passed by, and Joey was sitting in a hospital room shared with another patient. Frieda was sleeping with the help of drugs, and the doctor had just left. Joey was informed that if the knife had been off another half an inch, Frieda would be dead now. Taking a look at her pale face, he decided he desperately needed coffee.

Leaving the room, he made his way down a hallway to the coffee machine and lounge room. After making a black coffee, he wandered over to the couch and took a seat and picked up *The Birmingham News*. It didn't take him long to find the story of last night's events on page four. Scanning the article, he was disappointed more information about his place of work wasn't given out, but at the same time realized this was for his own protection. After all, he did kill two gang members. Hopefully by not splashing the details around, the gang would not want revenge due to embarrassment. Didn't matter, Joey would be ready. He had a license to carry at all times, and he was definitely not afraid to use the lead.

As Joey continued to sit in the quiet waiting room, reality really began to set in. He thought about his job and the constant danger he was in, as well as Frieda. Now, she was in there, barely alive, and his establishment was not so private anymore with his picture clearly displayed on page four. It was one thing to advertise as a private investigator, but another to splash a picture of your face alongside the logo. How was he gonna do undercover work now? It was the undercover work that paid 80 percent of the bills. Frowning, his thoughts turned toward the gang. Yeah, he wasn't afraid to shoot, but honesty filtered into his brain as he realized he couldn't possibly watch his and Frieda's backs 24-7. Placing his hands over his face he tried to block out the fact that it took only a few seconds to let your guard down, and *bam*! Dead, he concluded.

Maybe it is time to get out? How? Mathematically, he began to count up his assets and then frowned when he realized it just wasn't enough to quit. *Maybe I could sell the building and move to Miami. Frieda likes warm weather, and there is sure to be lots of work down there.* Again he remembered the gang. He would have to change his name as well as Frieda's identity. *Well,* he thought, *wouldn't be the first time.*

Closing the paper, he set it back down on the coffee table and began to stand up when something on the cover caught his attention and he quickly sat back down. On the lower left corner, there was a photograph of a mom and child. Joey picked up the paper and took a closer look and then shook his head and smiled.

Out loud he said, "I'll be damned. Man, is she clever."

Placing his coffee down on the table, he leaned back and began reading the story titled: Junior League Annual Golf Charity Event Still on Despite the Shadow of Grief.

After reading the article twice, Joey slowly put the pieces together, smiled, and slapped his thigh and said loudly, "Payday! And boy, it couldn't come at a better time!"

Late morning on Wednesday, Quinton was in his office looking over a case file when his secretary buzzed in. "You have a visitor by the name of Joey Franks here to see you."

Quinton frowned into the phone and said, "I don't know a Mr. Franks. Make an appointment. I'm too busy right now."

In a hesitant voice, she replied, "He said it is about your wife, Melissa."

Now that got his attention. Quinton stood up without responding, walked over to the door, and briskly opened it up to see why a stranger would show up at his office about his dead wife.

The secretary saw his expression and carefully slid the handpiece back down and opened her mouth to respond, but stopped when Mr. Franks stepped forward and extended his hand.

"I'm sorry to bother you without an appointment, but you are gonna want to see me, Mr. Pierson."

As Quinton shook his hand, he gave his secretary a hard stare and then stepped to the side and gestured his visitor into his office.

Once inside and away from others, Joey immediately got down to business. After researching Quinton Pierson, he had decided it would be best not to play games, and get right to the point.

As Quinton spread his hands wide for an explanation, Joey spilled the beans.

"Mr. Pierson, your wife and child ain't dead."

Chapter 33

Time stood still for Quinton as he felt the floor shift under him. Mumbling, "Who the hell do you think you are coming to my office and—"

Joey didn't back down. Instead, he produced his private investigator ID for him to view. Angrily, Quinton stepped forward and yanked it out of his hands as Joey continued.

"I met your wife and son a couple of months ago. She came by my office and said she needed my help."

Not taking his eyes off the ID, Quinton said, "Go on. This better be good."

Joey smirked and made his way over to the leather couch and said as he sat down, "Why don't you join me and sit down? Then I will fill you in on all the details of where I can go find 'em and bring 'em back."

Quinton felt his heart speed up, and tightness formed in his chest. He tossed the ID to Joey, but walked in the opposite direction, toward his bar area. With his back turned, Quinton picked up a glass with shaking hands and began to pour himself a shot of whiskey. As the alcohol stung down his throat, he turned around and glared at the man sitting on the couch who had just turned his life upside down.

Three hours later, Quinton was driving down the interstate toward Mallory Jane's home. He had missed her last three calls, and his secretary was becoming suspicious. Quinton refused to make his romance public despite the fact that Mallory Jane was now six months pregnant. She was doing a good job working from home and hiding it with the winter sweaters, but he knew his time was shrinking. The last thing he needed right now was to be seen with Mallory Jane. His circle of friends adored and loved Melissa, and no one would understand how he could just move on so quickly. Besides, there was a baby involved, and everyone could easily do the math. Mallory Jane wasn't backing down either, and she was starting to push his buttons, the wrong ones.

Pulling into Mallory Jane's driveway, he used his remote that she'd issued him a year ago and drove into the garage and then lowered the door behind him. The door had just closed as he emerged from his vehicle and walked over and opened the door. Inside, Mallory Jane was standing in the kitchen wearing another one of her oversized sweater jackets over a pair of dark leggings.

"Took you long enough! You know this isn't just about us. My business is beginning to suffer with your lack of interest and communication."

Quinton stepped within inches of Mallory Jane and whispered, "Fire me."

Mallory Jane pushed his chest with her hand and then spun around and headed toward the family room.

Quinton reached out and pulled her back around hard and said, "Don't walk away from me."

"Stop it! You are hurting me!" She took a deep whiff and asked, "Is that whiskey I smell at three thirty in the afternoon?"

"Yeah, but who cares? Everything is going to hell in a handbasket anyway." Then he slowly released his grip, and she stepped back with a frown on her face.

"What the hell is going on, Quinton? You know, I can do this on my own. I don't need you!"

"Ha! Is that why you call my office all day long every day?"

"That is not fair! You treat me as if there is no one else for you, pamper and spoil me, and then turn right around the next day and act like I don't exist."

Quinton turned away from her, walked into the family room, and poured himself another drink from her bar. This time, his hands were no longer shaking. After he gulped down the first drink, he quickly poured another. With a full glass, he turned around to face Mallory Jane and asked, "Would you like to join me for drinks?"

Shaking her head, she walked over within one foot, placed her hands on her hips, and very calmly said, "I'm done. Give me my remote and keys. I want you to walk out that door and never come back."

Quinton gulped down the second drink and just stared back at her.

She continued, "I mean it this time. We are through. I'm going to call another lawyer tomorrow and change firms for my business. I can do this alone, and I will."

"I'd like to see you replace me. You wouldn't know which way was up without me."

Mallory Jane took a step closer and said, "You really think so, don't you? This world doesn't revolve around you, Quinton. I was doing just fine before I stepped into your office, and I will continue to do so without you."

Mallory Jane broke eye contact and turned and walked away three steps. Quinton watched her from behind wearing her tall Italian boots and leggings with sweater that hid her belly. She no longer looked the same as when he'd first met her. A switch flipped in his brain, and rage began to build. Within seconds, Quinton picked up an unopened wine bottle, took four wide steps, and sent the bottle crashing down on Mallory Jane's skull. Falling forward, she hit the corner of the glass kitchen table and then went down and landed on her back in a crumpled position.

Blood oozed from Mallory Jane's cut eyebrow from the fall to the table, and more blood began to puddle around her golden hair sprayed out on the floor. As her ivory sweater turned crimson, Quinton just stood there and watched as she slipped away, never regaining consciousness.

Time stood still as Quinton remained standing there in his work clothes, holding what was left of a cracked bottle in his hands. Wine had splattered all over the kitchen table and floor, as well as the cabinets to the left of the table.

Dropping the bottle to the floor, Quinton took both of his hands and covered his face and turned around. Closing his eyes, he shouted, "Damn you, woman, and damn you, Melissa!"

At eight thirty, Quinton looked around Mallory Jane's home and looked for any hint of the disaster that had occurred earlier. Luckily for him, the floors in the living room and kitchen area were tile, and everything had cleaned up nicely with bleach and soap. Quinton had stripped down his clothing and washed and dried them as he went to work on planning Mallory Jane's disappearance. First, a flight was booked for New York, and then a few bags were packed with Mallory Jane's purse. Next, e-mails were sent from her home computer to her business associates, as well as one to himself. Last, he cleaned her computer of all traces of them for the last year.

Taking no chances, Quinton looked again over the house and frowned when he walked into the bathroom and realized he'd forgotten to pack her makeup bag. Quickly he pulled it out of the bathroom drawer and then shoved it into her luggage. Walking back through her bedroom one last time, he paused when he saw her large bed unmade. Deciding it looked out of place, he hastily made the bed up like he had seen Mallory Jane do so many times before. Placing the last pillow in place, he carefully sat down and then picked the pillow up one more time and pressed it to his face and inhaled deeply. He could still smell her, and his heart skipped a beat as memories came flooding back of them spending hours in this bed.

Finally, after another five minutes of sitting on the bed, he stood up and got his mind right and stepped back into reality. She was gone now, and it was time to get rid of the body, and fast.

Quinton left the same way he'd arrived, and he was carefully driving the speed limit with Mallory Jane and all her luggage packed away in the trunk of his car. At around nine o'clock, he finally pulled off a rural highway and took a small one-lane road that led to a lake that was rarely used this time of year by fisherman. No hunting was allowed within ten miles of the lake, so he knew he was safe from potential illegal hunters, and it was too cold for camping.

Quinton knew the lake well; he and Mallory Jane had visited it often and rarely saw anyone around as they took long walks, had picnics, and skinny-dipped on several occasions. Somehow, Quinton thought this would be a good place for Mallory Jane to have her finally resting spot. Slowly he backed his car into their favorite spot near the water. The ground was firm, and there was no risk of getting stuck. Popping the trunk, Quinton got out and then looked around, but only saw darkness with a touch of light from the quarter moon.

Carefully, Quinton reached in and grabbed a heavy stack of bricks that had a rope looped through the holes and tied it in a knot that would not come undone. Then he bent over and gently picked up Mallory Jane, who was wrapped in several sheets with ropes holding everything in place, and then carried her over to the edge of the lake and placed her on the ground.

Taking a deep breath, he said, "Damn it, Mallory Jane," then stripped down naked, picked her up, and entered the icy cold water, pulling the rope and bricks behind him.

Counting fifteen steps before he was completely submerged, he then threw her body forward another two feet and watched as she sank to the bottom. Quickly he turned around and made his way back to shore. He grabbed a blanket that he had taken from her house and immediately began to wrap up and pat himself dry. It took another two minutes to get dressed, and then he jumped in behind the wheel and cranked up the heat on high.

For the next five minutes, Quinton concentrated on getting warm before enacting his next move. Finally, he could feel all parts of his body again, and he opened up the door and walked back outside, toward the lake, carrying a flashlight. Shining the light over the water, he saw nothing disturbed or out of place. He got back in the car, shifted to first, and pulled away back into the night.

As Quinton drove back onto the highway, he contemplated his next move. He still had to dispose of the luggage as well as the blanket. Pulling into an empty parking lot, he found a large Dumpster on the side of a building and disposed of the blanket. Next, he drove into downtown Birmingham, into an area that was known for drugs, strip joints, and gangs. It took a while, but he finally found a dark alley behind an abandoned warehouse. He put his car in neutral, quickly popped the trunk, and threw Mallory Jane's purse and luggage into a half-empty Dumpster.

Turning around, Quinton closed the trunk, and then he heard a noise from behind the Dumpster and froze. He saw no one as he looked around. Reaching into his backseat, he grabbed a flashlight and then walked over to the side of the Dumpster and flashed the light. Instantly, a possum jumped down from the lid above and landed at his feet and scurried across the payment.

Mumbling, "Shit!" he jumped back into his car and peeled out of the deserted alleyway and quickly back onto the main street that would get him back onto the interstate in one piece. Smiling, he thought, *Yeah, getting shot or carjacked would sure put an end to this charade!*

Quinton finally pulled into his dark driveway around ten o'clock, physically and mentally exhausted. Entering his house, he threw his keys and briefcase into the nearest chair and climbed the stairs two at a time up to his bedroom that he had once shared with Melissa. Turning on the bedroom light, he went straight to her closet and turned on the switch. Everything was still there as she had left it, except for the wedding portrait leaning against the wall.

With flashes of Joey's story running through his mind, he began to tear into her walk-in closet searching for some clue that she had indeed faked her death and run off with Dillon under a new identity. Twenty minutes later, Melissa's closet was in complete disarray. He had found every piece of her wardrobe that she had worn so often. Bending over, he picked up her favorite pair of boots and began to poke holes in Joey's theory, thinking that the fake passports weren't for her after all, but some desperate single mom and child she had met through her countless charity events.

Sliding down the wall into a sitting position, Quinton twirled her boot and thought about how many times Melissa had gotten involved in people's dramatic lives. He could hear Melissa clearly, as if she was standing in their bedroom.

"Quinton, I met the saddest little thing today. She left her husband, who had started drinking…"

Slowly, Quinton placed the boot back down and rubbed his eyes to try to block her voice out of his mind. Opening his eyes, he immediately took sight of Melissa's blue evening gown that she had worn recently. She looked so beautiful that night. She had lost all of her baby weight, and she looked better than ever. How had he ever let Mallory Jane creep into their lives? She wasn't supposed to last, and sure as hell not get pregnant, he thought.

After scanning the clothing once more, Quinton finally got to his feet, walked out of her closet, flipped the switch, and closed the door. Walking over to their bathroom, he suddenly stopped at a memory of Melissa holding Dillon in their large garden tub. She was trying to convince him to leave his favorite bath toy, his little blue boat. Melissa didn't want him to take it with him to his room because it always leaked water from the small holes. He could hear them clear as a bell, as if they were standing right in front of him.

235

"No, Dillon, boat stays in tub. It is a bath toy. You have plenty of toys in your room."

"I want boat! I want boat!"

Quinton rushed toward the cabinet beside the tub and began pulling out all Dillon's bath items: his shampoo, soap, washcloths, and various bath toys. Sitting down on the floor, he reached all the way to the back, but found no blue boat. Quickly, he sprang up and ran down the hall to Dillon's room, but stopped cold when he reached the doorknob. He had been in Dillon's room only once since his death, and it felt like he was now on top of the highest mountain in the world and couldn't breathe because of the lack of oxygen. Closing his eyes, he took slow, shallow breaths and then slowly turned the knob and pushed the door open.

Turning on the light, he looked around, and everything looked the same. The housecleaner cleaned the room each week whether it needed a dusting or not. Walking over to his bed, he found his favorite stuffed animals all neatly sitting on the bed without a single wrinkle on the bed quilt. Picking up a stuffed bear, he placed it to his nose and tried to remember Dillon's smell. Melissa was always putting baby lotion on Dillon, and he swore he would forever have smooth skin regardless, of how much he liked to play rough and in the dirt.

Slowly, Quinton walked over to Dillon's toy box and opened the lid. Seeing the red fire truck, he immediately remembered Dillon on all fours pushing the truck and squealing with delight at the sound of the sirens. Instantly, Quinton placed the truck on the floor and gave it a push. Soon the room filled with noise, and he felt a tear roll down his cheek. He thought, *Could he be alive? Could she have found out about Mallory Jane, or worse yet, Rebecca?*

Leaning toward the toy box, Quinton pulled out more toys, until it was completely empty, but still no boat. Not giving up, Quinton ran to his closet and searched the floor for any sign of his boat—nothing.

Placing a hand upon his chest, he took a few steps backward until he found Dillon's bed and sat down. Anger began to take over as he pushed all thoughts of death and grief from his head. Reaching into his side pocket, he retrieved his phone and then dug in his wallet and removed a card and read:

Joey Franks, Private Investigator

No job is too big or small for Joey

Give me a call!

I can make all your troubles go away

With a smirk upon his face, Quinton dialed the number on the card and waited for Joey to pick up on the other end.

"Joey Franks."

"I'll get you your money, but I want their new name and location by tomorrow, five p.m. sharp. Do you think you can handle that, or do I need to look elsewhere?"

"No problem. You got the cash, I got the goods. See you tomorrow."

Quinton didn't respond and hung up the phone.

Chapter 34

Tired of tossing and turning, Joey finally sat up in bed. Sometime over the night, he seemed to have grown a conscience. All night long, he'd tossed and turned about what he had done. He couldn't get Melissa's beautiful face out of his mind. He kept seeing images of her all bruised and bloody, begging for her life, as Quinton pulled the trigger with her small son watching in the corner. Why did she go to such lengths to fake her death? She could have just left him and taken her share of the dough and house. Angry at himself, Joey yanked off the covers. He walked over to his computer, turned it on, and then looked over the paperwork of Melissa's new life, with all her details— her address, Dillon's day care, her workplace address, and the name of her bank. Looking over the phone numbers, he calculated in his head the time in Australia, fifteen hours ahead. It was a little after 2:00 a.m. Thursday morning in Alabama, so he calculated the time for Coolum, Queensland, where she lived.

With the computer on, he logged on to his Skype account and typed in the number for Teresa B. Smith.

After three rings, a female voice answered.

Melissa was sitting in a local pub in Mooloolaba at 5:15 p.m. Thursday when she got a call on her mobile phone. Melissa broke away from her colleagues and walked toward the corner of the pub and said again, "Hello?"

"Is this Teresa Smith?"

239

Thinking it was an important client calling her back, she said, "Yes. How may I help you?"

"Melissa, it's Joey Franks, the private investigator from Birmingham."

Instantly, Melissa dropped her beer to the ground, and all color drained from her face.

"Teresa! What are you doing?"

Melissa looked at the mess on the floor, and at the bartender who was frowning behind the counter, and her good friend Karen walking toward her.

"Melissa? Do you remember me? I gave you and your son a new identity."

She held up her hand at her friend. "I have to take this. I will be right back." Melissa ran toward the exit and answered in a trembling voice, "Yes, I remember you."

Chapter 35

Quinton met Joey Franks at 5:00 p.m. on Thursday evening at the designated place. It was a crowded establishment, and no one noticed as a folder was exchanged for a plastic shopping bag.

"Is it all here?"

"No. You will get the rest when I return from Australia and I've seen with my own eyes that they are alive."

Joey narrowed his eyes. "So how much is in the bag?"

"Two hundred thousand."

Joey nodded his head. "Don't screw with me, Pierson. You'll regret it."

Quinton leaned forward. "Don't threaten me. If what you say is the truth, there will be more."

Joey stood up. "Don't call me from Australia. Wait till you get back."

Quinton nodded, and then Joey turned and left. Quinton opened up the folder and found a few sheets of paper and began to read. It appeared that Melissa had done well with her new life in Australia. She was working and making good money and lived in a small community. Joey had produced five pages on Teresa B. Smith. Picking up the folder, Quinton left and then pulled out his phone once he was outside and dialed an airline.

Chapter 36

Melissa was sitting at her desk when she got the call.

"He arrives in Brisbane on Sunday morning."

"Wow, that was fast."

"Do you have everything set up there?"

"Yes"

"Good. Be in touch."

"Thanks, I will."

Melissa stood up then and walked toward her boss's office. Last night she had rehearsed once more her prepared story. She was disappointed. What started out to be a temporary job had gained her respect and recognition, and now she was going to have to decline if he offered her the full-time position.

Andrew Morrison greeted her at his door with a big grin on his face. "Come on in, Teresa. I've got some good news to share with you."

Hesitating briefly, she stepped inside and took the offered chair. Andrew walked around his desk and sat down, still smiling.

"Now, before I get started, I just want to say once more how impressed we have been with your work over the last few weeks."

"Thank you, that means a lot."

"Good. As you know, the team met earlier to discuss the possibility of bringing you on full-time. And, I am happy to say that we would like to offer you a full-time position and continue to complete our team as you have so nicely done."

Melissa felt heartbroken, and her expression must have shown it.

"Teresa? Are you not pleased?"

Melissa forced a warm smile and then began her well-rehearsed speech. "A few days ago, I got a call from a family friend in Florida. She has cancer, and I have decided to move back home to help her during this rough time."

Andrew's smile slowly faded into a slight frown. "I'm so sorry to hear that, Teresa. Do you anticipate coming back in the future?"

"I don't know. She has a small child, and there is so much to consider…"

Andrew held up his hand for her to stop. "Of course you can't make any long-term decisions. I shouldn't have pushed."

"Don't apologize. I understand your predicament, and I know how anxious you are to find a full-time replacement for this job."

Slowly he nodded his head. "So I guess today truly will be your last day with us."

Melissa forced a smile and responded, "Yes."

Andrew stood up and then walked around his desk and extended his hand. "Well, Teresa, if you ever find yourself back here in Australia and looking for a job, please don't hesitate to call us, even though we might have no advertised positions available."

Melissa took his hand and gave a firm shake. "I appreciate that, Mr. Morrison, and I will miss everyone around here so much."

Slowly Melissa turned and walked toward the door as he opened it up for her. Stepping into the hallway, she turned around once more and smiled. "Thanks again." Then hurried back toward her desk before she burst into tears.

Four o'clock seemed to never arrive. Melissa had been on edge all day with the thought of Quinton landing in Australia soon. He was coming here, to get her. The thought brought a cold shiver down her back, and she closed her eyes and sat back in her chair.

"Hey, you all right?"

Melissa looked up and found Karen standing in front of her desk.

"Yeah, just tired. I didn't get much sleep last night."

Karen tilted her head. "What is going on with you? Ever since last night at the pub, when you got that phone call, you've been on edge."

"I know. I told you, it is just some stuff back home. In fact, I'm gonna have to move back to Florida for a while."

"What? When were you going to tell me?"

Melissa looked away briefly to collect her thoughts. "Today, after work."

"Oh, Teresa, I'm going to miss you, and I hope whatever it is has you back out here soon."

Melissa met her eyes. "Thanks, and you were right, Morrison did offer me the job, and I had to turn it down."

"Well, maybe he can hire another temp and then, when you return, hire you full-time."

"It wouldn't work. My friend has a small child, and there are just too many unknown factors to predict, and I just couldn't put him in that position."

Karen frowned. "Well, I'm really bummed. Who am I gonna get pissed with now?"

Teresa laughed, "You won't have any trouble finding a new weekly drinking partner."

"Oh, it just won't be the same around here, that's all."

Looking at the clock, Melissa said, "Thanks. Are you ready to leave? I'll walk out with you."

Karen touched her purse and said, "Yep. Let's go, and how about I shout you one more drink before you leave?"

Melissa shook her head. "I can't. I have to go and pick up Dillon, but I wish I could."

Karen frowned again. "Well, okay, you just let me know if you need anything."

"Well, it helps that I was renting month to month in a furnished house. All I need to do is just pack up our few belongings."

The ladies reached the parking lot, and Karen reached out and gave Melissa an affectionate hug. "I will miss you, and I want you to e-mail me as soon as you get settled, promise?"

"Yes, of course I promise. Bye, Karen, I will miss you too."

Slowly, Melissa pulled away and headed toward her vehicle and barely got the door shut behind her before the floodgates opened up. As she placed her key in the ignition, she realized she was shaking uncontrollably. Removing her hand from the keys, she covered her face and cried at the nightmare that had found her once again.

Later that night, Melissa packed a few bags while Dillon slept peacefully in his room. When she was satisfied that she had packed enough of her belongings, she then began to clean and tidy up the place. Tying the garbage bag, she walked out her side door that led to the garbage carts on the side of the house. Lifting the lid, she tossed the bag inside and then jumped when she heard a noise behind her coming from the reserve. Spinning around quickly, she looked around, but saw and heard nothing. Spooked, she ran back into the house and locked the door and rested her head on the doorframe to catch her breath.

Damn it, Melissa, stop getting yourself worked up. You have a long night ahead, she said silently to herself.

Slowly turning around, she walked into the kitchen and opened the refrigerator. Justifying that it was just going to be one and it would help settle her nerves, she grabbed a beer. Twisting the top, she stepped toward the back porch and slid the door open. Unlatching the screen, she stepped outside and then pulled the screen back into place.

Taking a long swig, she walked over to the railing and looked out to sea. It was a beautiful clear night with many stars visible. The sound of the waves was loud, and it helped bring some peace and relaxation to Melissa. After another few sips of her beer, she took a step back and settled in on her hammock and waited for the call.

Chapter 37

"Welcome to Australia, Mr. Barnes, what brings you here?"

Quinton adjusted his fake reading glasses and said, "Business."

"And where are you staying and for how long?"

"Brisbane. Four nights."

"Tough turnaround. So what business are you in?"

Quinton had been well prepared. Joey had given him a fake passport of a man who ran his own drilling supply company. Joey explained how a lot of oil and gas people came to Australia for short business trips and assured him they would ask a few questions, but nothing to be alarmed about. It was normal.

"A drilling supply company."

The custom agent nodded his head. "Have a nice trip, Mr. Barnes."

"I will. Thank you."

It took another hour to retrieve his luggage and then go through another long line for his luggage to be scanned and more questions asked. When it was all over with, he was actually impressed with the entire system and no longer agitated by it all.

Walking outside the airport, he immediately hailed a taxi. "Hilton, downtown."

This was the first time Quinton had ever been to Australia, and he immediately liked the looks of things. Brisbane was an older city that was situated on a river that ran through the city. There were parks, botanical gardens, museums, and several water taxis along the river. The taxi made a few more turns down busy streets, and he finally arrived at the Hilton.

After paying the driver and retrieving his bags, he took an elevator up one level to the reception desk. Stepping out, he saw a large atrium with two restaurants and another set of elevators that took you up to the guest floors above. Walking over to the desk, he was greeted warmly, but was then informed he couldn't check in yet since it was only nine o'clock.

"When will my room be ready?"

"Sorry, we have a business conference here this week, so not until two o'clock. But we will be happy to hold your luggage." The young girl noticed his displeasure and added, "If you would like, you can browse our tourist info area, and someone will be able to help with a tour to fill the time."

Not wanting to cause too much attention to himself, he smiled and said, "That would be lovely"—he leaned in forward and looked at her name tag—"Benay."

Smiling, she walked around the counter and placed a tag on his luggage and then gave him a receipt and gestured toward the other side of the atrium to another set of elevators that would take him back down to the street level.

"Once outside, you will see the building with the yellow-and-blue *i*."

Taking the tag, he left and walked away, following her instructions. Once the elevator opened back up, he found himself on Queen Street, filled with shops, souvenir stores, pubs, and of course, the tourist information center. First, he walked over to a bakery and placed an order for coffee. Getting his to go, he walked back toward the information building and opened the door and stepped inside.

Instantly, he was greeted by an elderly lady who was overjoyed at the opportunity to help. "First time in Brisbane?"

"Why, yes, it is."

She smiled again. "Wonderful, welcome to our beautiful city. Now, how may I help you?"

Quinton returned her smile and adjusted his glasses. "I'm looking for something to fill my time before check-in at two."

"Great. I know just the tour." She extended her right arm toward a wall of brochures that read: Day Trips.

Following her gesture, he walked over to the wall that held many colorful brochures and watched as she picked up one.

"This is a river cruise that leaves at ten and returns at two. They will feed you a nice lunch and drop you off at the koala sanctuary for a visit with the koalas."

Taking the brochure, he read over the information and studied the dotted line that weaved over the river in a winding motion. The price was listed at the bottom, and it was one he could live with. After all, he told himself, he did come all this way, he might as well see Australia's famed fuzzy animal. Plus, he could share the story of his trip with Dillon, and maybe that would help ease the tension that for sure was going to come after months of their separation.

Looking back up, he found her blue eyes and said, "It sounds perfect. Sign me up."

Smiling, she motioned him over to the counter, filled out a sheet of paper, then took his offered credit card. "Check, credit, or savings?"

"Credit."

"Pin or signature?"

Hesitating for a moment, he reached back for his card. "Let me pay cash."

Smiling, she handed him his card and then took his money. The elderly lady, in her blue pantsuit, punched a few buttons on a computer keyboard and then handed him a receipt.

"Now, if you will follow me, I can get you going in the right direction."

Stepping out behind the counter, she headed for the exit door, and Quinton followed closely. The automatic doors opened, and both stepped outside. Once again, she used her hands to gesture more instructions.

"Do you see that sign that reads 'Edward Street'?"

Quinton looked toward their right and saw a sign mounted along the side of the red light and replied, "Yes, I do."

She continued, "Follow Edward Street for about five minutes, till you get to Eagle Street Pier. There you will see a white-and-blue boat with the words 'Koala Sanctuary Tours.' It should be ready for loading."

Looking down at his watch, he noticed he had only about twenty minutes before departure. Quickly he mumbled, "Thanks," and began walking as directed.

"You're welcome. Enjoy our beautiful city, and I hope you have a pleasant stay."

Quinton turned around briefly and waved and then continued onward.

Making his way down the street, he noticed the many beautiful buildings, some dating back to 1865. The streets were clean, people were friendly, and many were out just enjoying the day with a cup of coffee. Turning the last block, he saw the river up ahead and people gathered around the blue-and-white boat, waiting to board, just as she had promised.

After waiting in line behind a large group of Asians, he finally approached the young brunette attendant. He dug into his pocket, retrieved his ticket receipt, and handed it to her.

Glancing over it quickly, she tore it in half and then handed it back with a smile. "Welcome aboard."

"Thank you."

As he walked up the metal plank, he was greeted by a male attendant who ushered him toward a row of seats. Deciding to get a better view, he went up to the top floor despite the hot weather. As soon as he took a seat, they began to ready the boat for departure. In a few short minutes, they broke away from the dock and headed upstream. The next forty-five minutes were filled listening to a narrative of the city and eating various samples of seafood mixtures and a superb Greek salad.

Quinton watched the city go by and began to tune out the narrator as thoughts of Melissa and Dillon filled his mind. *Is this a hoax? Did she really fake her death and run to the other side of the world?*

Just then, a little blond-headed boy ran by with his dad a few feet behind him. He continued to watch as the father picked up the boy and placed him on his shoulders. Quinton looked away.

Hours began to move by quickly, and as the lady had stated, the koala sanctuary was nice, and it helped fill time that Quinton so desperately needed to block out thoughts of Dillon. The last four months without him was a void he couldn't fill no matter how hard he tried. Oh, Mallory Jane had tried, and promised him joy would return with the birth of their child and he could be happy once again. Blocking out the image of a pale-faced Mallory Jane as he carried her to her unmarked grave, he looked out at the families gathered today and thought, *She didn't have a clue. Dillon couldn't be replaced.*

Arriving back safely at the Eagle Street Pier, Quinton thanked the crew and stepped off the boat and headed back down Edward Street. He was tempted to visit the botanical gardens, but smiled as he decided he would bring Dillon here with him to enjoy it.

Finally, Quinton was allowed to check in, and he took a shower and then dressed for dinner. He was going to dine out tonight and then be back in by seven for bed. With the time difference and flight, he had gotten only six hours of sleep over the last thirty- two hours. Tomorrow was sure to be filled with a lot of emotions with seeing his son, and he wanted to be ready, mentally and physically, for what he had in store for Melissa.

Chapter 38

Quinton woke at 4:35 a.m. and couldn't go back asleep. After tossing and turning the next two hours, he finally got out of bed, dressed, repacked his luggage, and then checked out of the Hilton.

Catching a cab, he rode to the nearest car rental place and rented a car for two days with cash. He was amazed at how easy it was to rent a car with a foreign driver's license. Equipped with a GPS, he typed in the town of Dalby and was soon on his way. The next forty-five minutes was a little tricky with the roundabouts and traffic in Brisbane, but soon he got the hang of driving on the opposite side of the road without any mishaps.

According to his GPS, he would arrive in Dalby at 11:45 a.m., before lunch. His plan was to ride by the address given for Melissa and then check into a hotel and plan his next move. Melissa wasn't scheduled to be home from work till five fifteen, after having to stop and pick up Dillon at day care. The next several miles were filled with silence as Quinton thought about what he was going to say once he found her. Should he kill her immediately or make her suffer? Either way, he would have to ensure Dillon was out of harm's way and would witness none of it.

When he was fifteen kilometers away from Dalby, he saw his first kangaroos along the side of the road. So far, he hadn't hit any, but the chance would increase when the time approached evening. Pulling over at a service station, Quinton pulled out Melissa's file and then typed in her address. Apparently, she lived seven kilometers out of

255

town. Pulling back out onto the Warrego Highway, Quinton drove a few kilometers out of town and then turned left down a one-lane gravel road. There weren't many houses along the turnoff, and it was easy to find number 8 Bowen Street. Slowing down, Quinton drove past the white wooden house with a fenced-in yard with no vehicles in the driveway.

At the next house, Quinton pulled in and then backed down the driveway to turn around. Approaching Melissa's house for the second time, he came to a stop beside her mailbox. No cars were passing, and it was absolutely quiet along the street. Quinton tried to picture Melissa and Dillon living in this house in this small rural town, but for some reason, it didn't fit, and something seemed off.

Carefully, Quinton put the car in park and eased out of the driver's seat. He walked two steps over to the mailbox and opened it up. Nothing. No mail. With a sigh, Quinton got back into his vehicle and then drove away in search of the Best Western, where he already had a reservation for the night. Since it was still early, Quinton decided to drive around town some and find Melissa's place of employment. The information given stated she worked for a real estate company and they were located on Main Street, two blocks down from his hotel.

Checking into his hotel, he had a short conversation with the kind owner and then found his room and was pleasantly surprised when he opened the door. Looking around the place, he noticed how nice and tidy the room was kept. His stomach rumbled as he placed his suitcase down. *I need to eat*, he thought. Choosing something simple, he left his rental car in the parking lot and walked across the street to get a fast-food burger.

Twenty minutes later, with his stomach full, he decided now was the perfect time to go and spy on Melissa. He picked up a small map that he had taken from his hotel room and studied it. Immediately he found Western Downs Realty Company marked clearly in bold letters. Tucking it inside his pocket, he strolled casually down Main Street and soon found her work with no difficulty. Readjusting his glasses, he walked by and quickly took a glance inside. No Melissa. It was hard to see inside due to the small flyers showing properties for sale that were strategically placed all over the glass windows. He did, however, see a brunette sitting there talking on the phone, and she was clearly not Melissa.

Trying not to bring attention to himself, he continued on down the street and stopped. He thought, *Now what? Should I go back and take another quick look or head back to the hotel and prepare?*

Looking at the building in front of him, he immediately figured out he was at the town post office, which was four blocks from his hotel.

Realizing it was too risky, he fought the urgent desire to see her and headed back toward his hotel. Once back at his room, he looked at his watch. He had four more hours to wait. Quinton removed his shoes and settled onto the bed and rearranged his pillow for a nap. Closing his eyes, he thought, *Soon, Melissa, and I'm coming for you.*

Chapter 39

Quinton awoke to his alarm at five o'clock. After rising from bed, he quickly took a shower and changed into dark clothing. Now he needed to eat and wait another three hours before heading out. Deciding to keep a low profile around such a small town, he stayed inside and passed the time flipping through the channels on TV.

At 8:25, Quinton cracked the hotel door and looked around outside. He was a little surprised to see people, lots of people, hanging around outside having a smoke and a beer. All were men, and they were dressed in traditional blue-and-orange work clothing and steel-toed boots. He slipped out and took the four steps to his rental car; hoping most wouldn't pay him too much attention. The rental car was parked right outside his room and he remembered at the last moment which side to walk to, without making a classic mistake by foreigners.

Settling in the driver's seat, he looked around to see if anyone had noticed him. He had caught the eyes of two men, two doors down, but they quickly turned away and continued their conversation. Pulling away from the hotel, he pressed the button that stored recent destinations in his GPS and pressed Melissa's address on the screen.

Quinton noticed how his hands were sweating as he gripped the wheel tightly, too tightly as he drove out of town. Easing up, he rolled his shoulders and bent his neck side to side to try to work out some of the tension. It seemed to be working until he turned a sharp turn and was faced with two kangaroos on the road. Swerving and honking the horn, he was barely able to get past them without any damage to the car. *How the hell do people drive out here?* he thought.

Driving at a cautious speed, Quinton drove past Melissa's house and noticed one car parked outside. He continued on for another two kilometers and then turned around on a dirt road and drove back. There was only one other house along the way making his task easier. Passing her house once again, he finally pulled to a stop about four hundred meters away.

He turned off his GPS and then the engine. Carefully he stepped out and locked the car. Placing the keys in his pocket, he began to make his way through the dark to Melissa and Dillon.

With each step along the side of the road, Quinton could feel his heart rate increase. He couldn't quite decide if it was from the thought of seeing Dillon or the idea that he could be bit by one of the world's deadliest brown snakes. Focusing hard on his mission, he was able to regulate his breathing and prepare. After another few steps, he could finally make out Melissa's house in the dark.

Through the front window, he could see that the house was well lit, so she must be home. When he reached her driveway, he was able to see an old blue 4x4 parked to the side, just like the one described in the files Joey had given him. The house was old, and it had a wraparound porch along the front with several windows. Seeing a shadow walk by the window, he froze at the thought of finally seeing Melissa.

Careful not to make a noise, he slowly climbed the few stairs up to the porch and then paused to listen for any kind of noise from behind the front door before he proceeded again. He heard nothing. He continued on and stopped at the side window and peered inside. Looking around, he found a few toys—trucks, books, and a rubber ball on the floor—in what appeared to be the living room. He saw no one, however; he did notice a hallway that led away from the room. Carefully, Quinton walked around to the right side of the door and found another window to look through.

As he watched, he noticed movement at the end of the hall. It was darker than the living room, and he couldn't make out Melissa's face.

Leaving the window, he carefully walked back to the front door and twisted the knob. To his surprise, it was unlocked.

Not knowing if she was truly home alone, he left the front porch and made his way around to the back of the house. When he was almost there, he tripped over a log and fell forward to the ground. Catching himself before his face hit the dirt, he silently cussed and then got back up and dusted himself off.

Getting back on his feet, he moved at a slower rate, feeling around in the dark for more unknown objects. Finally he reached the corner and looked up to the windows above. The porch in the back was smaller, and he couldn't risk climbing the stairs without being noticed. For the next several minutes, he watched the larger window, but still could only make out a person moving back and forth behind the curtains. Noticing a tall white refrigerator through one of the partially uncovered smaller windows, he was able to conclude it was the kitchen. Deciding that Melissa was indeed alone and probably washing up after dinner, he made the final decision to enter from the unlocked front door.

Melissa was pacing back and forth with Dillon on her hip. The waiting game was beginning to get the best of her. She had followed Joey's instructions down to the letter, and now all she had to do was wait for the unknown to happen. Dillon was getting heavy, so she stopped in front of the worn chair and placed him down. He had been asleep for the last few minutes, but Melissa just couldn't seem to put him down. She was so frightened with the realization that Quinton knew his son was alive and his wife had tricked him. Sitting beside Dillon, she brushed his blond hair away from his forehead and just watched as he slept without a care in the world.

"Oh, my sweet boy, what has your mommy done?"

Suddenly Melissa heard a noise from outside, and she quickly bolted up and carefully looked out the small window to see if she could find the source. She saw it. A four-legged creature with its eyes low to the ground darted by. Realizing it was just a cat or a raccoon, she was able to take a deep breath and make her way back over to Dillon.

Chapter 40

Quinton eased back up onto the front porch without making a noise and peered through the same window that showed the kitchen from the end of the hallway. Seeing another shadow, he concluded she was still in the kitchen. Carefully, he took another step over to the door and then turned the knob and opened the door quietly as not to make a sound.

The room held a worn couch, two chairs and a coffee table placed in the center. He continued forward and noticed the back of a picture frame. Checking the floor, he carefully stepped around the toys and then closed the door without a sound ever made. Hearing music from the kitchen, he was relieved that it would hide any creaks the floor made due to its age.

Quinton was able to lose all doubt about Joey's omission as he saw the picture in the frame. Smiling at the photo of Dillon with Melissa at the beach, he thought, *It won't be long, Dillon.*

Focusing on his mission, he took a couple of steps, breathing deeper as his pulse increased. As he made the remaining few steps down the hall, he carefully twirled a cord around his wrist as Melissa's backside came into view as she stood in front of the sink washing a few dishes.

The room wasn't as well lit as the front, but he could see Melissa's long blonde hair flowing down her back. She was wearing jeans and a halter top that tied at the base of her neck. She looked a little heavier, but he wasn't surprised she had gained her ten pounds of weight back. It was such a battle for her after having Dillon. Watching her pick up the last glass to wash, he made his final step and raised his arms with the cord clutched between his fingers.

Suddenly, a noise was made from behind him, and thinking it was Dillon, he turned his head just in time to see a large object crushing down upon him. He fell hard on the floor. Next, he instinctually grabbed his head and felt moisture. He blinked away the wetness flowing down his forehead just in time to see a man leaning over, swinging again. This time Quinton lost consciousness.

"Babe, get the rope!"

Chris knelt down beside Quinton's crumpled and bleeding body as his wife handed him the rope. Quickly he tied his hands and feet together and then took a wet cloth and began to inspect the damage he had caused to the intruders' head.

"Is he dead?"

Chris looked at his wife and then back down at the man with blood oozing from his skull. "I don't think so. Pete said not to take chances, so let's just get him out of here fast!" Checking his pockets, Chris found the rental keys and tossed them to his wife, Sarah. "Go and get his car and bring it to the house."

"But, it's dark, and I—"

"Take the flashlight. It can't be far. We saw him pass by, remember?" Seeing his lovely wife hesitate, he caved. "Fine, you stay with him, and I'll go!"

With quivering lips, she shouted, "Oh no, I'll go! I am not staying here with him!"

Chris smiled. "Good girl!"

Chapter 41

Melissa woke up beside Dillon to a cold, semidark room. The cabin had no electricity, only oil lamps and a fireplace. Sometime during the night, while she slept, the fire had burned out. She found Dillon still snuggled up with his bear and sleeping as she turned her head. Easing off the couch, she got up and walked over to the small window and looked outside. The sun was starting to rise, but it seemed unable to stop the chill. The wind was blowing, and the tree branches were swaying. Feeling cold to the bone, Melissa walked back over to the fireplace and placed another log on the fire and struck a match. Soon, heat was filling the small room once again, and Melissa made her way over to Dillon and eased back down beside him and fell back to sleep.

Two hours later, Dillon began to stir and woke up Melissa.

"Good morning, my little man!"

Dillon rubbed his eyes and looked at her and giggled. Still clutching his bear, he sat up on the worn couch and looked around.

"Where are wee?"

Melissa looked around the one-room cabin and said, "Camping."

Dillon's eyebrows rose, and he asked, "Camping where?"

"In the woods."

Dillon looked around some more and then jumped down and walked around to check out the place.

Melissa got up and walked over to the little cupboard by the sink and pulled out a skillet and two eggs. Placing a little drop of oil in the pan, she walked over to the fire and placed the skillet on an iron rack. Dillon watched in amazement as she then cracked the two eggs over the hot skillet.

When he walked closer, she said, "That is close enough, Dillon. The fire is hot, and it will burn you."

Dillon stopped at the word "hot" and just watched as Melissa finished cooking their breakfast. Removing the skillet, she walked over to the small table and placed each egg on the only two plates in the cabin. Grabbing the only provided silverware, Melissa chopped up Dillon's egg.

"Come sit on the chair, and let's eat."

Dillon looked around some more and then followed her over to the only wooden chair and took a seat. Melissa got down on her knees to be shoulder high with Dillon and began eating.

After three bites he said, "I'm firsty!"

Melissa stood up and walked over to the small cabinet and removed one of the cartons of orange juice. Finding no cup, she walked back over and carefully held it to his lips while he drank.

After a few sips, he giggled. "No cups!"

Melissa tried to smile as she said, "No. No cups."

After they were done eating, Melissa took the two plates to the bucket by the cupboard and carefully wiped off the crumbs. Noticing only five large containers of water, she decided not to use the water for washing. Earlier, Melissa had made a quick inventory of what else she had. Two cartons of orange juice, four crates of eggs, five cans each of Spam, tuna fish, and pork and beans, and six cans of soup. In the corner of the room, behind a makeshift curtain, Melissa had felt nauseated when she found a six-pack roll of toilet tissue and one small portable potty. Inspecting it closer, she was only slightly relieved it was just dusty, not dirty.

Inside the cupboard was also one towel, a bar of soap, and one small bottle of cooking oil. It all gave the appearance of someone's bare essentials in a hunting cabin. Melissa had not yet ventured back outside since arriving by Jeep late last night, driven by some strange man who angrily stated, *"There is a stream outside, but stay indoors as much as possible. It is hunting season, and you could get shot."*

When Melissa gave him a concerned look, he only replied with, *"This won't last long, and you never saw me."*

When she opened her mouth to speak, he said, *"No more talking!"* and she'd closed her mouth and stepped out of the Jeep with her sleeping son in her arms.

"Mommy?"

Melissa broke free of her thoughts and turned and faced Dillon. "Yes?"

"Go outside?"

Melissa nodded. This was something she needed to do, to check out the place and see where the stream was located. "Stay close to Mommy and hold my hand at all times. This is going to be a very big adventure into the woods."

Dillon crinkled his face and whispered, "Woods scaary?"

Melissa gave her best smile. "No, not when you are with your mommy!"

He wasn't completely convinced as he walked over and quickly grabbed her hand. Melissa led him over to the door and slowly opened it up to reveal the small porch with one concrete step leading to the ground.

"Carry me, Mommy?" Melissa bent over and scooped him into her arms as he said, "Cold!"

Shutting the door behind them to keep the heat in, she replied, "We are in the mountains, so it is colder now."

"Moundtains?"

"Yes, mountains."

After looking around the ground and the surrounding trees, Melissa finally stepped off the small wooden porch.

"There is a stream nearby. Let's go on a scavenger hunt to try and find it!"

Dillon clapped his hands and squealed, "Scaveg hunt!"

It didn't take long to find the stream. It was behind the cabin, down a very steep hill. Melissa estimated it was about three hundred meters away.

"Dillon, we are going to get that bucket in the cabin, and then we are going to go down to the stream and fill it up with water." Dillon watched as she pointed down the hill.

"Sliiide!"

"Maybe, but not intentionally. Will you help Mommy carry it back up the hill?"

He nodded, and Melissa turned with Dillon and went back into the log cabin to get it. After shutting the door, she took the shorter direction behind the house. Rounding the corner, she instantly felt a huge sense of relief when she spotted the stack of firewood. The food was going to be much better if it was heated. Walking around the stack of wood, she saw a small table set up with what appeared to be dried blood. In the wood was knife scratches from cutting.

Turning away from the bloody table, she said, "Come on, Dillon, let's go slide." At the top of the hill, Melissa placed the large silver bucket on the leaves and told him, "Get in!"

Smiling big, he placed his little hands on the side and balanced himself and picked up one leg and climbed on in.

"Are you ready?"

"Go!"

Melissa slid alongside of him down the hill while holding on to the tub. By the time they got down to the bottom, Dillon was laughing hysterically. Melissa stopped about twenty feet from the water's edge and pulled him toward her.

Kaboom! Kaboom!

Melissa jumped and fell onto the ground and rolled on top of Dillon. With wild eyes, she quickly scanned the forest for hunters. Seconds passed, but they seemed like minutes to Melissa.

"Mommy, off!"

Leaning close to his ear, she whispered, "Stay. I'm going to get the water." Quickly she ran forward and dipped the bucket until it was one-fourth full and then turned and made her way back over. "Let's hurry back up, okay?"

Dillon tried to hold on to the bucket as both hiked back up the hill. By the time they made it to the top, he was physically exhausted, and she was mentally exhausted.

"Come on. Let's go inside and clean up the dishes."

Dillon followed willingly, and Melissa closed the door and locked it once they were inside.

"What noise?"

He had asked several times earlier, and Melissa said she would tell him once they got back to the cabin. "Gunshots from hunters."

"Hunting silly wabbits?"

Melissa laughed aloud. "Yes. Hunting silly rabbits!"

Chapter 42

MONDAY NIGHT, FEBRUARY 1
DOWNTOWN BIRMINGHAM

Joey Franks was sitting at his desk and finalizing the last details with the Pierson case when his phone rang. "Joey Franks."

Silence.

Joey glanced at his watch and noted the time, eight thirty. His business hours were over, and he assumed it was the wrong number. Hanging up, he leaned forward again and contemplated his last move. All was set in place, and Melissa should be able to return back to her normal life in just a few more days. He felt lousy about approaching Quinton and revealing she was alive.

Damn, why did I do that? he thought. He had met Melissa before through her charity organization and really liked her. She seemed truly dedicated to helping others. *Well, what is done is done. I have now made it right.*

Joey stood up and pushed his chair back and walked over with his cryptic notes toward the filing cabinet. Opening the drawer, he found the correct folder and slipped the paper inside. He then shut the drawer and raked a hand through his hair. He was tired. Hearing a noise he turned around and said, "Frieda, I got this case."

Bang! Bang!

Joey Franks fell to the floor with two bullets pierced through his forehead. A fifteen-year-old kid dressed in black and red quickly made his way through the small building, toward the back, in search of the one Joey called "Frieda."

Just as the skinny white kid rounded the corner, he heard a shot from the back and heard his sidekick yell out, "Yo homie, I got 'er, man. Let's get out of here!"

Together they continued out the back door and down the dark alley and into the night. Luckily for Frieda, the neighbor next door was home and quickly dialed 911.

Chapter 43

Melissa was standing by the window and looking outside into the night. Looking at her watch with the help of a small oil lamp, she could see that it was 3:00 a.m. *What the hell have I done?*

Days had turned into a week, and then another week went by without any word from the strange man who had dropped her off or from Joey. Thinking of the remaining food supply, Melissa began to worry that perhaps they had been forgotten, or worse, something had gone terribly wrong with the plan. Melissa had to make a decision, and soon. She was not going to stay here and run out of food. She hadn't heard a gunshot again since that day and could only assume hunting season ended at the end of January. But still, she had no clue where she was, and the ground had several inches of snow. She pulled the curtains back, walked back over to the small cot, and climbed in beside Dillon and prayed that this charade that had turned into a nightmare would end soon.

Virginia Leigh Mason was sitting in her living room, having coffee on her estate in Jackson, Mississippi, when the doorbell rang. Looking at the clock, Nana thought nine o'clock was too early for an unannounced visitor as she placed her coffee cup down and got up out of her favorite chair.

"I'll get it, Vera!"

After pausing at no response, Virginia Leigh continued toward the front door and smoothed her hair down as she walked. Already dressed for the day, but not expecting visitors, she glanced over her appearance and then finally opened the door. Immediately she was bombarded by cameras with flashes and news reporters shouting questions.

Taking a step backward and grabbing her chest, she made out the most important words: "Melissa and Dillon are alive!"

Melissa had held Dillon tightly as she was led gently out of the run-down cabin and into the back of an ambulance by two police officers. She had been bombarded by questions the last several minutes, but had remained very quiet except for a few spoken words. The paramedics had intervened nicely and given her some time to think and plan. Now, she lay on a cot with Dillon by her side, sleeping.

As the ambulance began to move forward, the young paramedic spoke. "I'm June."

Melissa looked up and met her big brown eyes and said, "How far are we from a hospital?"

"At least thirty minutes. Do you have any idea where you are?"

Melissa shook her head.

"North Georgia, the Blue Ridge Mountains."

Melissa tried to calculate the distance in her head from when she landed in Atlanta on Saturday, January 30. The day had been such a blur with the jet lag and layover flights once she landed in Los Angeles.

Soon, her thoughts were interrupted when June asked, "Do you want something to help you sleep?"

Melissa seriously considered it, but couldn't risk Dillon falling into the hands of strangers and being questioned, so she declined.

"Well, try to relax. Your blood pressure is a little high."

Melissa nodded and closed her eyes and rested her head to the side, against Dillon's forehead. The next several miles seemed to creep by as she thought about the last two weeks living in the cabin. Four days ago, they started running low on food, and Melissa had taken only one meal a day, where Dillon could have more. Trying to maintain the heat, they had stayed in the cabin and stopped going outside to the stream. Running out of firewood yesterday, Melissa had broken a small footstool to use as wood. Yes, something had definitely gone wrong with the plan, and she was beyond worry for her child's safety, as well as with the thought that Quinton was on to her.

Now, here she lay in an ambulance, hungry and slightly dehydrated, but alive with her son and hopefully going home as planned. With the thought of home, Melissa paled. June stood up, leaned over her, and checked her IV and then her vitals once more.

Melissa had no idea what had happened over the last two weeks. No one had been in touch as Joey had promised, and she had no idea what had led the police to the cabin to rescue her. *Is Quinton alive? Did he find out the plan?* More questions raced through her mind, with no good answers.

Melissa thought back on the events as they had unfolded. She remembered waking up early and then going back to sleep. It was voices outside the cabin that woke her from her sleep beside Dillon. Soon, the door was knocked down, and several officers came rushing in. Melissa had time only to cover Dillon's face as she found herself surrounded by lawmen wearing armored vests and swinging their weapons around the room as they swept the area for danger. When they saw her sitting on the bed, an officer immediately lowered his weapon and identified himself.

After the officers secured the area, a paramedic quickly arrived on the scene and rushed in to look at Dillon and Melissa. Questions were fired away, but she couldn't keep track of it all as nausea overtook her and she vomited on the bare cabin floors. Soon an IV was hooked up, and the paramedic informed the officers that she was dehydrated. It took only minutes for them to be whisked away, but seemed like an hour to Melissa. She couldn't think what to say as they asked questions.

"Are you two alone?"

"How did you get here? Do you know who you are?"

Melissa answered only one question. "Melissa Pierson, and I want to go home."

That had silenced their questions, and the paramedic had come to her rescue when he suggested, "Later, we need to get them to a hospital and checked out by a doctor."

So here Melissa was with Dillon, riding along a country road, and the only scenery from the back windows was trees. Not fighting sleep anymore, Melissa dozed off with Dillon in her arms.

Once at the hospital, a nurse tried to separate Dillon from Melissa, and she lost it. Soon she realized she was scaring him, so she finally gave in.

"Dillon, Mommy is going to see a nice doctor while you see a nice doctor also. I will be right here when you come back."

"No, Mommy! No!"

Two nurses took him away kicking and screaming as Melissa laid her head back down and a tear rolled down her face. The nurse continued taking her vitals as a doctor looked over a chart and then made his way forward.

"Melissa, I'm Dr. Young. I know this has been a traumatic experience for you. Are you okay with me giving you an exam and then running some tests?"

"What is today?"

"Friday, February twelfth. You have been missing since November."

Melissa closed her eyes.

"Melissa, may I examine you?"

She opened her eyes and responded, "Yes."

Two hours had gone by before Melissa was once again reunited with Dillon. As he slept, he was rolled into her room in a child's bed and placed alongside her bed.

With moist eyes, the nurse quietly said, "The doctor will be in shortly to go over his tests. Try to rest yourself. You are both safe now."

Melissa nodded her head, and then the nurse left the room.

Another hour passed as Melissa watched Dillon sleep soundly without moving. Just as she was closing her eyes and beginning to drift away, she heard voices from outside.

"Do you not know who I am? I am going in! Now let me pass!"

A smile crept across her face as she heard her Nana's sweet voice.

Soon the door was opened, and Virginia Leigh met her eyes. She ran forward with open arms and tears in her eyes.

"Oh, Melissa! I thought I had lost you!"

Holding on tight, Melissa hugged her as she wept in her arms. She saw the officer look around the room, and then he closed the door to give them some privacy.

"Where is Papa?"

Nana shook her head. "I'm sorry, Melissa, he is gone. Heart attack in January."

Now it was Melissa's turn to break down and sob as Nana held her tight.

Chapter 44

Melissa was sitting in her hospital bed reading the local Georgia paper. On the front page was a picture of Joey Franks and a family portrait of Quinton, Melissa, and Dillon.

The headline read: Melissa and Dillon Pierson Expected to be Release from Hospital Today, Outlook Looks Grim for Missing Husband and Father, Quinton Pierson.

Melissa scanned the article and reread twice the paragraph on Frieda, Joey's assistant and longtime girlfriend. Apparently, Frieda had barely survived her second gang attack in just less than two months. Once she recovered and was released from the hospital, she started going through their current files and came across the Pierson file. After going through it and noticing most of the notes were cryptic, she set it aside and then continued to go through the rest. A day later, when she was done, she returned to the Pierson file and questioned why Joey had written notes in a code that only he could understand. When removing all the papers from the file to break the code, she found a small handwritten address on a worn paper that had been previously folded. After hours of unsuccessful attempts to decipher his notes, she finally called the police.

The article ended with:

> Police are still investigating Joey Franks's relationship with a well-known gang, the Ripps, and whether or not he was involved with the apparent kidnapping of Melissa and Dillon Pierson.

Melissa folded the paper and closed her eyes. *My God, they think Joey masterminded my abduction.* Slowly, a tear rolled down her face as she opened up her eyes and found Nana standing in her doorway to her room.

With a worried expression, she asked, "Melissa, you ready to go home?"

She nodded and slowly got out of bed and walked over to the closet to retrieve the outfit Nana had brought her yesterday. "Is Dillon ready?" she asked over her shoulder as she walked into the bathroom.

"Yes, a nurse is going to bring him in any minute now. You go on and change, and I will wait in here."

Melissa nodded and closed the door. Slowly she turned and looked in the mirror at her reflection and thought, *What have I done?*

Three hours later, Melissa and Dillon were almost home to Birmingham. Nana was driving, while Melissa sat in the passenger seat asleep, with Dillon buckled in a car seat in the back.

Dillon clapped at his movie, and Melissa jumped, startled from the noise.

Nana glanced over. "You okay?"

Melissa looked around and then relaxed. "Yeah, there were some gunshots around the cabin from hunters, I...I..."

"It is okay now. You are on your way home and are safe."

Melissa tried to smile and then turned around and looked at Dillon and noticed how content he was with his movie playing. Turning back around, she asked, "Nana, what have the police told you?"

"Nothing they haven't shared with you."

Melissa didn't comment, so Nana continued.

"Two hundred thousand dollars was withdrawn from Quinton's bank account on Thursday, January twenty-eighth, the same day he requested time off of work, and now he hasn't been heard or seen from again."

"I know that part, Nana, but…but what do they think happened?"

Virginia Leigh looked over toward Melissa and then back to the road ahead of her. "Let's talk about this when we get home. Not now."

Melissa could see that she was getting upset, so she nodded and then laid her head back and closed her eyes.

Twenty minutes later, Virginia Leigh pulled into Melissa's home and was instantly surrounded by the media. Soon, a garage door was opened, and she was able to pull the car forward, honking the horn as she went. As soon as the door was lowered, she turned off the engine just as the kitchen door swung open, and out came Alison, running to greet them.

Again, Melissa was filled with emotion and quickly embraced her childhood friend. Virginia Leigh opened the back door to unhook Dillon, and he scrambled out of the car and ran toward Alison, screaming, "Alson! Alson!"

Alison let go of Melissa and bent down and scooped up Dillon in her arms. "I missed you so much, Dillon." And she hugged him tight.

Virginia Leigh came around the car and gently touched Melissa's elbow and guided her into the house with Alison and Dillon right behind them.

As if time had somehow magically rewound, Dillon ran up the stairs and straight into his room and found his toy box. Alison followed him up as Melissa slowly walked around the house and inspected every inch of it.

"Nothing has changed!"

"No. Quinton hadn't changed a thing. He was devastated when the police told us you were missing. We all were."

Melissa took a deep breath. "I'm sorry, Nana. I never meant to hurt you."

Virginia Leigh took a step toward her. "Oh, child, you were a victim. You are not at fault."

Melissa turned away to hide her shame. Virginia Leigh didn't back down.

"Melissa, do you want to talk about it?"

With her back still turned, she shook her head.

"What about seeing the psychologist from the hospital? You only had one session."

Closing her eyes, Melissa tried to push out the pain and guilt. *How can I continue with this lie?* she thought. *So many people were hurt and worried about me.*

She turned back around. "Nana, there is something I want—"

"Dillon sure is happy to be in his room. It's like he never left."

Both ladies looked up as Alison stepped down the winding staircase.

Melissa reached out and grabbed Nana's hand and whispered, "I love you!"

Squeezing her hand back, she said, "I know, dear, and I love you too. Now, how about I put on some coffee?"

Alison answered, "That sounds great, thank you."

Melissa watched as Virginia Leigh left the room, and then she ran to her friend and hugged her tight.

"Shh, now. It is going to be all right. You will see." Alison pulled back and looked into Melissa's eyes and continued, "You are home now, and you are safe. Quinton is gone."

Melissa pulled away. "But, I don't know anything. In a way, I feel like I was kidnapped. Staying cooped up in that cabin, not knowing if anyone would ever come, almost sent me over the edge."

Alison leaned closer. "Dillon talked about the beach while we were upstairs."

"Oh shit! I can't control what comes out of his mouth."

Alison pulled her over to the nearby couch. "Don't worry, most people will believe he made it up under the stress."

"You're right. I can just explain that I told him stories to fill the day." She laughed out loud. "I actually did. The days were so long, and there were hunters outside."

Alison grabbed the remote off the coffee table and pressed a button. "We need to hear the latest."

Melissa glanced at her watch and noticed it was twelve thirty. "Okay, you are right."

To no one's surprise, the news started with Melissa and Nana pulling into the driveway. As the garage door closed, an attractive brunette standing in the street smiled into the camera and began to give the play-by-play.

"Melissa and Dillon Pierson were released today from a hospital in North Georgia. Since November, the state of Alabama has vainly searched and prayed for their safe return. Today, yellow ribbons and flyers that have hung up around the community for months have now been removed."

A lady asked from the news station, "Has there been any word on Quinton Pierson?"

"I'm sorry, there has been no update released from the police. As you know, the whereabouts of Quinton Pierson, husband of Melissa Pierson and father of Dillon Pierson, has not been seen since January twenty-eighth, when he withdrew a large amount of money and requested time off from work. There has been speculation that Mr. Pierson received a ransom note, but the police have only confirmed their investigation of the private investigator Joey Franks and his possible connection with the notorious gang the Ripps."

"Thank you for that update, Maria. Now back to other news, there was a stranded—"

Melissa hit the off button and stared at Alison. "How long will the police search before they give up?"

Over her shoulder, Nana's voice was heard. "A long time. They didn't give up on you, thank the Lord!" Both girls watched as Nana put the platter of coffee down on the coffee table.

Alison smiled. "No, they didn't."

Melissa picked up her coffee cup with shaking hands as both ladies watched with a concerned look upon their faces.

Alison spoke first. "Melissa, it has been almost two weeks since anyone has seen or heard from Quinton. It doesn't look good."

Nana picked up her cup and took a sip. "As much as I hate to say this, I agree with Alison. We all need to prepare for the worst."

Melissa placed her cup of coffee down and then stood up. "I think I will go and lie down while Dillon is taking his nap."

"I'm sorry." Nana hesitated briefly before continuing, "You have been through plenty as it is. We can talk about this again in a few more days."

Melissa placed a hand on Virginia Leigh's shoulder. "No, you are both right. We will have to make arrangements. Just not today."

"No, not today," replied Alison.

Chapter 45

Three days later, Nana was sitting on Melissa's couch reading the newspaper. Frustrated, she folded the paper and placed it back down on the coffee table. "Birmingham is not safe. Have you given any more thought to moving back to Jackson?"

Melissa placed her magazine down. "Yes. It is just that Dillon has settled in so well here and I'm afraid to move him to a strange house."

"I know. You are right. But still, this town is not safe. There was another gang robbery last night, and two people were left dead in their home."

Picking up the paper, Melissa glanced at the headlines and froze when she scanned the article and, once again, Joey Franks's name was mentioned with the last gang robbery. "Oh my God, it looks like the same gang that killed Joey Franks."

Nana shook her head. "I don't believe his girlfriend, Frieda. I bet Joey was in on the gang that kidnapped you and Dillon."

Melissa sighed, "I don't know, Nana. I just want this nightmare to end," and she placed the paper back down on the coffee table.

"Are you okay?"

A moment passed before Melissa opened her eyes and spoke. "Yeah, I'm going to be just fine."

Virginia Leigh tilted her head and raised her eyebrows with doubt. "I have an idea. How about you and Dillon come home with me tomorrow, and we will see how he does for a few days away from the house?"

Melissa stood up and raked her hands through her long blonde hair. "Thank you, but I need to stand on my own two feet for a while." Noticing the sad look on her face, she continued, "But we will be there for sure on the Fourth of July."

"I understand. But, I had to ask."

Melissa took two steps toward the kitchen and then stopped when the doorbell rang. "I'll get it." She turned around and walked over and first looked into the peephole before announcing, "It's the police."

Melissa opened the door and immediately recognized Walter Craig, the detective who had worked Rebecca's case.

"I'm sorry, Mrs. Pierson, to stop by unannounced, but may I come in and have a word with you?"

Pulling the door back wider she announced, "You remember my grandmother, Virginia Leigh Mason?"

"Yes, I do. How are you, Ms. Mason?"

"I'm better now that I know Melissa and Dillon are safe, but...but I can't help think the worst for Quinton."

Melissa turned away from Nana and asked the detective, "Any news, anything at all?"

Detective Craig shook his head. "No, I'm sorry."

Melissa frowned and then realized her manners. "Oh, I'm sorry, please come in."

Stepping inside, he answered, "Thank you."

Nana stated, "I will get the coffee," and she turned and walked out, leaving them alone.

Detective Craig followed Melissa into the formal living room and took a seat. Taking out a notepad and removing a pen from his pocket, he asked, "How well do you know Mallory Jane Hawthorne?"

Melissa was taken aback. "Well, I mean, I haven't seen her since I've been back, but we served together in Junior League."

"And Quinton, how does he know her?"

Melissa narrowed her eyes as she spoke. "I introduced her to my husband's line of work a long time ago. They hit it off, and she became one of his biggest clients. Why?"

"Well, we received a call yesterday from her secretary, reporting her missing."

"Missing?"

"Ms. Hawthorne took a business trip several weeks ago and has failed to return home. Now, her secretary has officially filed a missing-persons claim after failing to find her anywhere."

Melissa, upset, stood up and walked toward the window and asked over her shoulder, "What does Quinton's office say?"

"They have nothing to offer on her whereabouts. They received an e-mail stating she was going out of town and would be in touch in a few weeks. Unfortunately, we haven't been able to question your husband."

Melissa sat back on the couch and crossed her arms. "I'm sorry, I don't know. As you know, I haven't been back to Junior League since... since—"

"Are you okay, Melissa?" asked Virginia Leigh.

"Yes. Detective Craig was just informing me of a friend, colleague, who is missing."

Virginia Leigh grabbed Detective's Craig's arm. "You don't think it is the same people that took Melissa and Dillon, do you?"

Melissa looked to the detective and waited for him to answer.

"At this stage, we honestly don't know. We are just asking questions to people she knew and worked with."

Nana shook her head. "What is going on in this city? I was just telling Melissa earlier that it is not safe here."

"Crime has continued to rise over the last several years, mostly due to an increase of gang activity."

"Mommy! Mommy!"

All looked up and found Dillon standing at the top of the stairs, holding his favorite bear.

"Excuse me."

Melissa got up and walked up the stairs, then picked up Dillon and took him back into his room.

Virginia Leigh looked at Detective Craig. "Is there something you need to tell me about Quinton? I mean, do—" She turned around to make sure they were alone and whispered, "Do you think he is dead?"

Detective Craig searched her eyes for a moment and saw that she was sincere. Finally he answered, "You need to help prepare her for the worst, ma'am, but until we have a body, we will continue the search."

She sighed. "How long does she need to wait and hold out hope? I mean, she has been through so much as it is. I just don't think this is healthy to continue—"

"Yes, ma'am. I'm sorry."

For the first time in a long time, Nana was silent.

"Well, I will leave you two now. Please tell Melissa to call if she has any new information on Ms. Hawthorne."

Walking to the door, she replied, "I will."

He opened the door, stepped outside, and then turned back around. "Thank you."

Hearing the door close, Melissa peeked around the hallway and found only Nana standing in the foyer. Relieved the detective had left, Melissa turned and walked back toward Dillon's room.

The next day, Melissa and Dillon waved good-bye from the driveway as Virginia Leigh pulled away in her town car and then honked the horn as she drove off. Looking around, Melissa saw no camera or news crew. *Finally, the circus has left town and found a new bone to chase.*

Picking up Dillon, she turned around and walked back into the garage and then hit the button on the wall for the door to close. As she turned the doorknob, she heard the house phone ringing. Quickly, she made it down the hallway and picked up just in time.

"Hello?"

"Melissa, it's Mitch. How are you?"

Closing her eyes, she caught her breath. She had been avoiding Mitch and hadn't returned any of his calls since returning home. How could she? How could she face him knowing what Quinton had done to Rebecca?

"Mitch, I'm sorry I haven't called. I've—"

"Oh, Melissa, don't apologize! That is the last thing I want you to do."

She remained silent, not knowing what to say.

"Look, Remi is at day care, and I would like to come over and talk. Is now a good time?"

Clutching the receiver tightly in her hand, she finally agreed. "Okay. Come on over."

"Great, I will be there in five minutes."

Melissa slowly lowered the phone down and disconnected. Turning around, she saw Dillon still standing beside her.

"Dillon, are you hungry? Do you want a snack?"

"No. I want vaves! Beach!"

"I know. We are a long way from the water, but I promise to take you back soon, I promise."

"Go now?"

Melissa knelt down to his eye level and smoothed out his golden hair. "How about we go tomorrow? Would you like that?"

"Carey come?"

Trying to fight back tears, she said, "He is working, but maybe another time."

Hearing the doorbell, Melissa stood back up and walked toward the front door to greet Mitch.

Dillon, not knowing who the visitor was, came running behind her screaming, "Carey, Carey!"

Melissa stood dead in her tracks and turned around to face Dillon. Picking him up, she whispered, "It's not Carey. It is Mitch from down the street."

Seeing the disappointment in his face, Melissa hugged him tight and then opened the door, feeling her web of lies slowly unwinding, and nothing she could do was going to stop it.

Chapter 46

Mitch was standing there patiently waiting for the door to open. Finally, a dead bolt twisted, and the front door finally swung open, and there stood Melissa, holding on to Dillon tightly.

Relief immediately washed over him, and he couldn't hold on to his emotions anymore. Walking forward, he threw his arms around her and Dillon and stammered, "Oh God! I am so glad to see you again."

Slowly pulling away, he watched as Dillon squirmed out of her arms and hit the floor running toward the opposite direction.

"I prayed every day, Melissa, that you two would return."

Melissa glanced toward Dillon and saw that he was settling in front of the TV. Then her eyes slowly found Mitch's, and she burst into tears and reached out and hugged him back.

"Oh, Mitch, I'm so sorry. I should have called sooner, I just—"

Holding her tight, he spoke in her ear. "Shh! Don't say anything. Just let me hold you and feel you to know you are for real."

Time stood still as Mitch and Melissa held each other tight in the foyer. Neither wanted to let go.

"Mommy!"

Mitch pulled away first and glanced over toward Dillon and saw him standing and looking at them with a puzzled expression on his face.

Wiping her tears from her face, she picked up Dillon and said, "You remember Mitch, Remi's dad."

"Where Wemi?"

Mitch smiled. "She is at day care. But maybe you can see her tomorrow."

"We go to beach!"

Melissa tensed and placed Dillon back down. "I promised him I would take him to the beach tomorrow."

"The beach?"

Walking away toward the kitchen, she said over her shoulder, "Come on, I made some tea earlier. We can talk in here," and then to Dillon, "*Blue's Clues* is on. Why don't you watch it while I have grown-up talk in kitchen?"

Dillon didn't answer. Instead he ran toward the living room and, like magic, the well-known tune filled the living room from the TV. Melissa never stopped walking until she pulled out two glasses and then removed the iced tea from the refrigerator.

"Please, have a seat. We have lots to talk about."

By the time *Blue's Clues* ended thirty minutes later, Mitch had filled Melissa in on all the neighborhood events of the last couple of months since her disappearance. Rebecca was only brought up once, and Melissa instantly thought of the engraved watch she'd intended to give to Quinton. Pushing the thoughts out of her mind, she focused on the newest news and discoveries of Remi. No doubt about it, Mitch was so proud of his daughter. It kept the mood light and refreshing.

Placing his empty cup down, Mitch looked into Melissa's eyes and asked, "Do you want to talk about it?"

Melissa broke eye contact and searched for Dillon. He was still settled on his beanbag, and his next favorite show, *SpongeBob*, was coming on. Looking back at Mitch, she struggled to find the right words and then settled on, "I'm a survivor, and so is Dillon. That is all that matters now."

Mitch slowly nodded and then reached out and touched her hand. "I understand. But remember, I'm always here for you. You and Quinton mean so much to me and have been such good friends."

Melissa tensed, as Mitch grabbed her hand. "Don't give up hope, Melissa. You came back."

Suddenly she removed her hand. "Well, I didn't withdraw a large sum of money, though, and agree to meet a stranger in the middle of the night."

Mitch's eyes grew moist, and he slowly nodded. "Have the police said any more or made any new leads?"

"No. All leads stopped cold when the investigator died."

"Oh, Melissa, thank God his girlfriend stumbled across your information where they could finally find you."

Melissa half smiled and looked down at her hands resting in her lap.

An awkward silence passed before he continued. "Melissa, you've been through enough. I will support whatever decision you make. I know how hard it is to move forward without the love of your life."

"Thanks. Honestly, I don't give a damn anymore about what people think, and besides, it's really not up to me. The police have the case still open, and they will decide when to close it."

"Will you be fine financially?"

"Yes. Um, I'm thinking about moving, though, and starting over somewhere else."

"Funny you say that. I thought the same thing after Rebecca died, but I had my job, and our house was Remi's home too, and I just couldn't take that stability away from her and move somewhere else."

Melissa looked around her kitchen and quietly said, "He is just everywhere I look sometimes. It's…it's just so…"

He reached for her hand again. "I know. I felt like I was living with a ghost, and swear some nights when I was watching TV I could hear her call out from the kitchen like she used to do." He shook his head. "Our imaginations sure have a way of playing tricks with our minds sometimes."

Melissa looked down at their hands and then slowly raised her head and met his eyes. He was so kind and truly cared about her, she thought. "I won't make any hasty decisions about the house. But I am going to the beach tomorrow with Alison."

Mitch pulled his hand away. "I think the beach is a good idea. Dillon seems really excited about it." Slowly he stood up. "Well, I need to get going. I have to pick up Remi."

Melissa stood as well. "Thanks, Mitch, for coming over. You've been such a good friend!"

He smiled and leaned over for a hug and a quick kiss to her forehead. "I will see myself out. But, call me when you get back, and let's set up a backyard barbecue."

Melissa smiled. "That sounds lovely. I will. Bye now."

"Good-bye Melissa."

Melissa watched as Mitch walked into the living room and ruffled Dillon's hair, then walked to the front door and turned back to wave. Melissa smiled and waved back as the door closed.

Turning back to the kitchen table, she removed the two cups and went over to the sink and placed them inside. Instantly she felt a sensation of Quinton right behind her with his hands wrapped around her waist and breathing in her right ear as he used to do as she cleaned up the dishes after dinner.

Jumping, Melissa dropped a cup, and it broke as it hit the porcelain sink. Spinning around, she saw no one. Quinton wasn't there, and he never would be again, she thought. She slowly picked up the broken pieces to discard in the trash.

"Mommy!"

Dusting her hands off, she left the kitchen in search of Dillon. She found him standing up with his back toward the TV and looking for her.

"I'm right here, sweetie. Did your shows end?"

Dillon ignored her question and asked, "Wherz Carey?"

Melissa quickly walked toward Dillon and picked him up. "You miss him?"

Dillon nodded. "Where is he?"

"Working."

"I want him to stop!"

Melissa smiled. "I know you do. But grown-ups have to work sometimes."

Dillon frowned. "Go to beach 'morrow?"

"Yes. We will leave early in the morning with Alison."

"Will we see Carey?"

Melissa placed Dillon back down and tried to remain patient. Taking his hand, she said, "Why don't we go upstairs and start packing?"

Dillon pulled away and started running toward the staircase, and Melissa stood there and raked her hands through her hair and watched as he bounded up the stairs. When he was at the top, he turned around and screamed out, "Come on, Mommy!"

Slowly, Melissa pulled herself together and climbed the stairs behind him.

Later that night, Melissa and Dillon shared a quiet dinner at home and then cuddled up together on his bed to read books. After several stories, Dillon's eyes couldn't stay open anymore, and he finally gave in to sleep. Several more minutes passed as Melissa sat there watching him sleep in the quiet house. She thought of Carey and how close they had gotten over the last couple of months. He was patient and such a good listener. Slowly she came to the realization that what she felt for him could very well be love. Closing her eyes, she rested her head beside Dillon and wondered what he was doing in Australia. It would be almost noon there on a Saturday. He was probably spending the day on the beach surfing with his mates after a long, hard week at work. It was still hot there, and she imagined the wind blowing his hair, and his bronzed body walking along their beach, holding a surfboard.

Is he thinking about me? Does he miss me as well? Oh, why did he agree to no contact when I forced him to promise!

Slowly, Melissa opened her eyes and carefully got off Dillon's bed. Leaning over, she tucked him in and then placed his favorite bear under his arm. He buried his head into his bear, stirring only briefly. She watched him a few more moments and then turned around and flipped the light switch and closed the door behind her.

Heading back downstairs, she made her way to the front door to check to make sure it was locked. She continued around the rest of the main floor and checked all the other locks. Finished with her task, she started up the stairs again, but stopped when she heard a noise.

Holding the banister, she slowly turned around, but saw nothing but semidarkness. There was a light on in her bedroom above that gave her just enough light to make out an empty foyer and living room. Reminding herself the doors were locked and the alarm set, she shook off the sensation and continued up the stairs toward her bedroom.

The bedroom she once shared with her husband was now empty and the only thing that remained were his ghost. Melissa closed her eyes and took a deep breath to steady her nerves. Closing her door, she walked toward her bathroom to turn on the water for a nice, relaxing hot bath. Minutes later, she was submerged in the warm water, relaxing her head back with her eyes closed.

Memories of Carey raced through her mind. There were so many nights they spent together talking on her porch while Dillon slept in his room. Stories were shared, lots of laughter, and many, many beers consumed. Slowly she opened her eyes and wished she were holding a XXXX Summer.

Melissa's eyes rested on the beach painting that hung on the wall over her large garden tub. It was a painting that she had picked up in Costa Rica on her honeymoon. It felt like ten years ago when she'd made that purchase, instead of just over three years ago. Studying the outline of the waves, memories of Australia, not Costa Rica, flooded her mind once more. Slowly Melissa smiled as she realized she was moving on and she was going to be just fine.

After another ten minutes of relaxation, Melissa began to wash. She had a big day tomorrow and told herself she needed to get to sleep versus spending more time wishing and longing for more nights on her old porch with Carey. Finishing up, she removed the plug and carefully stood up as water rushed off her body. Just as Melissa stepped out of the tub and reached for her towel, the house alarm went off with a shrill.

"Oh my God! What the hell?"

Quickly wrapping up in a towel, she ran forward, but slipped on some water and went crashing forward, hitting her head on the bathroom doorframe and landing hard on the tile floor.

Chapter 47

Dillon sat up in his bed and looked around the dark room as an awful noise continued to ring out. Frightened, he yelled out, "Mommy? Mommy, where are you?"

Soon, tears began to form and run down Dillon's face as he grabbed his favorite stuffed animal and worked himself out from beneath the covers and got out of bed. With the help of a faint glow from his night-light, he could barely make out his door. He quickly ran to it and opened up the door and found darkness. Standing on his tippy-toes, he turned on the hall light, which was located outside his door. He immediately noticed he was alone. Terrified, he ran toward his mommy's closed bedroom door and pushed it open. Scanning the bed, he didn't see his mommy, and he began to cry harder. Just as he was turning back around, he stopped when he spotted her lying on the floor in the bathroom.

Dropping his bear, he ran over and knelt down beside her and began shaking her and screaming, "Mommy!"

Melissa was in a fog, and someone was yelling at her and tugging on her arm. Instantly her eyes opened, and she found Dillon crying over her with the house alarm blasting away. She moved her hand and touched Dillon.

"Mommy, get up!"

Melissa instructed her body to do as Dillon requested. Slowly getting to her knees, she wrapped the towel back around herself and then leaned into the wall in a sitting position and held out her arms for Dillon.

Falling into her arms, he said, "Noise hurts my ears!"

Melissa heard the house phone ringing faintly and thought, *The alarm company.* "Dillon baby, go get Mommy the phone."

Dillon let go and ran toward the nightstand holding his ears. First, he stopped to pick up his bear, and then finally he grabbed the phone and ran back to Melissa.

Taking the phone as Dillon got back into her lap, she spoke. "This is Melissa Pierson."

"Ma'am, this is Demand Security. Your alarm has been activated, and the police have been alerted. Is everything okay?"

Melissa looked around her bedroom and saw no strangers rushing in with weapons, but somehow she didn't seemed relieved. Why was her alarm going off?

She finally answered, "I'm home alone with my son, in the master bedroom. I was in the bathtub when the alarm sounded. I-I don't know why it is going off."

"Ma'am, we would like you to remain in the master bedroom and lock your door and wait till the police to arrive."

Melissa tried to stand, but felt woozy. "Dillon, go close and lock Mommy's door."

Dillon quickly got up and ran to the door, and Melissa held her breath until she could see his little fingers twisting the lock in place. Just as she let out a breath, the alarm stopped.

"Ma'am, we don't hear or see your alarm activated on the computer screen. Did you turn it off?"

Melissa wrapped her free hand around Dillon and said, "No. I haven't touched the keypad."

The operator said something, but Melissa couldn't understand what was being said because images of Quinton coming home and punching in the code made her freeze motionless. As if the world had stopped, Melissa could visually see Quinton bursting through the door, grabbing her son, and then aiming a gun at her head and pulling the trigger. Melissa began to shake so hard she dropped the phone to the tile, and for a full ten seconds, she couldn't move.

Dillon picked up the phone, handed it to Melissa, and was saying something. Time began to speed up again. She found her voice, grabbed the phone, and placed it to her cheek. "I'm still—"

Suddenly, the bedroom door handle twisted, and a banging noise was heard. Melissa was trying to understand the voice when she felt Dillon wiggle free and run to the door.

"Dillon, no! Don't open the door!"

Dillon stopped just short of the door and turned around, confused. "It's Alson!"

Opening her mouth to speak, she tried to comprehend what he had said. She watched in horror as Dillon unlocked the door and it flung open, only to reveal Alison standing there with a remorseful expression on her face.

Melissa closed her eyes and tilted her head back against the wall.

Ten minutes later, Alison was tucking Dillon back into bed as Melissa watched from his bedroom door. The situation had been explained, a code given, and the police were called off. Melissa was now wearing a housecoat, and her wet hair was pulled up into a clip.

Alison kissed the top of Dillon's forehead and turned around to face Melissa once again. Mouthing, "I'm so sorry," for the third time, she walked toward her friend and closed Dillon's door behind her. "Why don't I get us each a glass of wine?"

Melissa tilted her head and just stared at Alison. Somehow, all the anger immediately disappeared. This was her childhood friend. Her only real friend who knew her darkest secrets. How could she stay mad?

"That sounds lovely, but why don't you bring it up here and we can have it in my room?"

Alison nodded and headed for the staircase as Melissa turned and walked toward her bedroom. Back inside the bathroom, she removed the clip and pulled out a hair dryer. Soon, most of the dampness was gone, and Melissa put the dryer away and headed toward her bed just as Alison came in with two glasses of wine. Both girls climbed into bed and sat up against the headboard and sipped on their wine. A few minutes passed before either spoke.

"I thought you were Quinton coming back from the grave to kill me and take Dillon."

Alison frowned. "No. He's not coming back. He is dead and long buried by now."

"How can we be sure? I mean, neither of us has been in contact." Melissa stared into Alison's eyes hard and asked, "Right?"

"Yes. I mean no, I haven't made contact."

Melissa took another sip of her wine. "I can still feel him. I don't think he is dead."

"Your mind is playing tricks on you. You do trust Carey, don't you?"

"Absolutely. But...but what if something went wrong?"

Alison took her last sip and then placed her wineglass down on the nightstand. "It didn't. It's over."

Melissa looked away and then finished her wine and handed the empty glass to her friend. Alison took the glass and placed it beside hers and spoke. "Let's get some sleep. Dillon will be up early tomorrow with excitement about our big trip."

"I hope so. Maybe he won't even mention tonight's alarm."

Alison laughed, "Don't count on it," and she reached over and turned off the light switch as both girls lay down to sleep.

Ten minutes of silence followed, and then Allison asked quietly, "Are you awake?"

Melissa was on her back with her eyes open, staring at the dark ceiling above. "Yes. Wide awake."

"Me too. Want to watch a chick flick?"

"Yes."

The next morning, all three were in the car and on their way to Orange Beach, Alabama, by seven o'clock. Dillon was buckled up in the backseat of Alison's Volvo, watching a video playing on the back of Alison's seat. Melissa turned back and looked ahead as they continued along the interstate.

"I wish the weather was going to be warmer."

Melissa looked out the window. "I don't. It would remind me too much of Australia."

"I think we should go, all three of us."

Melissa looked back to her friend. "That would be nice. At least I wouldn't have to explain Dillon's random remarks he makes."

"Oh, I know. Well, at least he is going to a beach. It will now make it a little easier."

Melissa explained, "You wouldn't believe the crock of shit I told his psychologist. I told her that I made up a fictional dreamland during our captivity."

"Do you think she believed you?"

Melissa gave it serious thought and said, "Yeah, I really do. I told her it was a way to cope with the boredom." Melissa laughed out loud. "She even praised me for being so creative!"

Alison smiled. "Creative you are, always have been."

Melissa frowned. "Yeah, well, Quinton gave me no choice, did he?"

Alison shook her head. "No, he did not. May he burn in hell!"

Several more miles went by before Melissa spoke again. "Any word on Mallory Jane?"

She watched as her friend tensed behind the wheel.

"Alison?"

Slowly, she looked over at Melissa and said, "What are the chances Quinton was seeing Mallory Jane?"

Melissa felt her face drain of color. "What? Alison, that is absurd. Why do you ask that?"

"Is it? Rebecca was a close friend. Why do you think Mallory Jane would be above it? We both know Quinton isn't."

"Just stop. Stop! I don't want to know where you are going with this."

Silence.

Thirty minutes went by listening to a country CD, then Melissa leaned forward and hit the off button. "Okay, Alison, why do you think Quinton was seeing Mallory Jane?"

"I saw them out to dinner one night."

"Well, they worked very closely. It wouldn't be unusual for them to have dinner. After all, Dillon and I weren't at home for him to come home to."

"This wasn't in Birmingham."

Melissa felt a shortness of breath. Inhaling deeply, she forced herself to ask, "Where?"

"Tuscaloosa. I was there on business and staying at the Holiday Inn. That is where I saw them together having dinner."

She struggled to get the words out. "A hotel?"

"Yes. I don't know if they were staying there on business. I tried, but I wasn't successful in finding out."

"So, they could have been. It really wouldn't surprise me."

Alison sighed, "Oh, Melissa, do you think we made a mistake? I mean, do you think he had something to do with Mallory Jane disappearing?"

Melissa turned away and faced the trees going by on the interstate.

A few minutes passed, and Alison continued, "Maybe we both should have gone to the police and had them arrest Quinton for murder and—"

"No. Then I would have been arrested and questioned for my attempted murder in Gatlinburg. Then where would Dillon be then?"

"What, Mommy?"

307

Melissa turned around and smiled. "Nothing, sweetie. Are you enjoying your movie?"

"Yes! We at beach now?"

Melissa watched as he looked out the window with a perplexed look on his face. "No, but not much longer, okay?"

Dillon looked back at his portable DVD player and began watching his movie again. Satisfied he wasn't going to ask any more questions, Melissa turned back around.

Alison checked her rearview mirror to see if Dillon was preoccupied, and then she continued again, "What if he did something to Mallory Jane?"

Melissa looked out the window. She couldn't face her friend. If she did, Alison would see the guilt she felt. If he had done something to Mallory Jane, then her blood would be on her hands. After all, she never went to the police about Rebecca or her tampered-with car. If she had, it would have ended there.

Damn it! she thought. *Why did I have to take matters into my own hands? Oh, why the hell didn't I let the mechanic call the police?*

Melissa placed her head in her hands.

"I'm sorry, Melissa. I was wrong to say we made a mistake. You did what you felt you had to do to protect Dillon and yourself. Look, it's over. Starting today, no more. Time to look forward and not backward."

Alison removed her right hand off the wheel and placed it on Melissa's hand that was covering her face. Feeling her touch, Melissa slowly looked up at Alison. "You are such a good friend. I'm so sorry I drug you into this mess."

"What are friends for? You would have done the same for me."

Slowly, a tear rolled down Melissa's face. "Yes. I would have." Then she smiled.

Chapter 48

After four days of building sandcastles and eating seafood, Melissa arrived home with Dillon. Alison said her good-byes and went back to work leaving Melissa alone once again. Starting the last load of laundry, the telephone began to ring. Melissa left the laundry room in search of the phone.

Once in the study, Melissa unplugged her phone from the charger and spoke. "Hello?"

No answer.

Melissa looked at the phone, and it read: Unknown Caller. She tried again. "Hello?"

Again, no answer.

Melissa pressed the end button, reconnected her charger, and went in search of Dillon. Scanning the living room, there was no sign of him.

Melissa hastily ran up the stairs, calling out, "Dillon?"

Rounding the corner to Dillon's room, she stopped when she saw him arranging his seashells on one of his shelves.

"There you are."

Dillon turned around, startled.

"I like all your shells, and they look good there."

He beamed with pride. "I love the beach. When we go again?"

Melissa couldn't help but smile. "You miss the beach, don't you?"

Dillon nodded his head and turned back around.

"We will go back again soon" she said as she stepped forward to stand by his side.

Dillon looked up and met her eyes. "Will Carey be at beach?"

"I don't know. He is still working right now."

"I don't like him working!" Dillon pouted.

"I know, buddy. It is what grown-ups have to do, though. Now, let's get you ready for bed. Have you brushed your teeth?"

Before he could answer, Melissa heard the house phone ringing from her bedroom. "I'll be right back."

Melissa made her way to her bedroom and paused beside the bed. Listening to the phone ringing again, she tensed. She thought, surely not another wrong number. After another ring, she finally picked it up.

"Hello?"

"Mrs. Pierson, this is Detective Walter Craig. I'm sorry to call so late, but do you have a moment?"

Color drained from Melissa's face as she took a seat on the bed because her knees had gone weak. "Um, yes, of course, what...what is it?"

"I tried calling today, but got no answer, and I didn't want to leave a message."

"Dillon and I were at the beach. We got home a few hours ago."

"I see. Do you have some time in the morning to come by?"

"Um, yeah, of course. What time?"

"Nine o'clock?"

"That's fine, but what is this about?"

"If you don't mind, I would rather wait to discuss this in the morning."

She hesitated briefly. "All right then, I'll see you then."

"Thank you, Mrs. Pierson, have a good night."

Melissa hung up the phone and sat there thinking about what he could possibly want. Did they find more evidence between Quinton and Joey Franks? Instantly she felt sick when the thought of Mallory Jane missing entered her mind.

Quietly she spoke aloud. "Oh please God, don't let this be about Mallory Jane."

The next morning, Melissa dropped off Dillon at day care and then drove straight to the station, arriving a little before nine. Immediately she was escorted back to Detective Craig's office, where she took a seat while he finished up a phone conversation. He motioned with his hands that he would be only another minute. Awkwardly, Melissa sat there and patiently waited and tried not to fidget.

Soon the phone was placed down on the holder, and Detective Craig spoke. "Thank you for coming in this morning."

"It was no problem. Now, what is this about?"

Detective Craig leaned forward and looked hard into her eyes. "We found your husband's wallet and vehicle."

Melissa grabbed her throat with her right hand and stared back at the detective for more news.

"The car surfaced down the Mississippi River yesterday. After the vehicle was drained, they found his wallet in the glove box and a black dress shoe in the trunk."

"What about Quinton?"

A kind expression formed over his face as he answered, "I'm sorry, we didn't find his body."

Melissa stood up and turned around toward a white wall lined with filing cabinets.

"I need you to take a look at the shoe."

Melissa slowly turned around and faced him as he pulled a box off the corner of his desk and then opened it and pushed it toward her. She stood still, with no emotion on her face, as she stared at the box with wet eyes. Willing herself to move, she picked up her foot and forced her body forward while taking a deep breath. Her eyes left the detective's face and found the box. Inside was a muddy shoe that resembled the ones Quinton wore. Nodding her head, she turned back around and cried into her hands.

Melissa heard the detective covering the box with the lid and making his way around the desk toward her. Soon his hand was on her shoulder in a caring gesture. Again, she took a deep breath and slowly turned around to play a role she had prepared for ever since receiving the call in Australia from Joey Franks.

Detective Craig looked into Melissa's eyes and spoke directly. "Yesterday, the decision was made to move your husband's case from missing person to murder. I'm real sorry, Mrs. Pierson."

Melissa's heart rate increased as she willed herself to try to process the information he was sharing. "I don't understand. Quinton is still missing. How can you...move it?"

"I'm sorry, Mrs. Pierson, but we don't have enough evidence to support that he survived the events that led to his shoe in the trunk and his car in a river."

"So that is it? You are just going to give up?"

"We are still investigating your abduction, but unfortunately, with the latest discovery and the death of Joey Franks, our investigation has hit a wall."

"So, what does this mean exactly? Are you declaring him" she asked with a broken voice, "dead?"

Melissa couldn't speak. She thought silently, *This is it. They think he is dead.* Quickly she grabbed a Kleenex from his desk and placed it up against her face and bowed her head.

"Mrs. Pierson, again, I'm real sorry. Unless something else comes up, we have no choice."

Slowly Melissa removed the tissue from her face and lifted her head to meet his eyes. "What do I tell my son?"

He responded with a saddened expression. "Can I call someone for you? Maybe one of the lawyers at Quinton's firm?" Placing a hand gently on top of hers, he continued, "There will be some legal issues that need to be explained in these situations."

She wiped a tear from her cheek and slowly nodded. "Yes, tell them to come over to the house."

Slowly she pulled away. "I'm going home to my son now." She turned away and placed a hand on the doorknob.

Quickly his hand seized hers, and he twisted the knob and opened the door for her to pass. Without turning around, Melissa carefully walked out of the police station with the thought of all eyes on her.

Detective Craig remained at his door and watched as she left and slowly shook his head side to side.

Chapter 49

"Quinton, I need some help in the stables!"

Quinton threw down his shovel and headed toward the voice calling his name. When he rounded the corner, Chris was standing there with his hands on his hips.

"I need this stable cleaned. We've got another tour group coming out tomorrow, and we will need six of the horses ready to go."

Quinton cut him a deadly stare and vowed silently, *This will be the last day, and tomorrow your blood will be on my hands.*

"Quinton, are you deaf? I didn't hear an answer!"

Quinton nodded his head. "I will work on it next. I'm almost done with the fence."

Chris smiled. "Good. Now just in case we don't speak again, you know the rules when we have outsiders."

Quinton walked over and grabbed one of the bowls of water and began drinking. Rubbing his mouth with his shirt, he finally replied, "How can I forget?" and he slowly turned around and walked away.

Chris continued watching until Quinton was well out of sight and thought, *Just what are you up to now, Quinton?*

Chapter 50

Melissa watched as Nana read Dillon a story in the living room. She had been so glad to hear that she wanted to visit again. Nana had been here for two nights and was planning on staying two more. She smiled at Nana's expression as she lovingly read to her great-grandchild. Melissa knew she had been lonely since Papa passed, and knew her visit would help fill a void. Oh, who was she kidding? Having her here helped filled a void she had in her own life.

Suddenly the doorbell sounded and jarred Melissa back to reality. Placing her well-thumbed magazine to the side, she got up and walked to the door to see who the uninvited guest was. When she was just two feet away, she saw through the side glass pane a shadow move. Knowing there could possibly be vultures from the media left over, she looked through the peephole and almost fainted at the sight of the man standing behind the door.

Melissa heard Nana's voice from behind her, but couldn't make out the words. All she could focus on was his face. Where had he come from?

Slowly turning to face Nana, she spoke in a quivering voice. "Where is Dillon?"

In a concerned voice, Nana answered, "Why, what is wrong?" She walked over, placed a hand on the knob, and spoke as she peered into the peephole. "For God's sake, it's not the damn tabloids again, is it?"

She slowly turned around to face Melissa. "They sure try to clean up nicely, don't they? Do you want me to get rid of him?"

Melissa had tears in her eyes as she faced her Nana. "No. I've got this."

"But Melissa darling, you're crying."

Melissa felt her cheeks and wiped the moisture from under her eyes. "I'm fine. Will you kindly go and watch over Dillon and I'll explain soon?"

Nana showed her uncertainty at the statement by frowning and placing her hands on both hips. Finally, at the sound of the doorbell again, she complied. Gently, she leaned in and kissed Melissa on the cheek and then stepped away, saying loudly, "Dillon, let's go into the kitchen and make some lunch."

Melissa watched them leave and then ran a hand down her long blonde hair and looked down at her clothing. She was wearing a gray lounge outfit with knitted house shoes. Breaking into a smile, she finally opened the door and faced the man she had given her heart to several months ago in the Land Down Under.

Epilogue

Carey was playing catch with Dillon in the backyard while Nana and Melissa sat in the gliding swing, sipping sweet iced tea. "So explain to me how you met someone so quickly in just four short days?"

Melissa took a swig of her tea and replied, "We met the first night in Gulf Shores and hit it off. Carey builds houses, and he is working on a few projects around the Tuscaloosa area."

"I heard about the shortage of builders after the tornado ripped through, but I had no idea they were bringing people in from Australia!"

Melissa smiled. "Yeah, I was surprised to hear as well."

"So, where is he staying tonight?"

Melissa looked at her Nana. "Well, here, of course. I have plenty of bedrooms."

Nana looked hard into her eyes. "Good. Let's show this Aussie what true Southern hospitality is all about. Wait till he has my famous breakfast! He is gonna think he died and went to heaven!"

Melissa smiled and squeezed her hand.

Later that night, Carey closed Dillon's bedroom door with Melissa by his side. "He has grown."

"Yes, he has."

Turning toward her Nana's bedroom, she could see the light was out and Nana had gone on to bed. "Would you like a glass of wine, or I have some beer?"

"Beer sounds good."

Melissa led him down the spiral staircase and into the kitchen area.

"You really have a nice home here. Did you design it?"

"No. But, I personally decorated it."

"You have extremely nice taste."

Melissa laughed, "In America, that is slang for expensive taste."

He met her eyes and held contact. "Yeah, that too."

Melissa grabbed two beers out of the refrigerator and motioned him over to the small family room with the oversized leather lounge set. Taking a seat, she whispered close to his face, "I've missed you. I'm glad you found me."

Carey didn't respond. Sensing something was wrong, she asked, "What? What's the matter?"

Looking away briefly, he took a long swig of his beer while she asked again, more urgently, "Carey, what is wrong?"

He set his beer down on the coaster provided on the coffee table, then reached out and grabbed her hands. "I couldn't tell you earlier with your grandmother around, and Dillon and all—"

Melissa looked hard into his eyes. "You are scaring me. What is it?"

With a grim expression, he stated, "Chris called me three days ago. Quinton escaped."

Color drained from Melissa's face as she tried to form the words to ask how.

"Chris said he had him out of his sight for two hours max! And then...then he was gone."

Melissa looked down at her hands, which were held tightly in his. "I...I don't...What do..."

"Look, Melissa, try not to read too much into this."

Melissa jerked away her hands and met his eyes. "Too much into this?"

Carey reached out and grabbed her hands again and pleaded, "Melissa, it is the outback. He is thousands of kilometers away from anywhere, with no water, food, or transportation. He will die soon, if he hasn't already."

When she opened her mouth to reply, he didn't give her a chance as he leaned over and kissed her sweet mouth, which he had longed for, for months.

Melissa felt the shock waves of his kiss and desperately tried to pull away, but was held tight by his strong, muscular arms. Finally, her heart took over, and she gave herself to him freely once more. Moments passed as they continued to kiss and fuel the fire between them.

Not wanting to waste another minute, Carey stood up, then leaned down, picked her up, carried her into the study, and closed and locked the door. Seconds turned into minutes, and finally, after an hour, they lay naked in each other's arms on the leather sofa, breathless.

"Carey, what next? I mean, how can we be sure?"

Carey smoothed back a golden lock that had fallen across her face and replied, "Do you trust me?"

Melissa hesitated briefly before answering. Searching his dark blue eyes, she knew in her heart, either way, he would protect her or die trying. Finally she answered, "Yes," and smiled when Carey took her into his arms once again.

Here is a sneak preview…

Fearless

(The sequel to *Just For You*)

Coming Soon

September 2012

Chapter 1

Jamie Conrad was running up the ship platform with a book in one hand and a beach bag slung across her shoulder. Her red, spirally hair was blowing in the wind, and her oversized black sunglasses were hiding her dark green eyes from a man holding open a door that caught her eye and winked.

"You got just one minute to spare."

Jamie showed her documents to the attendant and smiled her winning smile. "All I need."

Stepping across the threshold, she glanced back at an empty pier with no other late passengers trailing behind. She wasn't surprised. On day one, the cruise ship stated they waited for no one, and it was a constant reminder each day they docked at a new port.

Jamie stepped aside as a staff member passed her and began the process of dissembling the plank from the dock. Satisfied no one was following her and she was safe, she made her way down the hall toward the lift that would take her below three decks to her interior room.

Removing her key, she looked both ways and then opened the door and quickly locked it, placing her forehead back against the door. Closing her eyes, she tried to catch her breath and steady her breathing. After several moments passed, Jamie pushed back from the door and turned toward her small bathroom and began to remove her black sundress from her body. As her dress hit the floor, she froze at the dried blood on her stomach and thighs.

Instantly she removed her black two-piece swimsuit and then shut the door to look in the full-length mirror. Her eyes rested on her stomach first and then her legs. Slowly she turned around and followed the blood smear around her right thigh that ended at the back of her knee. Turning back around, she took a step closer toward the mirror at the sight of a smudge on her left cheek. As she pulled her hair back, the smear faded as it ran toward her neck. Frantically, she tried wiping it off with her right hand. Once it was gone, she turned her hands around and inspected her fingers. One of her nails was ripped, with something caught underneath.

Closing her eyes once more, she took a deep breath and then took one short step into the shower and turned the water on cold. Picking up the soap, she began washing her fair skin clean, but unsuccessfully washing the horrible memory out of her mind.

Chapter 2

Jamie stepped into the elevator behind her best friend, Becky Norris. As Becky pressed the button to the twenty-third floor, Jamie exclaimed, "I can't believe I'm moving into a high-rise condominium worth one and a half million dollars! Pinch me! 'Cause this is not happening!"

Becky turned to face her friend she had met during her freshman year at Central University. "I know, it is hard to believe. Just remember, we are only living here for one year, though, so don't get too comfortable!"

Jamie sighed, "I know, I still can't believe Robby's parents made us this offer."

Becky thought about her late boyfriend, Robby Singleton. It had been only eight months since his murder. With the help of Jamie, slowly she was able to pull herself out of depression and continue on the timely path for May graduation in the nursing program.

Ding.

Becky pushed the bad thoughts aside as both girls looked at each other, then stepped out into the hallway toward room 2305. Each girl was pulling two large suitcases with rollers, along with their handbags. Finding the door, Becky stood up her suitcase, removed her hand from the handle, and began to search for the key in her large pink Gucci purse.

Jamie was beginning to get impatient as Becky struggled to find the keys. "You should clean that thing out time to time."

Becky smiled. "I know."

Soon the key was placed in the keyhole and twisted. Taking a last look at Jamie. "Okay, let's see what this place looks like."

The door was opened to reveal a state-of-the-art furnished condominium. From the front door, one could see the floor-length windows that lined the exterior wall of the living room. Through the glass windows, two brown leather lounge chairs were set up, along with an outdoor lounge set, under a covered balcony. Both girls parked their luggage and handbags and ran across the room squealing like a bunch of school-age girls who just had been asked out by the hottest boys on campus.

Becky got to the glass door first. She unlocked it and slid it open for both to step out and check their view. "Oh my God, you can see all of Houston!"

Jamie pointed to the left. "Look, that is the hospital where we are going to work."

Becky nodded and added, "Check out the Galleria and all the shopping centers!"

Both girls bounced up and down and then hugged each other. "Come on!" screamed Becky. "Let's go check out our bedrooms!"

In a matter of a few short moments, rooms were picked, and then they both searched for the bathroom. "Wait, do we each have our own bathroom?" yelled Jamie.

"Yes. And a half bath for guests down the hall!" added Becky.

Jamie ran out of her room and through the living room to the kitchen. "Wow, a five-burner gas stove, Becky, I think we have died and gone to heaven!"

Becky saw a basket with a note inside on the kitchen island. She walked over, picked up the note, and read it while Jamie left toward the living room at the sound of her phone.

"Hello?"

"Hi, Jamie, it's Luke, um, Luke James."

Jamie turned her back toward Becky in the kitchen and answered, "Yeah, Luke, what's up?"

"I've been trying to get in touch with Bart this week, and he hasn't returned any of my calls. Have you talked to him?"

Jamie frowned at the sound of Bart's name, and a memory of an unpleasant sight filled her mind. "No. We broke up in March, and I haven't talked to him since."

"I'm sorry about that. I know Bart really liked you, and I was bummed to hear you guys ended it."

"Yeah, well, things can change."

"Yeah, they can. Look, do you happen to have his address in New Orleans?"

"I'm sorry, Luke, no."

Jamie lied. Bart had given her his address when he left town to take his new job offer. He had wanted Jamie to come with him, and that was the cause of their big split. She could hear him saying now, *"Just come check it out one weekend, any weekend. You'll love it, and they are also looking for nurses."*

She was adamant, no New Orleans. She thought it was a shit town, and no way was she leaving Texas.

Slowly her mind tuned back in to what Luke was saying on the other end. "Well, do you have my number in case you do hear from him?"

Hesitating for a moment, she finally responded, "Yes. I do."

"Okay, thanks, Jamie, take care."

"You too, Luke, bye."

Jamie pressed the end button and slid the phone into her hip pocket and walked back into the kitchen to hear about the note.

"So, what does it say?"

"It's from the Singletons. They left us a welcome bottle of wine and hope we feel welcomed here."

"Oh yeah, extremely welcomed."

Becky smiled and then walked over and opened up the large double-door stainless refrigerator and found the wine. Jamie opened up cabinets until she found two glasses and then pulled them down as Becky uncorked the bottle.

She poured the red wine, which was no doubt expensive, and both girls raised their glasses for a toast.

"To us!"

Becky touched her glass to Jamie's and added, "To us and our new jobs in the city!"

Jamie stared into her best friend's eyes and winked and took a sip.

Made in the USA
Middletown, DE
06 September 2024